TEMPTATION'S PRICE

"Kiss me," Elizabeth whispered. "Please, just once."

And Michael did, tenderly at first and then with fierce hunger. There was no subtlety in her desire, no holding back.

He kissed the soft skin at the base of her throat. Heat emanated from her, enveloping him in a sensuous, invisible cloud.

He dug his fingers into her hair and forced her to look at him. "I want more than this," he told her.

Elizabeth met his gaze unflinchingly. "We've already gone too far."

Also by Georgia Bockoven

A Marriage of Convenience
The Way It Should Have Been

Available from
HarperPaperbacks

Harper Monogram

MOMENTS

Georgia Bockoven

HarperPaperbacks
A Division of HarperCollinsPublishers

This is a work of fiction. The characters, incidents, and
dialogues are products of the author's imagination and are not
to be construed as real. Any resemblance to actual events or
persons, living or dead, is entirely coincidental.

HarperPaperbacks *A Division of* HarperCollins*Publishers*
10 East 53rd Street, New York, N.Y. 10022

Copyright © 1994 by Georgia Bockoven
All rights reserved. No part of this book may be used or
reproduced in any manner whatsoever without written
permission of the publisher, except in the case of brief
quotations embodied in critical articles and reviews. For
information address HarperCollins*Publishers*,
10 East 53rd Street, New York, N.Y. 10022.

Cover illustration by Jeff Cornell

First printing: March 1994

Printed in the United States of America

HarperPaperbacks, HarperMonogram, and colophon are
trademarks of HarperCollins*Publishers*

❖ 10 9 8 7 6 5 4 3 2 1

For
Sidney Grace Bockoven
and
Steve Stephens . . .
a beginning and an end.
I love you.

Prologue

The church bell sounded in the background—one ring for each of the seventeen years Elizabeth Preston had been alive.

Jennifer Cavanaugh stopped to listen and to count. She thought about the grief that had gripped the town for the past three days. Why did it seem so much worse when the prettiest girl in school died in a car wreck than when an overweight boy with acne was killed loading a grain elevator? Did beauty make a person more valuable? Or was it that Elizabeth was the daughter of the county's richest farmer while Tom had been the son of a mechanic?

Jenny's grandmother had told her that morning that it was a blessing Elizabeth's parents had died in the accident with her. Without their daughter they wouldn't have thought life worth living. Of course, Tom's parents had managed to go on. They weren't allowed the luxury of prolonged grief. There were bills to be paid and more children at home who needed them.

Jenny and Elizabeth had never had anything in common other than sharing the same birthday—but it wasn't as if they ever celebrated together. Colossus himself couldn't have spanned the social chasm that separated Jenny from the most popular girl in school.

According to Mr. Moore, the principal, that was the reason she'd been left behind to answer the phones in the office while the rest of the school went to the funeral. What he'd actually said was that since this was her normal hour to work in the office anyway, and since she wouldn't be missed—while the rest of them would—it naturally and reasonably fell to her to take care of things when everyone else was gone.

She didn't mind having him point out that she and Elizabeth hadn't been friends; it was the way he'd done it that hurt, as if she weren't good enough to attend the funeral. How important did you have to be to sit in a church to say good-bye to someone who had died? And who was this mysterious person who took note of the people who came and later chastised those who didn't?

The bell stopped ringing. She felt a twinge of guilt that she'd become too wrapped up in her own thoughts to keep count. It was the one way left to her to pay her respect, and she'd failed even that. Maybe Mr. Moore had been right after all.

She glanced down at the stack of mail she still had to open and sort and went back to work. She'd almost finished when she came to an envelope addressed to George Benson, the senior class counselor. When she'd first started working in the office, she had sometimes glanced at the mail as she opened it, even though that was strictly forbidden. It hadn't taken long to realize how boring most of the correspondence that came to the school really was. Today, however, something in the letter for Mr. Benson caught her eye. She stopped to read it through and immediately wished she hadn't. It was filled with the kind of irony that put a keener edge to sorrow.

It seemed Elizabeth Mary Preston had been awarded the Haddie Stephens Scholarship—four years, fully paid, to Safford Hill University. Elizabeth's parents could have sent half the high school graduating class to college and not suffered financial strain, and here their daughter had been given a free ride. But then, as the letter stated, it wasn't the money that counted, it was the honor of winning such a prestigious award. Jenny hadn't even known the scholarship existed. If she had, she would have applied, too. A prize like that would have been worth doing anything to win—even suffering the humiliation that came with asking her teachers and her grandmother's friends to write letters of recommendation and to please say something nice enough to give her a chance.

Her first year of high school she'd had a secret dream that she would get her own letter. Only hers would be from her parents—a note from her dad saying how sorry he was to have missed out on seeing his daughter grow into a beautiful young woman and one from her mother telling her how she'd thought of her every day they'd been apart and that she hoped the enclosed check, money they had saved to put Jenny through college, would help make up for leaving her behind with her grandmother.

The dream had died with her parents, then resurfaced midway through her junior year when it struck her that it was possible the money had been left with an attorney, to be sent when it was needed. As her senior year progressed, Jenny's dream had been taken from her in small, painful increments. She had begun looking for a permanent, full-time job, one that would pay enough for her to put money aside herself. She hadn't given up on college entirely, just on her ability to get there as soon as she would have liked.

"I'm back," called a disembodied male voice. George Benson rounded the corner just as Jenny hurriedly laid the letter back on the desk.

"Is it over already?" she asked. She liked Mr. Benson and felt especially guilty that it was his mail she'd been snooping through. He reminded her of one of the men at a safe house she'd stayed in with her parents just before they'd left her with her grandmother. That man had been tall and blond, too. Only he'd had a beard and she'd never seen him without a cigarette in his hand. He'd worn jeans and T-shirts, where Mr. Benson wore suits. But both had a way of actually looking at her instead of through her when they talked. Jenny liked that.

"There's still the graveside service," George Benson said. "I thought I'd come back to relieve you so you could go if you wanted."

"Thanks—but I don't have any way to get there."

"Didn't your grandmother go to the service?"

Jenny shook her head. "She put in an extra shift at the restaurant so everybody there could go."

"If you left for the church now, you could probably get a ride with one of the other kids."

He knew as well as she did there wasn't anyone she would ask; still, it made her feel good that he'd suggested it. "I appreciate the offer, but I should probably stay here. Mr. Moore wants me to get the filing done before I leave."

"If you change your mind, I'll be in my office."

Jenny glanced down at the desk and saw the letter. "I have your mail for you, Mr. Benson."

He gave her an amused look. "So that's what you were reading when I came in."

She swallowed. There was no use denying it. "I'm sorry. It's just that—" She held the letter out to him. "Well, you'll see."

He skimmed the text, frowned, and started at the beginning again. "God in heaven," he said wearily. "Of all days for this to come. What a waste."

"What are you going to do?" she asked.

"Send them a letter and a copy of the death certificate, I suppose."

"At least there's still time to give the scholarship to someone else."

He shook his head. "I wouldn't be surprised if the fall semester was half over by the time they got the paperwork processed."

"You mean the money is just going to sit there?" Every inch of her recoiled at the thought.

"That's the way it looks."

"If I knew who was next in line, I'd call and tell them what happened." Jenny picked up a stack of papers and headed for the file cabinet. "What if it's someone like me?" She pulled open the top drawer. "I wish it was," she added softly.

"I do, too, Jenny." George Benson folded the letter and tucked it back in its envelope. "If I'd have used half the sense God gave me, I would have had you applying for every scholarship we could find."

The apology in his voice took Jenny by surprise. A warmth flowed through her. It made her feel good that someone cared that she was being left behind. "It was my fault for not telling you that I needed help."

"I hope you haven't given up."

"Even if I wanted to, my grandma wouldn't let me. She's always saying things like 'Where there's a will, there's a way.'"

Fifteen minutes later Jenny was hunched over a file cabinet when George Benson came out of his office. "Jenny, I'd like to talk to you."

She stuck her hand in the file to hold her place and looked up at him. The expression on his face made her uneasy. "I'll be through here in a couple of minutes," she said.

"I think we'd better make it now, before everyone else comes back."

"Did I do something wrong?" The question would have made her grandmother angry. She was always telling Jenny she had to stop assuming everything that went wrong in the world was somehow her fault.

"Don't worry, you haven't done anything," he said. And then he added mysteriously, "But with just a little bit of luck and some careful timing, we're going to see what we can do to change that."

1

San Francisco, California—December 17, 1986

    "Excuse me," a male voice said.

Elizabeth Preston felt someone touch her arm. She started to turn—

"Don't I know you?"

—and then froze. After eleven years the inevitable, the unthinkable had happened. She'd almost stopped expecting it, but that didn't lessen the panic.

An agonizingly long second passed and then another and then, finally, her instinct for survival kicked in. Without any outward manifestations of her inner turmoil, she excused herself from the cigar-smoking chairman of Packard Industries and turned her attention to the man who had called out to her.

Of the six hundred people in attendance at Smith &

Noble's annual Christmas party, she knew, or at least recognized, half of them, either from business dealings or from past social functions. She was confident the man in front of her was not among them. Nor was he anyone she could place in her past. "Were you talking to me?"

The cool look she'd directed at him brought him up short. He appeared embarrassed when he said, "I know this sounds like a come-on, but I'm sure we've met somewhere."

She made a show of studying him before shaking her head slowly. "Sorry, but I don't remember you." It was the truth, but that didn't mean she was in the clear. There were too many people in her past to remember them all. Before he could say anything in reply, she offered him a quick, dismissive smile. "I have one of those faces people are always mistaking for someone else."

"I can hardly believe that."

It was meant as a compliment, but to Elizabeth it was more of a threat. She'd done everything short of surgery to change the way she'd looked when she'd left Farmingham eleven years ago. The short boyish-looking bob she'd worn in high school had been replaced with sleek, expertly cut hair that brushed her shoulders. And the intervening years had turned the color a much darker brown than it had been then. Glasses had been replaced with contact lenses; her five-foot-eight-inch body was fifteen pounds lighter; and the gap between her front teeth had been filled in with caps. Even time had become her ally. After twenty-eight years she'd finally passed the ingenue stage and had begun to look her age.

The silence had grown awkward between them by the time Elizabeth's practical side took over. Even though she knew what she was suggesting wasn't possible, she offered him an out. "Perhaps we've run into each other at Smith and Noble."

"No, that isn't it. I'm here as a guest of one of their clients. I live in New Jersey."

With her fear of discovery allayed, Elizabeth took a less direct route to extricate herself from the conversation. "Perhaps it was college?"

He brightened. "Cornell?"

"I'm afraid not." She managed just the right amount of regret. "Safford Hill."

"Well, I guess I should let you get back to your friends."

"Merry Christmas."

"Yeah, to you, too."

It was ridiculous, but she couldn't help feeling he'd given her a present. He'd let her see, without any of the danger or consequence, what it would be like to have to face someone from her past. Perhaps now the corner of her mind that refused to allow her to put the past to rest would finally loosen its hold on her psyche.

And maybe, if she just moved her arms up and down fast enough, she would lift off and fly across the room.

Why try to escape it? Her homegrown paranoia over being discovered was going to last as long as there were people who would be hurt if she was ever found out. She would do whatever it took, for however long it took, to protect her grandmother and George Benson. She owed them that. And so much more.

A whiff of cigar smoke reminded her she still had clients she hadn't greeted. She scanned the room and saw her assistant, Joyce Broderick, signaling to her. Elizabeth threaded her way through the partygoers to the tall, red-haired woman.

"Jeremy is looking for you." Joyce grabbed a glass of wine from a passing waiter and handed it to Elizabeth. "It seems Amado Montoya decided to grace us with his presence after all. I thought you should be prepared before you meet him."

There had been much speculation whether or not Smith & Nobles's newest client would make an appearance at the party. He was as noted for his reclusiveness as he was his wine and had hired the agency without going through the usual competitive process that pitted advertising companies against each other. As was to be expected, only the top people had been called in to help design the campaign. Neither she nor any of the other women at the agency happened to be among them.

Elizabeth took a sip of wine. "This is wonderful."

"The judges at three of last year's top competitions thought so, too. They gave it two gold medals and one silver."

"I'm impressed—and surprised. Serving it tonight was a stroke of genius."

"Thank you."

"This was your doing?"

Joyce held up her hand as if to ward off the praise about to be heaped on her. "It was nothing—merely a suggestion to the proper person. He took it from there."

"Keep it up and you'll find yourself working for one of those fine gentlemen on the top floor."

"Is that a threat?"

"Merely an observation." Elizabeth took another sip of wine and let it linger a moment on her tongue, seeking specific tastes and sensations that, as usual, eluded her. Her one foray into the world of wine tasting had been a disaster—after three months the instructor had pronounced her palate the most ineducable he'd ever encountered. She had a strong suspicion it was that she just didn't care whether a wine had a tutti-frutti aroma or tasted as if it had a bit of muscle. If she liked it, she drank it; if she didn't, it went down the drain.

Elizabeth nodded good-bye to Joyce, put her glass on a table, and practiced her smile on those she passed as she made her way over to Jeremy Noble.

He held his arm out in welcome. "Elizabeth, there's someone I'd like you to meet." He turned to the man beside him. "Amado Montoya, this is Elizabeth Preston, one of Smith and Noble's up-and-coming account executives." There was a bright energy to his speech that made it seem as though he were introducing a star circus performer.

She extended her hand. "Mr. Montoya, I've heard such wonderful things about you. I'm so glad we've finally had this opportunity to meet."

"Please, it's Amado."

"And I prefer Elizabeth." She was amused at the difference between the mental image she had created of Amado Montoya and the actual man. Somehow she'd gotten the idea he would be a little rough around the edges, as if he'd spent his life working fields of grapes and sequestered in caves filled with oak casks. The reality was a genteel-looking man who wore his tuxedo as comfortably as a farmer his overalls. She knew from office gossip he was fifty-eight; he could have passed for forty.

Jeremy beamed, bestowing a million-dollar smile on them both—which was several million shy of the amount he expected the agency would make from the account over the next five years. "Amado is here for the weekend, Elizabeth. He keeps an apartment in the city."

Elizabeth searched for something to incorporate Jeremy's awkward lead-in. "That must make your life a lot easier than staying in a hotel when you come here on business."

"Actually, I spend as little time as possible away from the winery," Amado Montoya answered. "But with the number of meetings Jeremy has scheduled for me to attend, I can see that is about to change."

"Having a client involved in the campaign can be . . . beneficial," Elizabeth said. Actually, it was a royal pain in the ass. Few businessmen understood the ins and outs of advertising. Almost always it was their insistent suggestions that would turn a campaign sour, and it was without exception the agency that took the blame. Even if the client owned up to the mistake, it was, "You should have stopped me. You're the professionals." Thank God she hadn't been asked to work on the Montoya account. Early reports had it that he was not the easiest client the company had ever had. Jeremy would see that heads rolled if anything happened that made them lose the account.

The man who'd been hired to oversee the entertainment for the evening came up to Jeremy and touched his elbow discreetly. Jeremy listened a moment and then, with a frown, excused himself. "I apologize, Amado, Elizabeth. I won't be gone long."

"Is he always so . . . how should I say this? . . . high strung at parties?" Amado asked when Jeremy had gone.

"I've never seen him like this before. Usually he's a rock." She glanced after Jeremy. "Solid, down to earth—" And as hardheaded as they come, she could have added.

"I'm glad. I was beginning to wonder about my decision to go with Smith and Noble."

Elizabeth met his gaze and gave him a slow smile. "You knew everything there was to know about the agency, and Jeremy Noble, before you ever picked up the phone."

He returned her smile, not the least nonplussed by her accusation. "Touché."

"Are you spending Christmas in the city?" she asked.

He nodded. "My youngest daughter and her children are here. And you?"

"Yes, I'll be here."

"Then you have family in San Francisco, also?"

She shook her head. "My parents died in a car accident when I was very young." She'd told the half-lie so many times, it seemed more real than the truth.

"I'm sorry."

She was never quite sure how to respond to the statement. "I'm sorry, too," seemed a little maudlin. And to thank someone for being sorry was not only inappropriate, it was fraudulent. Her parents, thanks to several well-trained sharpshooters employed by the state of California, had died as they had lived. If there had been a funeral, there would have been more joy than sorrow.

"It must be wonderful to have your grandchildren with you at Christmas. How old are they?"

"Six and ten. Both girls—the spitting image of their mother. Regretfully, I don't get to see them as often as I'd like. They are away at school most of the year."

"That's a wonderful age."

"Which one?"

"Pardon me?" She wasn't giving the conversation her full attention, a dangerous thing with a man like Amado Montoya, who for some reason wasn't content with the normal, inane chatter expected at a party.

"Which age were you referring to? Six or ten?"

"It was an observation," she said. And then, with uncharacteristic candor when it came to talking about her past, she added, "Personally, at the time, neither age held any special appeal for me."

"And looking back?"

Her sixth Christmas had been spent in a Volkswagen bus somewhere in Mississippi. Her tenth, in a black neighborhood in Philadelphia at a safe house. Because she was white and would have stood out if allowed to play outside with the other children, she'd been confined to her bedroom and the kitchen area in the apartment for over three months. "I'm afraid not even hindsight has improved them."

"That's unfortunate. Childhood is precious. It should be memorable."

"Oh, it was memorable."

"This must be a difficult time of year for you."

What had gotten into her? She had come perilously close to revealing a background clue that did not fit her Elizabeth Preston persona. "Not at all," she said a little too brightly. "There were more than enough good Christmases to make up for the one or two bad ones."

"I've made you uncomfortable. Please forgive me. It's just that I find it educational to hear of the family experiences of others. At times, I even find it helpful."

She was grateful when Jeremy rejoined them, making it unnecessary for her to respond. He was accompanied by one of the executives directing the Montoya account.

"Sorry to intrude, Amado," Jeremy said. "You and Frank know each other?" he added.

"Yes," Amado said, shaking the other man's hand. "Good to see you again, Frank."

Jeremy put his arm around Elizabeth's shoulders and gave her a hearty squeeze. "I can see the two of you have been hitting it off. But then I knew you would. Our Elizabeth has real potential in the advertising world. She's the pride and joy of Smith and Noble. One of our rising stars."

She'd heard the speech so often, she could mouth the words along with him. He used her, along with the three other women at the agency who had been allowed to reach the junior executive level, shoving them to the forefront whenever it suited him as proof positive Smith & Noble had a progressive attitude toward women.

Jeremy smiled expansively and gave her shoulders another squeeze before he let her go. "Now if you and Frank will excuse us, it's time Elizabeth and I did our thing."

For the past three years she'd been given the dubious honor of standing behind Jeremy as he gave out the traditional sterling-silver Christmas ornament emblazoned with S&N's logo. Two years ago when she'd suggested the privilege should be shared with some of the company's male junior executives, Jeremy had given her a blank stare and in complete innocence stated, "A man would feel strange doing something like that. The job is more suited to a woman."

She extended her hand to Amado. "It's been a pleasure."

"The pleasure was mine. I enjoyed our conversation, Elizabeth," he said. "But it was much too short. We must finish it one day."

"I'll look forward to it," she answered.

He touched her arm as she moved to leave. "Until next time," he insisted.

It was then she realized he was serious. He intended to see her again. She glanced up at Jeremy to gauge his reaction. Montoya Wines was his baby. He would not look kindly on her intrusion at any level. He seemed not to have noticed the other man's interest in her.

She took a step backward, widening the space between herself and Amado and forcing him to withdraw his hand from her arm.

"Now that you're with S and N, we're sure to run into each other again," she said. Polite enough not to offend, but certainly not encouraging. She hoped to hell it worked.

Three hours later, exhausted, a headache threatening and her feet killing her, Elizabeth opened the door to her apartment and went inside. The tiny rooms were a calm harbor after the storm of the party, a transitory comfort that would be gone in the morning.

God, how she missed Howard. Even though he'd chosen to ignore her as often as he acknowledged her, his presence had made the silence rejuvenating. With him she'd never minded the minuscule bedroom, where her king-size bed made it necessary for her to stand on the mattress to get into the closet, or a shower head so low she either became a contortionist or sat on the edge of the tub to wash her hair.

He'd been the constant male in her life, never objecting to the long or late hours she put in at a job she'd come to love.

Howard had left her that past May, almost ten years to the day the two of them had found each other. It was the sun that had awakened her that morning. Confused that he'd let her sleep so late, she'd put her hand out to touch him where he lay curled up on the pillow beside her. For the first time there had been no grumpy response.

She'd railed and told him he'd had no right to leave without telling her good-bye, but it made no more difference than it had when she was ten years old and her parents had left her at her grandmother's house.

If she could have foreseen the giant hole seven pounds of mangy fur and bad temperament would leave in her heart when it was gone, she might have left Howard in the alley behind the dorm where she'd found him digging in a garbage can.

Her grandmother would understand her grief over a cat. They were alike that way. And in so many other ways. Elizabeth would never understand how she and her grandmother could have so much in common and be as different as they were from their connecting link, Elizabeth's mother.

Without turning on the light, she removed her elegant gown, which had lasted longer than Cinderella's but had somehow managed to escape Prince Charming's notice, tossed it over a chair, and crawled into her unmade bed. A sense of accomplishment came over her as she drifted off to sleep. Even if the threat of discovery had only been a practice run, she'd handled herself okay. She had more confidence now. Maybe she'd stop worrying about everything so much.

2

Elizabeth took Christmas week off to drive up the coast to the Oregon border, staying at bed-and-breakfast inns along the way, stopping to walk through redwood groves and along deserted beaches.

She loved the northern California coast. It was about as far as you could get from Farmingham, Kansas, and yet somehow it still reminded her of the only real home she'd ever known, of the good times she'd had there with her grandmother. Time and distance had given her what she couldn't manage when she'd first left home—the ability to remember the good times over the bad. She could concentrate on the love that had gone into the chocolate-chip cookies her grandmother had baked, not on the taunting cruelty of the children who had refused her offer to share them at lunchtime.

Although they never discussed it, Elizabeth and her grandmother were poles apart on their views of Farmingham. As a lifelong resident of the community, Alice had experienced and been the recipient of all that was good about living in a small town, while Elizabeth had known only the bad. The town had rallied around Alice when she'd lost her husband and then, later, when she'd lost the farm. Elizabeth had come to them an outsider, a child of parents who were as alien to the beliefs and ideals of the community as a dyed-in-the-wool liberal or hard-line communist. A child like that had to be watched, especially around other children. You couldn't be too careful with tender young minds and negative influences. On the surface Jennifer Cavanaugh might seem the sweetest little girl God ever put on earth, but there was no getting around how she'd spent her first ten years, the kind of people she'd been exposed to, the things she must have seen. It was bound to have an effect, and there was no telling when or how it might come out. All in all, it was better to be safe than sorry.

Thoughts of her childhood were pushed to the back of her mind the next morning, when Elizabeth was forced to focus all of her attention on the hairpin turns of the coast highway. When she reached a straight stretch and could relax, she decided it was time she checked out the kittens at the SPCA. She'd never find another cat like Howard, but that didn't matter—at least she would be doing something positive for a change. The thought made her laugh out loud. Who in their right mind would want another cat like Howard?

*   *   *

On Monday Elizabeth was actually feeling good about being back at work when she got off the elevator and ran into Jeremy Noble. "Good morning," she told him. "I hope your weekend was as good as mine."

"We have to talk," he said. "Meet me in my office in five minutes." He headed down the hall to the stairwell.

Joyce Broderick saw Elizabeth and moved to intercept her. "Jeremy has been going crazy waiting for you to get here."

Elizabeth heard uncharacteristic concern in her assistant's voice. "Do you know why?"

"Rumor has it that Montoya is giving him some kind of trouble."

"So what has that got to do with me?" She stopped by her secretary's desk to pick up the morning's phone messages.

The young woman handed Elizabeth several notes and added, "Mr. Noble is looking—"

"So I hear," Elizabeth said. She flipped through the list of people who had called. There was nothing that couldn't wait.

Joyce took Elizabeth's coat and hung it up in the closet. "How was the trip?"

"Fantastic. I can't wait to go again."

"Next time you decide to take off, could it be when I'm on vacation, too? It's hell around here without you."

Elizabeth picked up her mail and immediately tossed it back on her desk. "Okay, if you need me, I'll be in Jeremy's office. But don't call unless it's an emergency."

"Are you sure?"

An appreciative grin appeared. "Don't tempt me."

When she arrived at Jeremy's office, the secretary gave her a long-suffering look. "Go right in, Ms. Preston. He's expecting you."

Elizabeth tapped lightly on the office door before opening it. "You wanted to see me?" she asked.

Jeremy was sitting behind his massive mahogany desk. He dipped his head to see her above his half glasses. Awkward seconds passed while he studied her. "Get in here," he finally said. "And shut the door behind you."

When she'd first gone to work for Smith & Noble, Jeremy's severe mood swings and management style had all but unhinged her. Since then she'd learned to wait out his tirade before attempting to take care of the crisis that had caused it. She crossed the room and sat down.

He tossed his glasses on top of his desk and glared at her. "What in the hell did you say to Amado Montoya?"

Elizabeth was taken off guard by the attack. "Party conversation—nothing more."

"Don't give me that crap."

"Why don't you just cut to the chase and tell me what this is all about?"

"It seems he wants you put in charge of the campaign for Montoya wines. Not included, mind you, but in charge."

"That doesn't make sense."

"Cut the innocent act, Elizabeth. What did you say that so fuckin' impressed him?"

She searched for details of the two-week-old conversation. "We talked about families."

He leaned forward. "Whose?"

"His . . . mine . . . families in general. What difference does it make?"

"And while you were doing this talking, I suppose you managed to flash a little tit just to make sure you had his undivided attention?"

She came up out of the chair and planted her fists on his desk. "Back off, Jeremy. You know damn well that's not my style. Besides, if I'd wanted to be a part of the Montoya account, I would have said something when it first came in. Why would I change my mind now?"

"Because Montoya would be one big fuckin' feather in your cap if you were thinking about leaving."

"You know as well as I do that there isn't an advertising agency here or in New York that wouldn't hire me on a phone call. I don't need the Montoya account any more than I need a letter of recommendation from you. Now would you like to apologize, or do I—"

"It has to be your body he's after," he said, as much to himself as to her. "Nothing else makes sense. He couldn't be impressed with your work. As far as anyone outside the business knows, you've never handled anything of any importance."

Something inside her snapped. "That's it, Jeremy. I'm out of here."

"I'm not finished with you yet."

"Let me see if I can make this simple enough even you can understand—I quit."

"You can't."

"Watch me."

He got up and came around his desk. "Look, if it was something I said—"

"I'm sick to death of your stupid, petty accusations." She headed toward the door.

"That's not fair. You never complained before."

His perverse logic stopped her. She pressed the palm of her hand to her forehead. "Jesus, that almost makes sense."

"If someone is doing something that bothers you," he went on, "you have to tell them about it. How else are they supposed to know?"

She sat down. Could she really be giving in this easily? Where was the righteous indignation that had put fire in her veins only seconds ago?

"Think about it. It's not only logical that I suspected you were up to something, it's reasonable. You've been in the game too long to start questioning the rules now."

"And after all this time, you should know me better than to accuse me of something like this."

"Where did this sudden streak of naiveté come from? For cryin' out loud, Elizabeth, I've been your mentor. Why wouldn't I think you had adopted some of my characteristics?"

She'd lost too much ground to make her point. Besides, she didn't really want to quit. Her reaction had been as knee-jerk as his. "Can we get on with this? I have work to do."

He went to his desk and picked up the file he'd been reading when she entered. "This is yours now, but I expect to be involved every step of the way."

"I told you I don't want anything to do with the Montoya account."

"And I don't want you to have it. The work load is going to be killing, and if something does go wrong, there's not going to be anyone to share the blame. You're going to be hanging out there all by yourself." He picked up his glasses and twirled them around nervously. "But it's out of my hands. I'm not pulling the strings on this, Montoya is."

She took the folder from his outstretched hand. "Tell me something, Jeremy. Are you having as much fun with this business as you seem to be?"

"It's my life's blood. I'd give up my family before I'd give up this agency."

"Do your wife and kids know that?"

"If they don't, they suspect."

"I hope I never—"

"Don't throw stones, Elizabeth. You may try to deny it, but we were cut from the same cloth."

It was a sobering thought. "I'll get on this as soon as I can."

She was halfway out the door when he said, "Next time you're feeling put upon, perhaps you should remember it's when you insist on making waves that your boat gets swamped and you drown."

"Is that why you made sure I knew how to swim before you hired me?"

A half smile pulled at the corner of his mouth. "When are you going to get it through that head of yours that being the boss entitles me to have the last word?"

She opened the door and cast a quick look backward before stepping through. "When you make me vice president."

Elizabeth canceled her trip to the SPCA and stayed in her office through lunch to try to catch up on the paperwork that had accumulated in her absence. Despite the circumstances and a real fear about being in over her head, she couldn't deny a growing sense of excitement over the prospect of taking on her first major client.

She was finally going to get the chance to prove herself. So what if it was in the most public way conceivable? Wasn't this what she'd been insisting she wanted? What was it her grandmother had said when she went to her with Mr. Benson's idea that Jennifer Cavanaugh trade places with Elizabeth Preston? *Time to put up or shut up, Jenny girl.*

By four o'clock, after a frustrating hour in the copywriting department and another with the art director, she acknowledged she wasn't going to get through the backlog of work facing her that day. She punched the intercom. "Would you see if Amado Montoya is in his office," she said to her secretary. "The number's in the file I left on your desk."

Several minutes later Amado was on the line. "Elizabeth, how nice to hear from you."

On the possibility he'd had second thoughts, she decided to offer him an easy out. "Jeremy tells me that you'd like my input on the campaign."

"I want more than your input. I thought I made it plain to Jeremy you were to take over."

"Are you aware that my coming on board this late could put the campaign back weeks, maybe even months?"

"Am I to assume that means you do not intend to go with the work that has already been done?"

"I don't know. To be honest, I haven't had a chance to go over everything yet. What I can tell you is that I believe creative work is signature work. Under normal circumstances I wouldn't want to take over someone else's idea any more than a reputable artist would want to try to finish a half-painted van Gogh."

"I'm pleased to hear that, even though I think your reasoning is based more in diplomacy than artistic integrity."

Obviously he was not happy with the preliminary report he'd been given. Everything was beginning to fall into place. Now she understood why Jeremy had agreed to go along with Amado's request instead of simply telling him she wasn't in a position to take on the responsibility of such a large account. Still, she decided to make one last effort to get him to change his mind. "Are you absolutely certain this is the way you want to go? The cost of tossing out all the work that's already been done is going to be steep."

"It doesn't matter."

"I'm flattered that you have so much confidence in me." It was the *why* she couldn't figure. "As soon as I can get some other things out of the way, I'll be able to give the project my full attention." She was taking a risk in making him wait, but she wanted him to know she felt loyalty to her clients no matter what position they held at the agency.

"And when would that be?"

"The middle of the month." She was being wildly optimistic.

"But that's only two weeks. I'd anticipated it would take much longer for you to clear your schedule."

Good grief, she just might end up liking him. "My schedule is never clear—just more or less full."

"Then maybe we should set up our initial meeting now?"

She flipped through her calendar. "How does the nineteenth sound?"

"Fine. What time should I expect you?"

"I'm afraid I've given you the wrong impression. I was setting something up for you to come here."

"Then the mistake is mine. I assumed you would want to see the winery before you started work."

"I do, but later."

"Why not now?"

She could give him a hundred reasons why not, the most compelling of which would be that she could ill afford the four hours' travel time it would take to get to St. Helena and back again. Meeting with him at the winery would shoot an entire day. She looked at her calendar again. "If I'm going to go there, it will have to be sometime near the end of the month—maybe the twenty-fifth or twenty-sixth."

"I have a better idea. Why don't you come here this weekend? I'm having a small party on Saturday. You'll have a chance to meet some of the other growers and perhaps pick up a few ideas at the same time."

"I don't—" She stopped. He was right about picking up ideas, and with the exception of meeting his friends, what he was suggesting was something she would have to do eventually anyway. The more she learned about a client and the client's product, the better the campaign. For her, inspiration didn't come from a lightning bolt, it came in slow, methodical stages, earned by immersing herself in the work. "Thank you," she said. "The party sounds like a wonderful opportunity to begin educating myself. I would love to come."

"Don't worry about where you will stay. I have a guest cottage on the grounds. It will be available for you whenever you come here on business."

"That isn't necessary."

"I know it isn't necessary," he said. "But it is the most practical. I live on a narrow, winding mountain road several miles from St. Helena. If you stay in town, you will spend half of your time traveling back and forth."

She couldn't argue with his logic, and she didn't blame him for his aggressiveness. After years of struggle to gain a place in the elite world of the wine connoisseur, the decision to mass-market Montoya Wines must have been a difficult one for him to make. While courting the masses, he could easily lose the position he had fought so hard to gain. Her challenge was to see that didn't happen. She didn't believe for a second that he was as patient as he claimed about getting started. "I'll be there Saturday morning."

"I'm pleased that we will be seeing each other again so soon."

Elizabeth was smiling when she hung up. For a man who had lived his entire life in California, Amado Montoya was far more old world than new. He was undoubtedly the kind of man who was put off when a woman opened her own door, and personally offended if she said "fuck."

She was going to have to watch herself around him.

So much for spending her weekend playing with a new kitten. Perhaps next week there would be time. If not, surely the week after.

3

Amado Montoya stood on the hillside in the midst of vines that were little more than gnarled stumps with outstretched arms. They had been stripped of their summer splendor by skillful pruners, men who listened to what each vine had to tell them, ignoring the distractions of red-shouldered hawks circling in a brilliant winter sky or a fog so cold it ate through the warmest wool.

Where the canes grew thicker than a man's thumb and trailed ten feet or farther on the ground, the vine said more buds must be left this year. Where the canes were plentiful but thin and spindly, the vine said too many buds had remained the year before, the pruning must be harsher. Canes that had grown in the shade were flat; those that had found the sun were round.

Amado's gaze swept the valley, noting where remnants of fog clung to vineyards and where it had burned away. Such things contributed to the microclimates that had helped to make the region famous. Unlike their European counterparts, the growers in California believed it was the climate, not the soil, that produced the ultimate wine grape. Amado had seen it happen over and over again on his own land. The same types of vines planted within yards of each other would produce grapes so different that one would bring medals in competition while the other made a wine that was average at best.

A man only had to listen.

Amado had learned this from his father, Domingo, who had believed the old Spanish saying that the best fertilizer for any crop was the owner's footprints. Domingo had been the fourth generation of Montoyas to grow grapes on the hillside where Amado now stood, and when fortune had smiled on him, he had been the fourth generation to make wine from those grapes.

Prohibition and then the Depression had almost ended the Montoya legacy, but Domingo had held on, doing whatever he could, selling some of his grapes to Italian families to make their allotted two hundred gallons of wine each year, some for juice and some for sacramental wines. When things were at their worst, three of the vineyards had been turned into orchards. Bitter, heartbreaking work it was to tear out the vines, but Domingo had done whatever was necessary to hold on to the land, for it was the land that had been entrusted to him by his father, not the vines. He was the caretaker, no more. For only his lifetime was the land his to love and care for. Then it was to be passed on to his own son.

But Amado had broken the five-generation-long chain. God had not seen fit to bless him with a son. Instead he and Sophia had been given two daughters, Felicia and Elana. They were beautiful and intelligent and, for a time, had been eager to follow their father into the fields each day.

Had they stayed with him, either could have taken the place of the son he'd been denied. But the joyful Sophia whom Amado had met in Spain when he was touring vineyards had become sorrowful in her adopted land. Nothing Amado did could keep her from slipping into a depression so deep she had come close to ending her own life.

The sleeping pills she'd taken in her loneliness for her homeland had finally convinced Amado he had to let her go. At the time he'd been so frightened, he'd been willing to agree to anything, to give her anything, including his daughters, to protect her from herself. He'd had no way of knowing the daughters he'd nurtured and loved would be taken from him permanently.

Divorce was out of the question, as was a formal separation agreement. They had simply parted, giving loud voice to the lie that it was only temporary. Each summer Sophia sent the girls to California, but by the time they had begun to feel at ease with their father and his home, it was time for them to return to Spain. It always seemed they had hardly arrived before they were packing to leave again. There was never enough time to teach them about the land or their heritage.

One day, as Amado was testing the grapes for their sweetness and thinking how he would pass the skill on to his daughters, he tried to remember how old he had been when his father had taught him. But as in all things he had learned about taking care of the vines and making wine, there had been no set moment for teaching. His knowledge and skill had come day by day, hour by hour, from watching, from listening, from smelling and feeling. He knew what it was to experience joy as the buds that would later be grapes opened to the beckoning call of spring, and he knew the despair that came when those buds were turned black from a late frost. He knew these things because he had been there and felt them, not because he had been told.

With a heavy heart, he'd come to realize that the things he knew were not things that could be taught in a summer; they needed all the seasons. By then it was too late. The time for his daughters to learn their love of the land was already past.

When they were old enough, both of the girls chose to go to college in California. For a brief shining moment, Amado had believed he'd been given a second chance—until they'd arrived and made it clear they were not running to, but away from. They were ready to burst free of the binding Catholic cocoon their mother had spun around them, and unwittingly, he provided the means.

Once they tasted freedom, they never looked back. Ironically, Sophia blamed Amado for taking them from her. Her bitterness became her sustenance. She was ancient at forty and incapacitated with mysterious ailments by forty-five. Her illness left her unable to travel to see her grandchildren born or, as they grew, to allow them more than a brief visit to see her. And then, two months shy of her fiftieth birthday, she had taken too many pills again. Only this time no one had been there to rush her to the hospital. Felicia, who'd been there for a visit, had not come back from the party she'd attended that night as early as she'd promised. By the time she did arrive, it was too late.

By church law, her death had freed Amado. But her passing made little difference in his life. He continued to live the way he had for almost the entire length of his marriage: alone.

Amado loved his daughters, but he didn't try to fool himself about the kind of women they were. Unless he succeeded with his plan to make Montoya table wines as well known as Gallo, when he died the land and the winery would be sold to the highest bidder.

If, in the ten or twenty years he had left to him, he could make owning the winery not only a financial but a social asset, he had a chance with his daughter Elana. She had climbed as high as she could in San Francisco society without more power or wealth, and it galled her that she could acquire neither as the appendage of her mercantile husband, Edgar Sullivan. Amado had convinced himself that if he could get her to take over the winery to achieve her own ends, she would never sell. Nor would she allow inattention to destroy something that would eventually belong to her children. Surely if his daughter was forced to operate the winery and oversee the vineyards, eventually she would grow to love the land and understand her heritage. In this slim possibility, this last hope, Amado was investing everything.

Felicia could not be had so easily. She had been force-fed her mother's bitterness. After graduating from Stanford, she'd stepped directly onto the corporate ladder at Chase Manhattan Bank. Within a year she had become more "New York" than the natives Amado had met in his own travels. She now considered anything Californian hopelessly second rate, including the wine. The few times she'd visited in the past five years for holidays and family celebrations had been painful experiences for them all, even more so after Sophia's death.

Amado's gaze swept the horizon, settling on the small section of land owned by the Logan family. For three generations the Montoyas had coveted and tried to buy those most precious acres, almost succeeding during the Depression when the Logan family fortune had fallen on even harder times than most. Harold Logan had saved his farm by selling a twenty-year option on future harvests to a San Francisco investor who wanted to get into the business of making wine. With the Logan grapes, the new winery eventually became one of the best in the valley.

For the past ten years the Logan harvest had belonged to Montoya Wines. But even more important than the grapes was the man who turned them into wine, Michael Logan, a man Amado believed to be the finest wine master in California—the man Amado would give five years of his life to call his son.

In the distance a crow cawed before taking flight. Somewhere in the valley a dog began to howl in response to a siren. And then another sound came to Amado. Someone on the hill above him was calling his name. He brought his hand up to shield his eyes from the brilliant winter sun. Although the figure was backlit, putting features in shadow, Amado saw a leanness and grace of movement that told him he was looking at a woman.

"I'm early," Elizabeth announced as she approached him. "I hope you don't mind."

He'd been so caught up in indulgent reminiscences, he'd forgotten for the moment that she was coming. "I apologize for not being at the office to meet you. I assume someone told you how to find the house?"

"A woman I ran into at the winery drew me a map. I thought the traffic out of San Francisco would hold me up, but it turned out there wasn't any." She came up to him, tugged off an expensive leather glove, and held out her hand. "So here I am."

He was startled at the change in her appearance. Had they passed each other on a busy street, he doubted he would have recognized her. Gone was the elegant creature seemingly born to drawing rooms and designer gowns. The woman before him, dressed in faded jeans and a heavy, oversize sweater, looked as if she'd never set eyes on a city bigger than Santa Rosa. "It's a pleasure to see you again." He was as taken aback by the firmness of her handshake as he had been at the Christmas party.

She looked around her. "I guess it's only appropriate that the nectar of the gods be produced in a place like this." When she looked back at him again, she had a mischievous twinkle in her eyes. "After the week I just put in, I was more than a little tempted when I saw that sign you have out front."

"Sign?"

"The one for pruners. I can't imagine a more beautiful or peaceful place to work." She let out a sigh. "But then I suppose you're looking for skilled workers. All I have to offer is enthusiasm."

"That sign isn't for us." With his mind still steeped in the melancholy of his earlier thoughts, he unwittingly took offense at her light-hearted banter. What had attracted him to Elizabeth Preston was her single-mindedness when it came to her career. His sources had told him she was a woman willing to do whatever it took to succeed in a man's world, not someone whose level of sophistication and dedication changed with her clothing. "It's the winery across the road that's doing the hiring. However, I don't think it's enthusiasm they're looking for. To do the job correctly takes a great deal of skill." He saw that he had her attention. At least she wasn't slow. "Are you always this, uh, exuberant in the morning?" he added.

She reacted to his coolness by perceptively withdrawing herself from him, giving him a quick smile that was professional and impersonal. "I apologize. I have a tendency to get carried away when I'm starting a new project, especially if it's as challenging and exciting as this one promises to be."

It was as if the fog had returned to block out the sun. Amado felt the loss in the pit of his stomach. He was confused and angry. What in God's name had prompted his churlish remark? Since when had élan precluded competence? "No, it is I who am sorry. I have this regrettable tendency to scowl and to suspect anyone who isn't scowling. Please forgive my—"

"I'll tell you what. Instead of falling all over ourselves to see who can apologize first and best, why don't we just start over?"

He would do whatever she wanted to see the spark return to her eyes. "All right," he told her. "I yield to your enthusiasm. You can start on the vines next to the road. There's an extra pair of shears in the barn." At her surprised laughter, an unexpected, intense swell of pleasure washed over him.

"I'm tempted to give it a try, but since we have so little time as it is, we probably should get started on the real reason for my being here."

"You're not staying the weekend?"

"Ten weekends wouldn't be enough for what I have to do. But for now, before I even begin thinking about the campaign, I want to know as much as you can teach me about wine and the wine business."

"That's a tall order, Ms. Preston." This time he worked harder to hide his annoyance. There were men who had spent their entire lives learning what she wanted to know in her ten weekends, but it would be counterproductive to belabor the point. "I'll do what I can," he said instead. "There are also many books I can loan you."

"I appreciate the offer, but what I want to learn from you, I can't get from books. I'm here to find out what makes Montoya different from all the other wineries in the Napa Valley, but I also need to know what makes it the same. I have to know what it is you really want from this campaign, and whether or not you have a sense of the marketplace that I can work with, or if I'm going to have to become the teacher."

He gave her a slight bow. "Shall we go up to the house and get started? I'll have Consuela fix coffee."

"If you don't mind, I'd just as soon we skipped the coffee and that you let me tag along with you while you do whatever it is you would be doing if I weren't here." She looked around. "What were you doing before I came?"

He wondered what she would say if he told her the mornings he spent in the fields were the only times he felt truly alive anymore. Here he could feel a continuity coursing through the vines and could make himself believe the chain of Montoya ownership was too strong to be broken. He gave Elizabeth a part of the truth, the part that was easily spoken. "I came to check the pruning skill of a man I hired last week."

"And?"

"He has a good ear."

"You mean he listens to the vine before he cuts."

Several seconds passed before he replied, "I see you've already started your homework."

"The research department at Smith and Noble is the best in the country. I look out for them, they look out for me. What's next?"

"The winery. We received a shipment of oak barrels from a new supplier yesterday, and I want to look at them before they are filled." He motioned her toward the house. "We'll take the truck." He waited for her to proceed him up the hill. When she didn't move he asked, "Is something wrong?"

"I appear to be stuck."

"I should have warned you. After a heavy rain, the ground can be like quicksand."

In her effort to free herself, she lost her balance and grabbed a gnarled stump to steady herself. "Why am I the only one in this predicament?"

"I know where to stand." He bent down in front of

her, took hold of one ankle and then the other, and freed her from the mud. "Now the trick is to keep moving."

"That I can do." With long strides, she headed back up the hill.

Amado waited a moment before following, taking more pleasure than he cared to admit in watching the way she moved as she walked away from him. A quick, private smile flashed across his lips. It had been a long time since he'd let himself indulge in the simple pleasure that watching a beautiful woman could afford.

It was almost midnight before Elizabeth and Amado parted company for the day. After the party he'd walked her to the cottage, told her good night, and said something about seeing her the next morning. She leaned against the elaborately carved door and uttered a quick prayer of thanks that the day was over and there was no need for her to be upright any longer. Pain shot through her arches. She let out a groan as she stepped out of her black patent-leather heels.

Amado Montoya had the restless energy of a bear two hours out of hibernation. Every time she'd stopped to take notes that day, she'd looked up to discover he had moved on to something else. The physical setup of the winery was much larger than she had imagined, and by the end of the day she'd been worn out from chasing him.

The showroom was the focus of the operation, and while it had been enlarged and modernized two years earlier, Amado had seen to it that the building retained the charm and warmth of an old Spanish villa. Even in the middle of winter people were lined up to take the guided tour.

After being introduced to what at times seemed like an endless stream of employees, Elizabeth did some mental calculations and concluded Amado's payroll was probably as large as, if not larger than, Smith & Noble's.

At the small gathering Amado had arranged in her honor that night, he'd abandoned the business persona and again become the urbane, deliberate person she'd met at the Smith & Noble Christmas party. She wondered which man would be the one to judge and respond to her work. The same campaign would not appeal to both.

Ideas had begun to form the minute she saw Amado in his fields, some so powerful and compelling that she had to remind herself to pay attention to what was going on around her. At every turn her mind had taken off in a new direction.

This was the exciting time, where the rush of ideas kept her on a constant high. With a little luck there would be an afterglow that would see her through the long months of grinding work ahead.

She glanced at her watch as she moved across the thick Persian carpet that covered the living room floor. Twenty hours had gone by since she'd crawled out of bed, and although she was more than ready to crawl back in, she decided to take a couple of minutes to enjoy the fire that had been built in her absence. She opened the glass doors and sat down on the wing chair beside the fireplace to let the heat envelop her while the flames bathed the Victorian room in a soft, welcoming light.

The "cottage" Amado had referred to was in reality the three-bedroom house he had lived in as a child. It was currently maintained and used exclusively for guests, an extravagance that was difficult for Elizabeth to fathom.

When she'd made a comment to Amado that she liked that he'd kept the old house rather than tearing it down, he'd laughed and told her it was a family tradition. There was a third house on the property—his great-grandparents'. The current wine master for Montoya Wines, a man Amado told her that he considered more friend than employee, lived there.

Elizabeth had met wealthy people through her job, but she'd never met anyone on Amado Montoya's level. Yet he had seemed as comfortable and unassuming with the woman who cleaned the winery showroom as he had with the guests he'd invited to his home that night.

Elizabeth stared into the fire as she pulled the backs from her earrings and massaged her earlobes with her thumb and forefinger. What she needed was a hot bath, bed, and three or four chapters of the book she'd brought along to distract her from the stimulation of all she'd seen and heard that day. Sometimes the trick worked; more often it didn't. Wearily she pushed herself up and headed for the stairs.

A half hour later she was sitting beside the fireplace again, her book propped open on her lap. A soft knocking on the front door drew her attention, and she looked up, glad she hadn't been reading Poe. The summons seemed purposely uninsistent, giving her the option to answer or not.

It was Amado. He was still dressed in his dinner jacket; his only concession to the late hour was his missing tie. "Is something wrong?" she asked.

"I saw your light and assumed you were still up working. But I can see that I was wrong, so I will say good night and we can talk in the morning."

"I work in my bathrobe because it's more comfortable." She told herself the small lie was to put him at ease and had nothing to do with her reluctance to see him go. "What is it you wanted to tell me?"

"There is a meeting tomorrow—"

"Please come in." She burrowed deeper into the thick terry cloth. "It's cold enough out there to freeze the . . . uh, never mind." He moved inside, but only far enough for her to get the door closed behind him. "Now what were you saying about a meeting?"

"It's a breakfast, actually. I wasn't going to go, but Consuela suggested you might find it useful. Michael usually attends, but he isn't here."

"Michael?"

"I'm sorry. Michael Logan is my chief wine master. The outside world believes I am the one who made Montoya Wines what it is today, but in reality the credit belongs to Michael. Had he not been tied up with other matters, you would have met him earlier."

Elizabeth noted the unmistakable pride in Amado's voice. "What time would you like me to be ready?"

"Seven-thirty—it is a half-hour drive from here." He started to leave.

On impulse she stopped him. "There's something I've been meaning to ask you ever since I was told you wanted me to take over the account. I have a feeling the answer will dictate the direction I go with the campaign."

"You have piqued my curiosity. But then you've been doing that all day." He shoved his hands in his pockets. "Would you like a cup of coffee? I'll call and have some sent over."

"That's not necessary. I have yet to make a soufflé that didn't fall, but I can handle coffee."

He followed her into the compact kitchen, gathering the mugs, cream, and sugar while she measured the water and coffee and plugged in the machine. When she was finished she joined him at the table.

"Now then," he said. "I believe you had something you wanted to ask me."

There were a dozen ways she could approach the subject. She opted for the most direct. "Why me?"

He leaned back in his chair, and his jacket fell open. He was a spare man, his waist narrow, his stomach flat. "I was wondering when you would get around to asking me that."

"And?"

"I was also wondering how I would answer." He shoved his hands in his pockets. "It's difficult for me to put feelings into words. I just knew when I met you at the Christmas party that you would understand what I'm trying to do with Montoya Wines and why. That was important to me."

"Important enough to risk going with an account executive who has yet to handle an account of this size?"

"You should have been given more important clients a long time ago. You were the best copywriter Smith and Noble has ever had."

Elizabeth got up to pour the coffee. "If you listen to everything my assistant tells you—"

"Please, don't do that." He reached for his cup and held it up for her. "Modesty is an overrated, time-consuming virtue."

"All right, so you've done your homework on me. That still doesn't answer my question." She eased back onto her chair, picked up her cup, and looked at him over the rim.

"The expansion Montoya Winery is undergoing has nothing to do with profits or market share, it is about continuity and tradition. A Montoya has lived on our land in the Napa Valley for five generations. I do not want it to fall to me that I am the last."

A man like Amado did not let go of his private thoughts easily. "I take it your daughters are not interested in assuming control of the winery the way it is now?"

"They have built lives of their own. The business, the land, are of little consequence to them. I have failed to make them understand. I am hoping my efforts will entice them back."

Elizabeth wondered what it would feel like to be a part of a family with generations-old traditions. The closest she'd come to a sense of family was with her grandmother. She'd never even met her father's parents. She had no idea whether he had brothers or sisters or where he'd grown up or why he never talked about his childhood. All she knew for sure was that no one had cared enough to come forward when he died. Alice had put off the state of California as long as she could about what to do with her daughter's and son-in-law's bodies, hoping one of his relatives would appear and help pay to transport them back to Kansas. In the end Alice had decided it would be wrong to separate them and reluctantly let her daughter be buried in a grave so distant that it would see no loving care or fresh flowers.

"But back to your question." Amado tilted his mug and gazed at the steaming black liquid inside. "Jeremy Noble was willing to give the campaign his mind." He looked up and met her eyes. "I knew you would give it your heart."

4

Michael Logan walked through the cool, dark aging room, absently checking the bungs at the tops of the barrels, making sure the corks were snugly in place. They were getting ready to fine the wines, to remove the solids and suspended particles that kept the reds from showing off their color and clarity. Tests were being conducted now to determine the optimum dosage of the fining agent. The process itself would take several days to a few weeks. This particular chai, or storage room, was where they aged the best of the best premium reds, the ones that would win the blue ribbons and gold medals for Montoya Wines. Michael kept close watch on everything that happened here.

The whites were in another building, farther up the hillside. He would go there next to check the progress of a Chardonnay he'd been watching for several days, concerned about the off smell being produced in several of the barrels.

After a quick backward glance, he headed for the stairs, taking them two at a time. Lately he'd fought an excess of energy that had him feeling like a constantly coiled spring. He'd added another mile to his morning run, thinking if he started the day on the tired side, it might help with the restlessness that came over him as he made his daily rounds at the winery. But only the hours he spent in the lab, where he became lost in whatever problem needed his attention that day, were free from his gnawing sense of discontent.

Out in the sunshine again, he stopped to let his eyes adjust and saw Tony, the field manager, headed toward him.

"Have you seen Amado this morning?" Tony asked. "I need to talk to him about that new tractor salesman he sent to see me."

Pausing to run his hand across the stubble on his chin and to scratch the itching skin beneath the week-old growth, Michael was again reminded that for the life of him, he couldn't remember making the bet with Amado that he wouldn't shave for a month if the 49ers didn't make the playoffs. "He's at some breakfast with that woman from the ad agency. He told Consuela to expect them back around eleven."

Tony shoved his hands in his pockets and brought his shoulders up, fitting his jacket collar closer to his neck in a gesture meant to ward off the cold. "Rosa said she thought she saw you up on the ridge yesterday morning when she was on her way to work. I told her that it couldn't be you because you were in Petaluma, but she insisted I ask anyway."

"It was me all right. I took the back way out of town." He hoped Tony wouldn't press the point.

"Damn. I should've known not to question her. That woman's got eyes a hawk would envy." He shifted his stance and started down the walkway. Michael fell in beside him. "She said they finally sold the old Taylor place—but if you were up there, you probably knew that already."

Michael nodded. He was still trying to put reason to the disappointment he'd felt when he'd come around the corner and discovered the SOLD sign tacked to the front gate. Only then had he realized how deeply he'd let the fantasy of buying the place himself insinuate its way into his thoughts. Someday he would figure out why he never recognized how much something meant to him until it was taken away. It was a hell of a way for a man to live his life, always blind to his true feelings.

Tony bent to pick up a discarded candy wrapper and absently stuffed the piece of trash in his pocket. "The way Amado's been going after land lately, I wouldn't be surprised if he was the one who—"

Michael stopped listening. The thought that Amado had bought the Taylor place had already occurred to him. Hell, he'd lain awake half the night thinking about it, his frustration nearly consuming him. Inevitably the feeling yielded to anger, the target as logical as it was unreasonable. There was no way Amado could know Michael had been dreaming about owning that particular piece of land—or that it wasn't Montoya wine he wanted to make from the vines that grew there; it was his own.

Saying he wanted to talk to the crew he'd hired that morning to prune the north field, Tony left Michael with the promise to pass on Michael's greeting to Rosa. Instead of heading uphill to check on the Chardonnay, Michael took a minute to watch the hawk that circled overhead. It was one of those clear winter days that brought everything in to sharper focus, like putting on a pair of glasses.

Too bad he couldn't do the same thing with his relationships. How could Amado know that Michael had grown to resent the loyalty that made him put aside his own ambitions in favor of Amado's? And that the resentment had produced a guilt so powerful, it kept Michael from admitting openly how he felt and finding a way to deal with it?

As much as he would have liked to escape it, there was no way Michael could deny that everything he was, everything he hoped to be, he owed to Amado. Without the old man's support and encouragement, Michael would never have reached the position he now held.

When Harold Logan had been diagnosed with lung cancer, medical bills used up the money he had set aside to put Michael through school. Harold lasted several months longer than the money, and it haunted him to the end that he had broken the bargain he'd made with his second son—an education in exchange for his interest in the farm. Michael had known all along the farm would go to his older brother, Paul.

When Amado discovered that Michael was looking for a job instead of leaving for school that fall, he'd stepped in and offered to pay Michael's tuition if he would agree to come to work for Montoya Winery after graduation. Michael had received his master's in enology from the University of California at Davis, and within a year of his return to St. Helena, Amado had turned the operation over to him, putting his trust in the instincts of an all but unproven twenty-five-year-old kid.

How much easier it would all be if the coin hadn't flipped, if the need and dependence had stayed as lop-sided as it had been in the beginning. Instead, in the nine years Michael had worked for Montoya Wines, he had made it his own. Amado himself insisted that every award, every medal, they had won in the last half decade was a direct result of the aggressive and innovative oper-ating style Michael had brought to the winery.

Only the winery wasn't really Michael's, and it never would be.

It didn't matter that Amado needed Michael as much as Michael had ever needed him or that Michael's love of the land and the business had grown until it was the equal of Amado's. He could work for Amado, he could be treated like the son Amado had never had, he could even see the sorrow in Amado's eyes that he was not his son; none of it made any difference. In the end it all came down to family. Real family. Felicia and Elana. Never mind that neither of them gave a damn about their father or the winery.

Once, in the early years of their relationship, when Michael still fostered the dream of someday working for himself, he had naively approached Amado about the possibility of buying into Montoya Winery. After all, by Amado's own admission, he had no real hope of con-vincing Elana or Felicia to eventually take over. Michael had believed Amado would welcome knowing there was someone who cared who had a vested interest in keeping the winery out of corporate hands for at least one more generation. But the question and Amado's negative and embarrassed reply had produced the only awkward moment that had ever passed between them. Although there had been times since then when Amado seemed to be encouraging Michael to ask again, he had never said another word on the subject.

The intrusive sound of one of the loudspeakers that were planted throughout the grounds shattered the silence. "Michael Logan—please call the operator."

He fought the urge to ignore the summons and returned to the building he'd just left. Without waiting for his eyes to adjust to the darkness, he felt for the phone beside the door, punched a series of buttons, and said, "Christine—it's Logan. What's up?"

"You have a personal call on line four." She paused. "I know, I know, you'd rather I take a message, but she sounded so . . . oh, I don't know, *nervous*, I guess . . . that I didn't have the heart to make her wait."

"You're a pushover, Christine. You wouldn't last a day in the White House."

She laughed. "They wouldn't even let me through the front door." She cut him off before he had a chance to say anything more.

"This is Michael Logan," he said when the connection was made.

"Mike . . . hi," an enthusiastic, high-pitched voice answered. "This is Diane Amberdine."

He struggled to place the name or the voice.

"We met at Linda's party last weekend," she prompted. "I was wearing a blue sequined sweater. You said the color reminded you of a stream you used to fish in when you were a kid."

A vague memory surfaced. "Oh, yes, of course. You have long blond hair."

"Yes." She sounded inordinately pleased. "I'm sorry about calling you at work, but your home number wasn't listed in the phone book and—"

"That's all right. What can I do for you?"

"I know it's really late notice and all, but I was wondering if you were doing anything tonight? No, that's not the right way to do this—" She stopped and took a deep breath. "What I meant to say is that there's a movie playing in Napa that I've wanted to see for several weeks now and I'm afraid if I don't get to it soon it will be gone and I was wondering if you would like to go with me tonight?"

His first impulse was to find an excuse to get out of it. Any excuse that would let her down easy would do. But he'd been in this situation too many times to be able to fool himself that there was anything he could say that would take the sting out of a refusal. "A movie sounds like a terrific idea. What time should I pick you up . . . and where?"

There was a long pause, as if she were too stunned by his reply to immediately answer. "Uh, six-thirty? No, why don't you make it five-thirty—I'll fix us something to eat first."

"Don't do that. We can stop for something on the way. There's a new pizza place in Yountville I've been meaning to try." As much as he appreciated a simple home-cooked meal, he had consumed too many horrendous attempts at gourmet cooking to trust casual invitations. Besides, eating dinner at Diane's would make more out of the evening than he wanted. The last thing he needed was to give her the impression he was either ready or looking for a long-term relationship.

"I guess it's all settled, then."

"Except you telling me where to pick you up."

"Oh, right." She told him how to get to her apartment. "See you at five-thirty?"

"I'll be there." The thought occurred to him that if he knocked on the wrong door and a friendly, willing blonde answered, he could end up going out with the wrong woman. He resisted the impulse to ask her what she would be wearing.

An hour later Michael was on his way back to the lab when he spotted Amado's car pulling into the parking lot. He started toward him, wanting to share the good news about the barrels of Chardonnay he'd just finished testing, when he saw the door on the passenger side of the car swing open and a woman step out. He watched as she moved around the car and joined Amado. There was something disconcertingly familiar about her, something that hit him viscerally. He tried to place her but couldn't.

She could be anyone from a new distributor making an informal weekend call to someone Amado had met on one of his annual trips to Europe. Either way, Michael didn't want to be included. He didn't have time to waste socializing, and his news wasn't so important that it couldn't wait a couple of hours.

As he turned to head toward the lab again, he heard Amado call his name. Stifling a groan of frustration at being caught, he swung back around and acknowledged the greeting. The expectant look Amado sent his way ended all hope of a quick escape. Michael fixed a smile and started down the hill.

The feeling of unease increased as he drew closer. Another glance at the woman told him why. Her resemblance to Susan was startling. Not Susan as she was now, the wife of his brother, the worn-out mother of four stair-step children—but the Susan who had lived in his high school jacket, the one who had made love to him in a sleeping bag in the back of his pickup, the one who had proudly slipped the diamond chip he gave her for graduation on her finger and announced to the world that she and Michael were officially engaged.

Amado came forward. He was smiling broadly. "I did not expect you to return until tomorrow."

"There wasn't as much to do as I thought."

Placing a hand on Michael's shoulder, Amado guided him back to the car. "There is someone I want you to meet."

At first Michael tried to avoid looking in her direction, but then he found he was perversely compelled to take a closer look. He focused on the differences, spying and noting them with an almost audible sigh of relief. She was slightly taller and thinner than Susan, her breasts less full, her hips not as rounded. The thick hair that framed her angular face was a darker brown, and she had a wide, unreserved smile that was nothing like the small flirtatious one Susan used to charm strangers. Intense, questioning eyes gazed back at him, letting him know his scrutiny had not gone unobserved.

"Elizabeth Preston," Amado said, "Michael Logan."

Michael reached for her outstretched hand. When he tried to break the contract—a fraction of a second too soon—she tightened her grip. Plainly she was not someone who tolerated being given short shrift.

"Elizabeth is with Smith and Noble," Amado went on. "She came for the weekend to familiarize herself with our operation."

Michael almost laughed out loud. Elizabeth Preston might give him the creeps personally because of her uncanny resemblance to Susan, but that didn't mean he couldn't appreciate that she was a hell of a prize for opening a new account. "I wasn't aware advertising was such a hands-on business."

"It isn't always," Elizabeth told him.

"Will you be available to join us for dinner?" Amado asked. "I am sure Ms. Preston would find your thoughts about the day-to-day operation invaluable."

Michael tried to look disappointed. "I'm sorry, but I have other plans for the evening."

"Perhaps we can get together the next time I come up."

"Do you have any idea when that will be?"

"I'm afraid it will probably have to be a spur-of-the-moment trip."

He didn't have an answer.

5

Mor
he wish
woman's
some o...
"Th
on Sun...
such nice...

...had
slight...
toand...
could...
breasts...
under...

It

The telephone rang just as Elizabeth was opening the door to leave her apartment for work. Already late, she vacillated on whether to answer it or not, then dumped her briefcase and purse on the sofa and picked up the receiver.

It was Amado.

"I was afraid I had missed you," he said.

He had never called her at home before. Fleetingly she wondered how he'd gotten her number, but then she'd learned he frequently did things that seemed impossible. He had more sources than a seasoned reporter. "Another minute and you would have."

"I find that I have to come to the city today, and I was wondering . . . I thought you might like to go to dinner with me tonight. If you don't already have other plans, of course."

The invitation took her by surprise. "Do we have a meeting I forgot about?"

He rushed to reassure her. "No, my business is with someone else. I just thought if you were available, we could go over the papers I sent you last week."

The "papers" Amado had sent were the reports from the University at Davis on some wine samples Michael Logan had submitted to them for analysis. Without the covering letter from Amado, she wouldn't have understood any of it. As it was, the material was interesting but of questionable background use for the campaign. Just in case she'd missed something, she'd made a note to ask him the next time they talked why he'd sent the report.

She glanced at her watch. It took twenty minutes to get to the office, and she had a meeting in fifteen. "What time?"

"Seven?"

"Great. I'll see you then." She started to hang up, then realized he'd never been to her apartment. "Amado?"

"Yes."

"You don't know where I live."

He laughed. "A minor detail, to be sure."

She gave him her address and waited just long enough for him to repeat it before hanging up and racing out the door.

At six-thirty that night, Elizabeth was standing on the edge of her bed in her postage-stamp-size bedroom staring into her closet, at a loss for what she should wear. She had evening gowns, business suits, an assortment of Levi's jeans that went back to her college days, and not much else. Someday soon, time or no time, she was going to have to do some shopping.

She pulled out a green knit dress, examined it, and put it back when she remembered she'd already worn it—twice—on separate weekends she'd stayed at the winery.

Damn, she hated wasting energy over stupid decisions. She reached for the dress and slipped it over her head. Amado didn't care what she wore; he probably wouldn't even notice.

The downstairs bell sounded in Elizabeth's apartment at precisely seven o'clock. After buzzing Amado up, she tossed the feather duster she'd run over the flat surfaces into the kitchen cupboard, straightened the pillows on the back of the sofa, and glanced at her reflection in the window. She was startled at the woman who stared back at her. On impulse, she had decided to wear her hair down instead of caught up in her usual severe French twist. The effect was hardly the casual one she'd been seeking.

She forced the unsettling image from her mind as she went to the door in response to his knock.

"Elizabeth—" He seemed startled to see her, or at least this version of her. "How different you look."

She almost laughed. "Please, come in. If you'll give me a moment, I'll fix my hair and we can leave." It was then she noticed the single rose he held at his side. There was something disconcertingly intimate about the lone flower. She would have been more comfortable if he'd brought a dozen.

"Please don't change your hair on my account. I like it the way it is—very much."

"Thank you." She self-consciously tucked a strand behind her ear. "How did your meeting go?"

He seemed puzzled by the question.

"You said you were coming into the city for a meeting. I assumed it was business."

"Yes."

Something peculiar was going on here. She and Amado had never had trouble talking to each other before. That morning she'd had an easier time communicating with a German client through an interpreter. She tried again. "Did you have any trouble getting dinner reservations on such short notice?"

He smiled. "Such things are never a problem when you are fortunate enough to carry the same name as a winery." And then, as if only at that very moment becoming aware of the flower he had brought her, he extended his hand. "I saw this and was reminded of you."

She touched the crimson velvet petals to her nose and gave him a mischievous look as she drew in the fragrance. "But there are no thorns."

"Is that how you see yourself?"

"I think you could probably find one or two people at Smith and Noble who see me that way, too."

"It is because they are jealous of your talent and afraid of your ambition."

She laughed. It felt wonderful. "If I didn't know better, I'd think you'd been talking to my grandmother."

"Someday you must tell me about her."

She'd intended her statement as nothing more than a

meaningless cliché. But for the first time since leaving Kansas, Elizabeth felt as though she had found someone she could talk to about the woman who had been more of a mother than a grandmother to her. She moved to the kitchen alcove and took a bud vase out of the cupboard, filled it with water, and put the rose inside.

Her back was still to Amado when she spoke. "When I was in sixth grade the teacher had us write an essay on our goals in life. I wrote something I knew would get me a good grade, but that had nothing to do with who I was or what I dreamed for myself. My grandmother read what I'd written and told me I'd done a fine job and that I would probably get the A I wanted. And then she had me write another paper, one that told the truth. I decided to turn in the second one."

"And it was the one that earned you your A?"

Elizabeth brought the rose into the living room with her and put the vase on the coffee table. "Not even close. The teacher said if I didn't lower my expectations, I was headed for a life of disappointment."

"Such people shouldn't be allowed near children."

"She had a point—how many women presidents have we had in this country?"

"I am sure it has something to do with the number of little girls who have been raised to believe they could do the job."

"Now you really do sound like my grandmother. She was furious when she saw what the teacher had written on my paper. Two weeks later I came home from school and discovered she'd framed the essay and hung it in the living room next to the medals my grandfather received in the Second World War."

"Everyone should have a grandmother like that."

"She was certainly an anomaly in that town. A dreamer among pragmatists."

"I would have known that without being told."

"How?"

"I can see her dreams in you." He paused. "Something tells me you've traveled more than miles to get where you are today."

The conversation had become too personal, and it disconcerted her. "I just realized how hungry I am."

He seemed disappointed at the abrupt change but went along. "I hope you like Chinese. I've made reservations for us at Dong Lai Shun."

It was one of the finest, most expensive restaurants in the city. "When I first signed on at Smith and Noble, Jeremy warned me that it was against the law to live in San Francisco and not like Chinese food."

"If it isn't, it should be." He picked up her coat from the chair and held it for her.

She slipped her arms into the sleeves. It seemed his hands lingered at her shoulders a fraction longer than necessary, but she put it off to her imagination.

Elizabeth laid her chopsticks across her plate and sat back in the plush booth. "I'm stuffed," she announced.

Amado laughed. "I'm not surprised."

"Shame on you. You aren't supposed to notice things like that."

"I notice everything about you."

During the two months they had been working together, their conversation had rarely strayed into anything personal. Tonight they had talked of little else. It was as if they were engaged in a peculiar emotional dance while each tried to figure out the cadence of the music being played. Elizabeth decided it was time to sit one out. "Would you like to hear about the campaign?"

"Yes, very much. But wasn't it you who insisted I should wait for the presentation?"

"I changed my mind." She'd decided Amado would need time to get used to the idea she'd come up with, and if he was going to reject it outright, she had to know as soon as possible.

He motioned for the waiter to clear the table and bring more tea. "I am more curious than you could ever know," he told her as he poured the amber liquid into her cup. "I've tried to figure out what you were planning by going over the questions you've asked, but I've learned I have no imagination when it comes to such things."

"Unless you are a mind reader, Amado, you couldn't have second-guessed me on this one." She paused to sip her tea while she tried to decide which approach was most likely to win him over.

"I knew from the beginning that I wanted to find a way to infuse the campaign with your enthusiasm and love for winemaking," she began. "At the same time the mystery and the magic of the process have to remain intact because that's part of what makes the customer spend his money. Here's where it gets tricky. We also have to make that customer feel he isn't being talked down to just because he doesn't understand what it takes to make a really good bottle of wine."

"And you think you've found a way to do all of this?"

"I have—or at least I think I have. It's vital we have someone the public feels it can trust. Someone who will act as the private sommelier to the entire nation whether they are buyers of premium wines or ordinary table varieties. In short"—she paused and took a breath—"I want to make you the on-camera spokesman for Montoya Wines."

She was keenly aware how small her window of opportunity was to convince him and went on before he had a chance to say anything negative. "I realize that at first glance there doesn't seem to be anything new in this kind of campaign. The idea of using a company executive as spokesman is as old as the advertising business. Hell, people over forty still talk about the Schweppes man.

"That's part of the problem with proposing something that's been done before—because the idea is so familiar, it's easy to reject. I have to admit I groaned myself when the thought first came to me. And, yes, I am aware that there have been some not-so-successful campaigns for wines that were similar to what I'm proposing.

"But the harder I tried to reject the idea, the harder it was to erase the image of you as spokesman from my mind. Once the picture was there, everything else we came up with seemed second rate."

She locked her hands together and put them on her lap to keep from reaching out to him in her enthusiasm. "This will work, Amado. I'm absolutely convinced of it. No one, nothing, can sell Montoya Wines the way you can."

He sat very still for a long time and then leaned back and folded his arms across his chest. "I assume the reason you decided to tell me about this tonight was to try to win my cooperation before you took the idea any farther."

"That's part of it."

"And the other part?"

"I didn't want to spring something like this on you in front of everyone. What I have in mind could work with an actor—it's done all the time. But I don't care how good the actor is, he can't talk about Montoya Wines the way you can. No one can fake the emotional integrity you have."

"It's easy to speak from the heart to another person. I would feel ridiculous saying those things to a camera."

"We would find a way to make you forget that the camera was even there."

"And what would you have me talk about? Do you really think anyone is interested in how the summer sun affected the sugar content of grapes at harvest?"

"No," she answered honestly. "But they are interested in knowing they can trust you to give them the very best of those grapes in your wine. What they want is someone to tell them which wines to serve at elegant dinner parties and at a picnic. What goes with turkey at Thanksgiving, with spaghetti, with Sunday supper at the relatives? How do you pick a good table wine? What would be a 'knock your socks off' wine to serve to your fiancé when you've arranged an intimate firelight dinner?"

"These are simple things," Amado said.

Elizabeth leaned forward, her enthusiasm spilling over to her body language. "Not to people like me.

The majority of people in this country know that wine comes in red and white and jugs and that's about it. I want you to give them inside information they know they can trust. If the campaign works as well as I believe it will, the public will feel as comfortable about their choice of wine as they do their beer."

"And how do you see me doing this?"

"Our print and television ads will correspond to the seasons. If it's summer, we'll show a picnic or a wedding or maybe even a backyard barbecue. If it's winter, Christmas or a perhaps a small dinner party. Occasionally we'll show the winery at harvest or the fields in spring when the ground is wearing a blanket of yellow mustard. We'll show them you put as much care into your table wines as you do your premium varieties.

"The whole thing will be low key, just people enjoying themselves, each other, and the moment. When glasses are raised in toast, you will enter the picture without entering the action and, in as few words as possible, tell the reader or listener which wine you have chosen for the occasion and why. The way I plan to present you, the customer is going to believe you would rather recommend another company's wine than have them choose the wrong one for the occasion."

He stared at her a long time. "Do you know what I like best?"

The stiffness left her spine and she was able to relax, but only a little. He hadn't said yes. "No, but I could guess."

He smiled. "Don't—let me tell you."

"All right."

"I'm not sure how to say this. The thought is so new it is still coming together in my mind." He paused. "I only just tonight realized that part of what has been holding me back, the part that makes me walk the fields and question what I am doing, is that I was afraid that if I took Montoya Wines to so many people, they would think I wanted them to drink more than was good for them just so that I could become a wealthier man." He shook his head. "I'm not expressing myself very well."

"But you are," she said. She saw him in a wonderful new light and liked him immensely.

"There is a problem, though. I am a private man, Elizabeth. I can understand why you want me to be the one to tell people about my wines, but I have trouble imagining myself in that role."

She'd known it would be an uphill battle to get him to participate. What she hadn't expected was her own reluctance to talk him into it. His life was certain to be changed with the loss of his anonymity. If the campaign was only half as successful as she anticipated, there would be few places Amado could go without being recognized. "Would you at least think about it?"

"What about Michael Logan?"

She frowned. "What about him?"

"He understands the grape even better than I do. And he is closer to the age of the people you are targeting."

"And he's handsome and personable and articulate— but he isn't you, Amado. What happens if he gets a better offer from a rival winery? Our credibility would be destroyed."

"That would never happen, but I understand what you are trying to tell me. What about an actor?"

"Who could get arrested for drunk driving?"

He reached for the leather folder that contained the bill and slipped a credit card inside. "I will think about it," he said at last. "It is all I can promise."

"Amado, it's important to me that you know I would never have approached you with this idea if I didn't think it was going to give you everything you were after when you made the decision to aggressively market Montoya Wines." As much as she believed in what she was doing, she had to allow him an out. "There are other ways to go with this campaign," she admitted reluctantly. "We can talk about some of them tonight if you'd like, but I don't think any of them will come close to the success we'll have with this one."

"When will you need an answer?"

If the answer was no, it was already too late. "I don't want to pressure you, but we're scheduled to make the presentation in two weeks."

"Will it look bad for you if I decide not to do it?"

"Of course not." Ideas were rejected all the time in advertising. After all, no one could be expected to get it right every time. At least that was the way it was if you weren't one of only four female account executives in a company where half of your male counterparts suspected you'd gotten where you were by sleeping with the boss and the other half were sure of it.

"I don't believe you."

She offered him a grateful smile and reached out to touch his hand. "I know it goes against your nature, but chivalry has no place in this. You have a business decision to make." He turned his hand to clasp hers, and she became intensely aware of the warmth radiating from him. "No, it's more than that. I can't lie to you about this, Amado. If everything goes as well as I think it will, your life will never be the same."

In a touching show of old world charm, he kissed her hand before releasing it. "Thank you, Elizabeth. As always, it is your honesty that captures my attention."

The twenty-minute cab ride to Elizabeth's apartment passed in a thoughtful silence. It was everything Amado could do to keep his gaze from wandering to her. He wasn't sure whether it was the green dress that made her dark eyes so compelling or her enthusiasm over the campaign. It hardly mattered why she appeared as beautiful to him as she did, only that he was careful to do nothing about it.

He should have known what was happening to him. It had been years since he'd looked forward to being with someone the way he did Elizabeth. He thought about her all the time, in intimate, disconcerting ways. Michael would be talking to him about the acid content of the wines in the new barrels they were using, and Amado would be thinking about how the sunlight made Elizabeth's hair shine. He could not walk through his own house without thinking how alive it seemed when Elizabeth was there.

His thoughts embarrassed him. This woman who charmed him like no other could be his child. His own daughters were older. Still, he could not get her out of him mind.

The cab pulled up in front of Elizabeth's apartment. She turned to Amado. "You don't have to get out. I can see myself up."

"Please—I would feel more comfortable seeing you to your door."

She smiled. "You'd think I would know better by now."

He stepped onto the curb and extended his hand. "I will only be a minute," he said to the driver.

When they were outside Elizabeth's apartment, she surprised him by giving him her key and stepping back to let him unlock the door. She smiled her thanks when he returned the key. "I'm learning," she said, and then laughed. "Of course there isn't another man I know that I would let open my door for me."

He frowned. "I don't understand."

"We'll talk about it another time. It's too complicated to get into tonight." She stepped inside and turned to him, her hand still on the doorknob. "If you have any questions, or you just want to talk about the campaign, I'll be home all weekend."

"Thank you for telling me." He moved to leave. "Elizabeth?"

"Yes?"

"Until today there has always been honesty between us." He felt as if he would choke on the admission, but was compelled to tell her. "I did not have other business in the city. The only reason I came was to see you."

Her mouth opened. A soft exclamation rode on a sigh. "I don't know what to say."

He could see by the surprised look in her eyes that she had not guessed as much for herself. "There is nothing for you to say. I simply wanted to correct the wrong impression I'd given you this morning." He headed for the stairs, not wanting or waiting for a reply.

6

Elizabeth swung her chair around from her desk and stared out the window. Her gaze skipped from Alcatraz Island to the Golden Gate Bridge—or at least what she could see of the bridge. Half of the city was bathed in sunshine, the other half was lost in a rapidly incoming fog. Were the people happier on one side than the other?

Which moments in life were worth fighting for, worth canceling plane reservations to capture, worth risking security to gain? If it was true that most lives were lived closer to sorrow than joy, how important was it to stand fast with arms outstretched when a little happiness happened by?

What in God's name had gotten into her? Today was not the day for staring out the window, her mind adrift in useless speculation. The campaign presentation for

Montoya Wines was less than five hours away, and Amado would no doubt arrive early.

Elizabeth pulled a folder out of her desk and leaned back in her chair. The file contained a collection of scribbled notes, charts, and photographs that she'd gathered since taking on the account. Most of the information was useless, scattered thoughts that had come to her at odd moments. Periodically she went through the collection and, in the process, discovered one or two ideas with staying power. Today she was looking for reassurance that she'd chosen the right direction.

Even though she was convinced the campaign she'd designed for Amado would give him everything he'd come to Smith & Noble to gain, she still felt occasional twinges of guilt at the dramatic change it could bring to his life.

He had kept a low profile since their dinner, calling her twice on business; both times his tone had made it clear he would not welcome anything personal. She didn't understand his change in attitude and wasn't sure how she felt about it. It was obvious his decision to go along with her idea about becoming spokesman for Montoya Wines had been a difficult one. If he blamed her for putting him in the position, he kept his feelings hidden.

To try to reassure him that he was making the right choice, she'd told him about the countless psychological studies that had been done on the importance of image. The way a product was perceived by the public was far more important than the product itself.

The campaign she'd created for Montoya would make his wine some of the most coveted in the nation while still within the price range of the majority of people who walked into a liquor store. The ultimate combination—snobbery and affordability.

Her intercom buzzed. She leaned across the desk and punched the button. "Yes?"

"Mr. Noble's on line one."

"Thank you." She picked up the phone. "What can I do for you, Jeremy?"

"We need to talk."

"Now? I have a dozen things—"

"It's important. And it won't take long."

"I'll be right up."

As requested, Elizabeth had kept Jeremy apprised of her progress, sending him weekly updates, reducing the blizzard of paper from the research department to a gentle, intelligible snowstorm and acting as a buffer between him and the copywriters. She'd expected more input, but he'd been peculiarly restrained throughout the almost three months she'd been working on the account.

Jeremy's secretary was on a break when Elizabeth arrived. She looked inside his office. He was sitting at his desk, his head bent as he studied the papers strewn in front of him. "Getting ready for this afternoon?" she asked. She tried to match Jeremy's nonchalance, but it took a concerted effort to keep the excitement and anticipation she was feeling out of her voice. She was looking forward to that afternoon more than she wanted to admit, even to herself.

He looked up. There was no smile of greeting. "Come in," he said. "And close the door behind you."

"Is something wrong?"

He motioned to the chair across from him. "Sit down."

When she was seated and he still hadn't told her why he'd asked to see her, she nervously prompted again, "I repeat—is there something wrong?"

"I've been going over the presentation."

Her throat went dry at his lack of enthusiasm. "And?"

"I'm afraid it just won't do, Elizabeth."

"What do you mean, 'won't do'?" she asked carefully.

He tossed his pen on the desk and leaned back heavily in his chair. "This folksy stuff you've come up with is not the way to sell alcohol anymore. It's been done to death. People want to feel sophisticated when they're holding a wineglass even if it's plastic and filled with seventy-nine-cent rotgut. The public just isn't going to buy the sentimental crap in this campaign. If we go with what you've got here, we're going to be the laughingstock of the industry right along with Montoya's wines. Besides, you're never going to get Montoya to go along with being the spokesman."

He'd caught her completely off guard. She didn't know how to defend herself. "Why did you wait until now to say something? Isn't it a little late in the game?"

He was clearly uncomfortable. "I was hoping I wouldn't have to, that you would figure out for yourself how wrong you'd gone."

Her mind raced, trying to make sense out of what he was telling her. Finally bits and pieces began to fall into place. It wouldn't have mattered what she'd have come up with. He'd never intended to go with her ideas. "Does Montoya know you've canceled today's meeting?"

He shifted position and fixed his gaze on the papers in front of him. "I didn't have to. Luckily we have a backup plan ready to go."

Having her suspicions confirmed did nothing to ease the blow. "Oh?" she said softly. "And what would that be?"

"When you took over the account, I decided it would be prudent to let the original team continue working on the project, just in case it proved to be more than you could handle. After all, Montoya dumped a hell of a responsibility on you when you'd never—"

"You bastard. You didn't have to go behind my back. You could have told me what you were doing." The conspiracy of silence necessary to pull off something like that hurt almost as much as the lack of trust.

"It isn't as bad as it sounds, Elizabeth. If you'd come up with something interesting, we might have—"

"I can't believe I could have been so stupid. All that work for nothing. How could you string me along this way? You've made me the joke of the entire agency."

"No one is laughing at you, they all sympathize."

"Yeah, sure." She stood. "What's the real reason you wanted me to think I had the job, Jeremy?"

He looked agitated and shifted position on his seat again. "We had to convince Montoya he was getting what he asked for. If we'd told you what we were doing, you might have slipped up. Bottom line is we just couldn't take the chance. The agency needs this account."

A bubble of laughter welled inside her. She fought to keep it contained. "So now the plan is to convince him that the campaign you're presenting this afternoon is actually mine?"

"That's why I wanted you here this morning, to go over the presentation. You have four hours to prepare yourself."

She looked down at the papers on his desk. At first glance she could see nothing compelling in the artwork, nothing to catch the eye or make the ads stand out from a dozen others that had been turned out by the agency. They'd played it safe, taken a route that wouldn't offend anyone, but it sure as hell wouldn't excite anyone, either. "You expect me to pass this stuff off as mine?"

Jeremy tried to intimidate her with one of his infamous looks. "Are you saying you need more time?"

"No, I'm saying I won't do it."

His voice dropped to a menacing whisper. "Don't get it into your head that you're indispensable, Elizabeth."

"You've made it abundantly clear that I'm not," she countered. "I'll be out of my office by this evening."

"You'll be sorry. I'll make sure every agency in this town hears about this."

She gave him a slow, deliberate smile. "Just be sure you spell my name right."

That afternoon Elizabeth was in her office packing the last of her personal belongings when there was a knock on the door. After fielding questions from half the office, she'd finally told Joyce to hold everyone off for twenty minutes so she could finish clearing out her desk. It hadn't been ten. She was still trying to decide whether to answer the knock when the door opened.

Amado came inside, closed the door behind him, and leaned against it. "Would you like to tell me what's going on?"

She couldn't read his expression. "There was a difference of opinion on how your account should be handled." She tossed the spare pair of panty hose she kept for emergencies into the box. If she was nothing else, she was prepared. God forbid she should show up at a meeting with a run in her stocking or, worse, with bare legs. "But I'm sure you already figured that out for yourself."

"At what point did Jeremy decide he didn't like the campaign you had developed?"

"Are you trying to find out how much I knew about what he was going to do and when I knew it?"

"Basically."

"Why?"

"Because I have the impression you have been as used and lied to about all of this as I have."

"I'm sorry, Amado. If I'd had any idea this was going to happen, I would never have—"

He held up his hand to stop her. "What will you do now?"

She came around to the front of her desk and sat on the edge. "I made some phone calls this morning after my run-in with Jeremy. Now all I have to decide is which job offer I want to accept."

"I'm pleased to hear there are wiser men in this business than Jeremy Noble. It must be refreshing to deal with people who recognize your talent."

"The reason they're hiring me doesn't matter," she said. "It's the change I'm looking forward to. I've only been to New York twice, but I think I'll like it."

He looked as if she'd hit him. "You are going to leave San Francisco?"

"There's nothing to keep me here. I moved to San Francisco because of the job with Smith and Noble and then put in so much time at the office, I don't have any real friends outside work. The lease on my apartment will be up next month, so there isn't even that to hold me back." She shrugged. "If you think about it, the timing couldn't have been better. I'm just sorry you got caught in the middle."

"You have nothing to apologize for."

She got up and went back around her desk to finish packing. "What are you going to do?"

He seemed agitated and confused. "About what?"

"The campaign."

"I don't know." He waved his hand in dismissal. "I have to give it some thought."

"You didn't like the presentation?"

Anger flashed from his eyes. "It would be a kindness to call it mediocre."

"Perhaps it was because your mind was already set—"

"Did you look at what they showed me?"

"Only fleetingly," she admitted.

"Montoya Wines could have been removed from the ads and another winery substituted and it would have made no difference. There was nothing clever or memorable. I made it clear to Jeremy in the beginning that I wasn't interested in a hard sell, and still he—" Amado raked his hand through his hair. "I'm sorry. My quarrel is with him, not you."

"Perhaps you could—"

"I don't want to talk about this anymore, Elizabeth."
His hand went to the doorknob. "I should go now.
There are some things I must think about."

She nodded. "I'll be in town for another week or two
if you need to get in touch with me."

"You are leaving so soon?"

"The people I talked to at the agencies said if I wanted to live in the city rather than commute, I should give
myself plenty of time to find an apartment."

He started to open the door and then closed it again.
Several seconds passed while he looked at her, his
expression unreadable. Finally he crossed the room and
held out his hand. "I have enjoyed our time together,"
he said.

His fingers closed around hers, and for a moment she
felt as though they were sharing a hundred unspoken
thoughts in the touch. "Thank you," she said. "I'll think
about you with every glass of wine I drink from now on."

He smiled. "Let us hope it is always a Montoya
wine."

She returned his smile. "Is there any other?"

When he was gone she had trouble remembering
how, only minutes earlier, she'd been excited about the
prospect of starting a new job and a new life. Now it
seemed what she had lost was greater than what she
hoped to gain.

Elizabeth arrived at her apartment that afternoon
full of good intentions. During the cab ride home, she'd
planned precisely what she was going to do. As soon as
she changed into her jeans, she would begin going

through her closets and drawers, deciding what was worth packing and what should go to Goodwill.

Somehow, the minute she closed the door, her good intentions disappeared along with her energy. She pulled a TV dinner out of the freezer and put it in the oven, not even bothering to look to see what it was.

She was worn out—mentally, physically, emotionally.

Perversely, as she had grown and matured, the person she'd fought so hard to leave behind had become more and more important to her. Under all the trappings of education and background, for good or for bad, she was still Jennifer Cavanaugh, not Elizabeth Preston.

There were times she ached for that lonely little girl, when her arms cried out to hold her and her voice longed to tell her she was not forgotten.

But she could never go back. She and Jenny were part of a web of lies so tangled that every attempt at freedom had only wound the silken threads around them tighter.

When she was in college the need to maintain her persona was fueled by the fear of discovery and prosecution. She'd never tried to kid herself about that. No matter how compelling the motivation that had put her there, what she'd done was fraud, pure and simple. The school would be compelled to take action against her, if for no other reason than to protect future donations to their scholarship programs.

From the day she'd walked on campus, she'd had no choice but to stay. If she abandoned the scholarship, her high school would be informed. The ensuing investigation would inevitably lead to George Benson. His job, his reputation, his life in Farmingham, would be over.

Her one other chance to stop being Elizabeth Preston had been when she'd graduated. But to do so would have meant abandoning the degree she'd worked so hard to earn as well as turning her back on the sacrifices her grandmother had made to keep her in school and the risks George Benson had taken.

Besides, it was made perfectly clear to her when she was recruited by Smith & Noble that they were hiring her because she'd graduated at the top of her class. And she'd needed a job that paid well to take some of the financial pressure off her grandmother.

Elizabeth took a bottle of wine from the cupboard—the last of the case Amado had given her when she'd taken over the campaign. Back into the living room, she kicked off her shoes and sat down on the sofa. With the bottle of wine in one hand, a crystal goblet in the other, she began to drink.

7

Elizabeth leaned her elbows on the kitchen table and pressed the palms of her hands to her temples. What idiot had told her she wouldn't get a hangover if she drank good wine? And what had made her believe him? After several minutes she reached for her coffee. Her stomach lurched. A groan followed. She had to find a way to clear the cobwebs out of her head. There were decisions to be made. She was no closer to making up her mind about which job to take than she had been when she'd received the offers. And she'd promised an answer by five o'clock that day—New York time.

She gingerly turned her head to peer at the kitchen clock. It was eleven-thirty. She had two and a half hours to make a life-altering decision with a brain that felt as fuzzy as her tongue. Yuck.

The thought of sticking anything in her mouth, even a toothbrush, made her gag. She shuddered at the idea of subjecting herself to a pulsing shower, but she got up and headed for the bathroom anyway. It was that or crawl back into bed, pull the covers over her head, and try to come up with a creative, believable reason why she hadn't called the agencies back when she'd promised she would—hardly an auspicious way to start her new life.

To her amazement, the shower worked. The cold water and vigorous scrubbing actually made her feel as though she could handle some breakfast. With luck, she might actually keep it down. After that, she would make her phone calls to New York, contact her landlord to tell him she would not be renewing her lease, and then try to find a mover who wouldn't charge more than her furniture was worth to transport it across country.

She was pouring herself a cup of coffee when the downstairs buzzer sounded. After crossing the room, she leaned her head against the wall above the intercom and said, "Yes?"

"Elizabeth, it's Amado. May I come up?"

Her hand went to the towel wrapped around her head. She looked down at her bare feet and terry-cloth robe. "Amado, I—sure," she said, and pressed the button to release the lock.

She threw on jeans and a T-shirt and met him at the landing.

"I can come back another time if it would be more convenient," he said when he saw the towel.

"Don't be silly." She motioned him inside her apartment. "Would you like a cup of coffee—"

He put his hand on her arm. "No, please don't go. I'm afraid if I wait any longer to tell you why I've come, I'll find a reason not to."

"All right," she said. A strange feeling came over her when she saw the look in his eyes. It was as if the invisible barrier that had formed and defined their relationship when they were working together had disappeared, and they were back to the night he had come into town for the sole purpose of taking her to dinner.

Amado released her arm. "I have been thinking about this new job of yours in New York," he said. "Is this change of cities something you were planning to do someday eventually, or are you leaving San Francisco because of what happened yesterday?"

"It was inevitable that Jeremy and I would have a confrontation one day. It didn't matter what kind of work I turned—"

"Please, Elizabeth, just answer me."

It wasn't like Amado to ask personal questions, let alone insist she answer. The little he knew about her, she had volunteered. "At one time, New York was a dream. Now, it's a job. I'm going because to stay would be difficult"—Why was she constantly trying to scatter rose petals over fields of fertilizer?—"if not impossible. Jeremy would see to that." Joyce had called that morning to tell her how apoplectic Jeremy had become when he'd learned Amado intended to pull the account.

"But you would remain here, or at least in California, if you could?"

"What are you asking me?"

He shoved his hands in his pockets. "I'm not doing this very well." A nervous smile flickered across his lips.

"And it isn't for lack of practice. From St. Helena to your doorstep I said the words over and over again in the car. And now you are standing in front of me and have said to me what I told myself I needed to hear, and still I cannot express what is on my mind."

Amado could be taciturn and difficult to reach when he was thinking about something that concerned the winery, but the rest of the time he was one of the most eloquent men she had ever known. "Look, if you've gotten the idea that my run-in with Jeremy was somehow your fault, and you came here to apologize, you couldn't be more wrong."

"That isn't it at all. I came here to make you an offer—a proposition—no, that isn't the right word, either. I want you to come to work for me." As if afraid she would give her answer before he had a chance to finish, he went on quickly. "The campaign you designed is brilliant. I admit, it took me a few weeks to see what you were trying to do, but now I understand. Since then your enthusiasm has become mine. Nothing else but the campaign you designed will satisfy me."

She was both pleased and flattered and a little bowled over at his high praise. "I'm glad—"

"Wait, there is more." He hesitated, swallowed, started to speak, and then swallowed again. "As much as I want you to come to work for me, I also want you to be my wife. No, I didn't say that right. I want you to be my wife even more."

Elizabeth blinked. A peculiar feeling came over her. She knew the words and understood their meaning, but she couldn't conceive they were meant for her. She was tempted to look over her shoulder to see if someone was standing behind her. It was as if the world she lived in had suddenly tipped, not enough to make her fall, just enough to make her lose her balance.

"I realize I have taken you off guard," he went on. "You're probably thinking I sampled too much wine this morning, and I don't blame you."

In a flash all of the subtle and not-so-subtle clues came tumbling back—the rose, the dinner, the protectiveness, the caring, even the way he touched her, as though she were somehow special to him, not just the recipient of a gentleman's courtesy. God in heaven, how had she been so blind? "I don't know what to say, Amado."

"I know. It is what I expected. You were not prepared for what I wanted to tell you, and that is my fault." He reached for her hand. It was as if by releasing the words, he had released himself, too. "You may find this hard to believe, but I am as surprised by all of this as you are. It wasn't until I was faced with the possibility of losing you as a friend that I realized you had become so much more. The thought I might never see you again has been like an echo in my mind and in my heart since I left you yesterday."

Elizabeth adjusted the towel that had begun to slip from her head. "I need some time to think about this."

"When did you promise the agencies in New York you would get back to them?"

She'd discovered Amado was at his best when faced with problems that seemed insurmountable. An aura of confidence surrounded him that was incredibly appealing. "Today," she answered.

"They will understand your need for another day or two to make such an important decision." He let go of her hand and touched the side of her face.

The gesture was as intimate as a kiss. A blush of warmth blanketed her chest and moved up her neck. "You have to remember, I went to them, they didn't come to me."

"Anyone so eager to have you they would hire you on a phone call isn't going to change their mind because you make them wait until Monday for your answer." He grew bolder with his touch; the backs of his fingers traced a line from her chin to the neck of the T-shirt. It was as if by not immediately rejecting his proposal, she had made acceptance not only possible, but probable. "Spend this weekend with me, Elizabeth," he coaxed. "Let me tell you about the job you would have with Montoya Wines. Give me the same chance to convince you that you would give to them."

If she took his job and it didn't work out, where would she go then? And what was the marriage thing all about? Did he think proposing to her was the only way to get her to go to work for him? "I have a feeling what we both need is some time alone to think. You're not the kind of man who does things on impulse, Amado. What happens if you wake up next week and decide you've made a mistake? Then what? We need a cooling-off period before this goes any—"

He gazed deeply into her eyes. His hand moved with confidence to the back of her neck. He held her as much by the intensity of his look as his grasp. With an arresting assurance he came forward and touched his lips to hers. When the kiss was over, he leaned back and locked eyes with her again. "It isn't cooling off we need, Elizabeth."

She caught her lip between her teeth to contain the response that welled inside her. The warmth that had started in her chest sent out tentacles that reached to her groin. It had been a long time since she'd responded to a man with an intensity that put desire above propriety. How could she have forgotten how incredibly exciting the feeling could be?

"All right," she said almost involuntarily. "I'll go with you. But it has to be strictly business." She almost laughed aloud at how prudish she sounded.

Instead of answering, he brought her to him and kissed her again. This time his mouth was open and encouraging in unmistakable invitation. She felt herself sway toward him. Without conscious thought her arms slid up his chest and around his neck. Her tongue flicked to meet his. She tasted a hint of coffee, smelled a trace of spicy cologne, and felt a body that was hard from a lifetime of physical work and filled with a longing that was a match to her own.

"So much for the strictly business," she said, and pushed away from him. "This is moving too fast. I don't understand what's happening here." She threw her hands up in the air. "Goddamn it, Amado, would you please explain this to me?"

He laughed. "In my fifty-eight years on this earth, if there is one thing I have learned, my beautiful Elizabeth, it is that some things cannot be explained. They just are."

She considered her own life, the seemingly arbitrary twists and turns, the bizarre coincidences. Perhaps it was time for a little joy that hadn't been planned or fought for, either—something that just was.

Two days later, on Sunday morning, Elizabeth was standing on a verdant hillside above one of Amado's vineyards, caught in a mental struggle to put words to feelings. The tractors had tilled the fields, turning under the brilliant mustard and subclover and Dallas grass and leaving clean rows of dark soil to frame and showcase the tender, almost translucent green of the newly opened vines.

Amado had brought her here the previous morning to watch the day break over the mountains. When the sun had finished staking its claim on the sky, he'd told her that she'd come to the valley in the flush of the three-week period when the vines did most of their growing, and that if she would stop and listen with her mind and her soul, she might actually hear them.

She'd dismissed the fanciful notion but had been reluctant to tell him. Instead she'd acquiesced to his wishes and stood beside him in the middle of a row of vines, her feet planted squarely in the freshly plowed soil, her eyes closed to the distractions surrounding her.

She'd heard crickets and crows and grackles and cars on a distant road. She'd even heard her own breath and the cacophony of thoughts in her mind. And then slowly, as she'd shunted aside the obvious, she'd become aware of other, less identifiable sounds, tiny pops and cracks and soft whisperings. Thinking it must be the wind sighing through the tender shoots, she'd opened her eyes and seen there was no wind. There hadn't even been a breeze to rustle the leaves.

She hadn't said anything to Amado, but he'd known by the look of wonderment on her face that she'd heard. He'd smiled contentedly and put his arm around her as they'd walked back to the house for breakfast on the deck.

He had been brilliant in his pursuit of her, knowing precisely where she was most vulnerable, where she would become defensive if pushed. Not once had he suggested that it would be an easy decision for her to abandon her career. What he had done was insist that he could not carry out his new marketing plans successfully without her.

He had touched her physically, but only in friendly, tender ways, holding her hand as they walked through a field, brushing a lock of hair from her forehead. There were moments when she would look up to see him staring at her, a naked longing in his eyes he did nothing to disguise, and then he would smile and she would be enveloped in his warmth.

He'd been most clever in sharing his love of the land with her, in his telling of the Montoyas who had walked the fields before him and his fear that their legacy might end with him. Somehow he'd recognized in her the need for roots and continuity and family, and it was this he appealed to. In marrying Amado, she would become the link that allowed the Montoya legacy to continue, if only for her lifetime. She would finally, actually, belong someplace. More important, she would be not an appendage, but a necessity.

With her in his life, Amado would not have to cling to the fragile hope that Elana could be lured back to her childhood home if he succeeded in making the winery an asset to her.

Amado was offering Elizabeth everything she had come to believe she would never have. That he was fifty-eight to her twenty-eight only meant that their lives together would be shorter, not less fulfilling. He might not live to see their grandchildren born, but he would have another chance to instill his passion into a child of his own.

She was acutely aware that despite the business acumen she would bring to the relationship, her identity would be based on being the wife of a powerful man, rather than a woman who had succeeded on her own. There would never again be a reason for anyone to pry into her college records or check her high school background. Being Amado's wife would not only give her credibility, it would give her the anonymity she'd once believed becoming Elizabeth Preston would bring.

Her children would never want for anything. They would never know the isolation she'd experienced from being on the run with her parents. And they would never know the feeling of abandonment that came with being left behind. As sons and daughters of Amado Montoya, they would never feel the stigma of being outcasts. No mother would tell her children not to play with them. Her children would grow up strong and confident and proud of who they were. They would never have to cheat or lie or steal to fulfill their potential.

And they would never find out who their mother really was or what she had done to escape her past.

The direction of her thoughts brought her up short. When had she gone from fighting Amado's proposal to siding with it?

She turned to look at the rambling Spanish mansion sitting imperiously on an outcropping overlooking the valley. It seemed that from some hidden part of her psyche, her decision had been made for her. When she thought about the sensitive and quiet-spoken Amado she had come to know, it was disturbingly easy to forget the wealth and position and power of the man who occupied that house on the hill. If all went according to plan, within five years Montoya Wines would be one of the best-known and most successful mass-market wineries in California.

She brought her hand up to shield her eyes from the sun as she looked at the house. A feeling of deep contentment came over her, and she knew with sudden surety that in time she and Amado would come to love each other and it wouldn't matter what outside influences had originally prompted their marriage.

A smile formed. If love was indeed a journey, it would find her an eager traveler.

Amado took Elizabeth into St. Helena for brunch. It was unseasonably warm for late March, and the outside tables had been set up in anticipation of an early spring.

The waitress brought a bottle of champagne to their table for Elizabeth's inspection. She yielded to Amado.

"It's perfect," he said. "However, I didn't order it."

"I did," said Elizabeth.

"Are we celebrating?" he asked cautiously.

She smiled. "I hope so."

Without taking his eyes from her, he motioned to the waitress to pour. "Tell me how I convinced you. Which words were the ones? I want to remember them."

"You don't have to. I won't change my mind."

"You know me better after three months than Sophia did in twenty years. It is one of the things I love about you."

The sentiment startled her. Until that moment he'd said nothing about loving her. Could he have thought it was too soon, that she would feel overwhelmed? "There's more than one?"

He held his glass up to her. "Shall I count the ways?"

"I was teasing."

"But I am not."

She didn't know how to answer.

"I love your spirit, it reminds me of myself when I was young and gives me hope that through you I will feel that way again. I love the simple things, too, like watching you, the way your hair shines in the sun, the way you walk and smile and say my name. Most of all, I love your honesty and your integrity, something rare and beautiful in today's world."

A sharp pain cut across her chest. She sat straighter on her chair and took shallow breaths until the pain had eased. For one brief moment she had considered telling him about her past, had thought how wonderful it would be if they could start their lives together with everything out in the open. But even as the thought had surfaced, she'd known it was a fantasy. Amado loved the woman he imagined her to be, not the one she really was.

"You have restored my enthusiasm for life, Elizabeth. There are no words to thank you."

She might not be able to tell him everything, but there had to be this one honesty between them. "Right now, at this very minute, I can't tell you . . . I can't say I love you."

He reached across the table and took her hand. "I do not believe you would agree to marry me if you didn't think you would come to love me in time. I can wait, Elizabeth."

He looked at her with such tenderness and longing, she let herself believe what he told her. How could she not come to love this man?

8

Amado stood at Michael Logan's side as he went over the results of the experiment they had been conducting on altering the temperature of the wine during fermentation. "What do you think?" he asked when Michael looked up at last.

"I'm sold on it. Everyone agrees we're getting a lot more subtlety from the musts."

"Then let's do it."

Michael grinned. "I knew you were in favor of the change, so I've already set it in motion." He put out his arms, stretched, and then stuck his fingers under his reading glasses to rub his eyes. "It's been a long morning. If you don't have something else in mind, I think I'm going to take the afternoon off."

"You're welcome to what's left of it." It was typical of Michael to become so intent on a project that he was unaware of everything else around him, including the passage of time. "But I would appreciate it if you didn't stray too far. I came to invite you to a dinner party I have arranged for this evening—just a few friends and Elizabeth."

"I thought you said the thing with the agency was going to be wrapped up this week at the presentation." He began to gather the papers that were spread from one end of the counter to the other.

"Oh, it was wrapped up all right—in a fashion."

Michael shot him a questioning look. "Good God, don't tell me you didn't like what she came up with. Not after all this time."

"I liked Elizabeth's ideas very much, but there has been a change in plans. I will explain everything at dinner. You will be able to join us?"

He laughed. "You know me better than to ask. I'd give up a date with the Robinson twins for one of Consuela's home-cooked meals."

Later that evening Elizabeth and Amado were on the deck that ran across the back of the house, enjoying a quiet moment before dinner. She smiled her thanks as Amado handed her a cracker topped with Brie. Shade was provided by a massive oak; its branches covered a quarter of the sprawling house. A breeze caught the hem of her dress, and she put her hand on her thigh to keep her skirt from traveling higher.

"You look especially beautiful tonight," Amado said.

"Thank you." Luckily she'd thought to pack something besides slacks. She brushed her hair from her shoulder and wished she'd worn it up in her usual twist. Whenever she was nervous, she had a tendency to fiddle with a strand, a dead giveaway for anyone observant enough to notice such things.

"Out of the people invited tonight, I think Michael will be the most surprised by our news."

"Are you worried by what he might think?"

"Not at all."

She didn't believe him. She hadn't been around the two of them together very often, but she'd picked up that theirs went beyond the simple employee-employer relationship. "Tell me about him. How did he come to work for you?"

Amado set his glass on the railing and stared out at the horizon. "The Logans and the Montoyas have been neighbors for generations. Look." He pointed to the distance. "Their vineyard is not far from here."

She moved to stand beside him. She didn't have the slightest idea which of the thousands of vines belonged to the Logans, but then it really didn't matter. Amado wasn't priming her for a quiz, just sharing another part of who he was with her.

"Fortunately," he went on, "or depending on how you look at it, unfortunately, there were two sons born to this generation of Logans, both of them interested in farming. As you can see, there is hardly enough land to support one family. By tradition, the vineyard went to the oldest son, Paul." He paused. "I have never told this to another person, but secretly, in my heart, I harbored a hope that at least one of Harold's boys and one of my daughters would somehow find each other. But it was not to be."

"So Michael wound up with nothing?"

"If I were to be honest, had I been faced with the decision Michael's father had to make, I do not think I could have come up with so fair a solution. Somehow, with barely enough land to feed his family, Harold managed to set aside the money to send Michael to college."

"So Paul got the land, but Michael got the education." Someone else had paid a higher-than-normal cost for college. She was surprised to discover she and Michael actually had something so life-altering in common.

"It turned out to be a little more complicated in the end, but Michael did finally get to go away to school. He chose very well—the University of California at Davis. It is the greatest wine university in the world. The knowledge Michael acquired there and his God-given skill have made him one of the finest wine masters in California. I do not exaggerate when I say he is the heart of Montoya Wines."

Elizabeth put her hand on his arm. "If Michael is truly the heart, Amado, then you are the soul." She doubted he would have spoken with more pride if Michael were his own son. It had not escaped her notice that while Amado had made a point of inviting Michael to share the evening, he had not asked his daughter Elana to drive up from San Francisco. "How long has he been with you?"

"Ten years. He came to work for me the day he graduated."

The woman hired to help Consuela with the party that night appeared at the doorway. "I am sorry to disturb you, Mr. Montoya, but Consuela would like to see you in the kitchen."

"Tell her I will be right there." He turned to Elizabeth. "Is there anything I can get for you before I go?"

"Amado, you must stop waiting on me. I'm perfectly capable of taking care of myself."

"Of course you are." He brushed his lips against her cheek. "But then you would deny me the pleasure."

She watched him walk across the deck and disappear inside the house. Was that what it was like to be in love? Was every thought, every action, centered around the other person? She envied Amado. She wanted to feel the way he did. But then if liking someone truly was a precursor to loving him, she was only a heartbeat away.

She wandered over to a wicker chair, sat down, and spotted Michael Logan standing in the living room, watching her. Although Amado had told her that he and Michael attended the same parties and traveled in the same social circles, this was only the second time Elizabeth had seen him out of his customary jeans and chambray shirt. An expression her grandmother had used came to mind—he cleaned up real good. She decided it was probably as much the way he carried himself, with a quiet, unassuming self-confidence, as it was his earthy good looks that gave him the ability to make anything he wore seem a personal fashion statement.

"Amado isn't with you?" he asked.

"He should be back any minute."

He came out on the deck, walked over to the table, and picked up a cracker, adding cheese. "I'm a little surprised to see you here," he admitted. "Somehow I got the impression you wouldn't be working so closely on the campaign once it was all set."

She detected a peculiar undercurrent in his statement. It was tempting to give in to the impression Michael didn't like her, but once she did, she knew the thought would linger and color her feelings toward him. Instead she ascribed his stiffness to the difficulty of trying to find something to say to someone he hardly knew. "There are a few details that need to be taken care of before we can begin work."

"I know Amado likes your ideas."

"That's nice to hear." Especially since he'd paid Jeremy a handsome sum not to try to lay claim to the ideas she'd come up with for the Montoya account while she was working at the agency.

"So when do you think you'll be getting started?"

If she told him about launching the campaign on her own, he would counter with questions about her leaving Smith and Noble, and those were bound to lead to the reason for the party that night. Amado's surprise would be ruined. Which meant she had to lie or hedge. "I'd like to have something ready for the fall to take advantage of the holidays."

"I had no idea these things took that long."

"There are a lot of people involved when you blanket the media. We're going to be coordinating television, radio, and print when we start out."

"And you think if all goes well, what you're doing is going to accomplish everything Amado wants?"

The way he asked the question gave her the impression he had doubts. "There's no guarantee, of course. But I've never felt more confidence in a campaign."

"Let's say you're right and we have a runaway success on our hands. What happens if the demand is greater than the supply?"

"It could irritate the consumer to the point they wouldn't buy Montoya Wines at half the list price or put it in such demand that the retailer could charge anything he wanted and get away with it. You never know."

"Is there a possibility the campaign won't be ready until next year?"

"What are you getting at, Michael?"

"Nothing."

"I was under the impression there were contracts with other wineries to produce Montoya table wines if the demand was too great."

"If we used every one of our backup wineries, we're still a long way from being able to handle what you've got in mind to do to us."

What she had in mind to do to them? Elizabeth bristled at the accusation. Michael made it sound as if she'd done the pursuing, as if she'd been the one who dictated the expansion, as if she—

A third voice entered the conversation when Amado appeared at the doorway Michael had just left. "If necessary, we'll have the Ivanski brothers handle any overflow."

"And take a hell of a chance on both the quantity and quality."

Elizabeth looked from one man to the other. This was not the first time they had had this discussion. But why bring her into it? Michael couldn't possibly believe she'd had anything to do with Amado pushing himself as hard as he had been.

"We can't fear success," Amado said.

"You know damn well it isn't success I'm worried about—it's the loss of control."

The doorbell sounded inside the house. Amado took a deep breath and ran his hand down the front of his shirt, smoothing his tie. "It appears our guests are arriving, Elizabeth."

She felt herself pale at the "our." The first public step into her new life was about to take place. She glanced at Michael as she rose from her chair. He was studying her through narrowed, questioning eyes.

Amado held out his hand. A broad smile covered his face. "Are you ready?"

In her mind a single word cried out—No!—but she refused to give it voice. Instead she took his hand and returned his smile. If Amado's friends were going to give her grief over the marriage, it was better she find out now.

Not wanting to overwhelm Elizabeth at her first outing as his wife-to-be—even though he had wanted to shout his news from the streets of St. Helena—Amado had kept the guest list small. Seated around the table were the owners of the three other wineries in the valley, members of the extended family of vintners and personal friends who had been at his side for the good and the bad for half his lifetime, and Michael.

The dinner dishes had been cleared, and Consuela was putting the final touches on dessert. Amado decided now was the time for the toast with which he would finally share his excitement and happiness. He stood and personally filled the Lalique glasses he had reserved for the toast. The Cabernet Sauvignon he'd chosen was the recent winner of a blind competition against the best burgundy France had to offer. It was young yet, perfect for the occasion, a reflection of his own attitude and feelings.

He returned to his position at the head of the table. "It is not unusual for us to come together when there is a reason to celebrate." His gaze swept those gathered at the table, ending with Elizabeth, who sat at his right. "This evening, however, is for me far more special than most. As you all know, I believed it was my destiny to live the rest of my life alone. I have brought you here tonight to share the news that this is no longer true. Elizabeth and I"— he withdrew a small velvet box from his pocket, opened it, and took out a ring—"will be married in August."

There was a collected, audible gasp at the table before congratulations tumbled out of stunned mouths. A clinking sounded as the Lalique crystal came together in the completion of the toast. Amado took Elizabeth's hand and slipped the three-carat diamond on her finger.

She held up her hand, visibly taken aback. "Amado, it's . . . so big."

Out of the corner of his eye, Amado watched Michael. Michael's expression was one of disbelief and then, as his gaze shifted to Elizabeth, questioning anger. Amado said a silent prayer that she had not noticed, but then he saw her flinch and was reminded that there was little she didn't see.

The silence that followed the obligatory drink verged on becoming uncomfortable when Connie Robertson spoke up. "Elizabeth, let me be the first to welcome you into what can admittedly sometimes be our overwhelming family of vintners." She laughed happily. "This news is going to knock them on their ears. I hope you're prepared to be feted morning, noon, and night. There isn't a person in this valley who is going to rest until they've seen you for themselves."

"Amado warned me that his friends might be a little incredulous," Elizabeth said.

"To say the least," Michael added in a low tone.

"This has got to be the best-kept secret this valley has had in years," David Robertson said. "How long have you two known each other?"

Michael unobtrusively laid his napkin on the table, as if preparing to leave.

"We met at the Smith and Noble Christmas party."

"This past Christmas?" the woman across from Elizabeth asked.

Elizabeth could almost hear the mental calculations. Why, that means they've only known each other . . . gasp, *four* months!

"When Amado makes up his mind about something, there's no holding him back," Michael said as he stood.

"Certainly not when I'm as sure about something as I am about Elizabeth."

With the initial surprise over, the couples who were still seated around the table broke into animated conversation. Michael made his way to Amado. "I apologize for leaving so soon after your announcement," he said. "But I promised Tony I would stop by after dinner tonight. He's having problems with one of the courses he's taking at night school."

Like the fog that struggled to cling to the mountains on a sunny morning, Amado felt some of the joy that had suffused him only moments earlier slip away. "I'll walk you out."

Michael put up his hand to stop him. "That isn't necessary." He turned to Elizabeth and made a slight bow. "Best wishes."

"Thank you," she replied.

When Michael was gone, Amado exchanged glances with Elizabeth. He could not answer the question he saw in her eyes. It was inconceivable that two people he loved would not like each other. All he could do was hope that in time Michael would see Elizabeth as the blessing she was and not the divisive force he obviously perceived her to be.

9

Amado didn't believe in long engagements, or so he told everyone who stood still long enough to listen. At times Elizabeth wondered whether he was rushing their wedding because he was afraid he might get cold feet or whether he worried she was the one who might change her mind. One day, in small, thoughtful ways, he would gently tell her that he would understand if she was having second thoughts. The next day, he would face her with a look of determination and insist he would kidnap her and carry her off to a deserted island if she so much as showed a sign of wavering.

The four and a half months that had passed since the dinner party where Amado announced their engagement had disappeared in a blink. Between working on the campaign and helping with the wedding plans,

Elizabeth had cut her sleep almost in half. She was in a perpetual state of exhaustion and loving every minute of it.

Elizabeth stood on tiptoe to read the revised arrival time on Alice's bus. Her grandmother would be there any minute. She'd sent Alice enough money for an airplane ticket, but as always, her grandmother had chosen the more economical bus. Years of pinching pennies had created a habit that refused to go away. Besides, Alice had insisted, how was she to explain the sudden affluence to her nosy friends?

In the twelve years Elizabeth had been gone from Farmingham, she and her grandmother had seen each other an average of two weeks every year. Once Elizabeth was out of school, they either met somewhere to vacation together, or, if Elizabeth couldn't get away, Alice came to San Francisco to visit. To try to explain more frequent absences would not only have entailed complicated lies about where Alice was going and whom she was seeing, she would have had to come up with the way she was supposedly paying for her trips. Keeping a secret in a town like Farmingham was tantamount to telling a woman in labor to delay giving birth until the doctor arrived.

Elizabeth had gone back to Farmingham only once. When it was time for her to leave, she and Alice had agreed it was just too dangerous for her to come back again. The questions were too many, the chance of discovery too great. She couldn't even risk driving her car. What if she were in an accident or pulled over for a burned-out taillight and someone got a look at her driver's license?

Had Elizabeth known at the time that by leaving Farmingham she would be cutting herself off from free access to the one person who loved her unequivocally, she would never have gone, no matter how intriguing the promise of an education and a better life. But at the time, neither she nor her grandmother nor George Benson had looked far enough ahead to foresee what the intricacies of guarding her identity would entail.

They had been blinded by the opportunity.

Elizabeth stepped outside and peered down the street as if she could will the bus to arrive sooner. She could hardly contain herself at the thought of being with her grandmother again. Finally the fumes from all the other buses coming and going got to her and she went back inside.

Jenny had been ten years old and small for her age when she'd looked up from the bottom step of her grandmother's porch at a woman with black hair and blue eyes who was as tall as her father. She would have looked even more forbidding had she not been wearing a waitress's bright pink dress, white apron, and ugly, thick-soled white shoes. Another ten minutes, her grandmother had said, she would have been at work and they would have missed her.

There'd been no hugs or kisses or happy greetings as Jenny and her parents entered the house. It wasn't until later that night that Jenny learned their visit had been a surprise. But, as her grandmother later told her, not the biggest one—that was saved for Jenny herself. Alice hadn't known she was a grandmother. After twelve years of silence, her daughter had simply appeared, child in hand.

As soon as they entered the house, Jenny's mother pointed to a high-backed chair in the living room and told her to sit there while she and her grandmother went into the kitchen to talk. Her father stayed with her for a few minutes and then went outside to smoke a joint.

Alone, Jenny sat with her hands clutching the arms of the chair and looked around the room slowly. She'd never been in a house as nice as this one. The brown sofa opposite her had white lacy things on the arms and across the back, but it didn't look as if they'd been put there to cover holes. At least she couldn't see any stuffing showing through. A television stood at an angle in the corner, and behind it was a whole wall of shelves that were filled with books. A piano with photographs on top was pushed up against the other wall. Jenny's gaze fell on a picture of a young woman with long hair and a big smile. She stared at it for several seconds before she realized it was her mother.

But she looked so different—like one of the people she made fun of and called "Establishment pigs." The picture confused Jenny. She twisted to look out the window at her father, careful always to keep a part of her body in contact with the chair. She never knew when disobeying orders would make her mother mad enough to hit her. Unless it was something really important, like getting up to go to the bathroom because she'd wet her pants if she didn't, when she was told to stay somewhere, she stayed. According to her mother, their lives could depend on whether Jenny was a good girl or not. If something happened that caused them to get caught and taken away, or if the men came with guns and shot them all dead, it would probably be because Jenny hadn't listened carefully enough or didn't do something she was supposed to do.

It hadn't seemed as though she'd been there very long when her mother and grandmother came back from the kitchen. Her mother didn't look at her, but Jenny could see by the happiness in her eyes that things had gone the way she wanted.

No one said it was all right for Jenny to get up, so she stayed on the chair when her mother crossed the room and went outside. Through the window she could see her father nod as he listened to what her mother told him. When she finished he smiled, let out a whoop, and picked her mother up off the ground. He swung her around several times before he put her down again. Right after that they got in the car and drove away.

Jenny watched and waited, but her mother and father never looked back at the window where she was sitting. Later she convinced herself that her mother had waved good-bye, that the only reason she hadn't actually seen her mother's hand come up was that the sun was reflecting off the windshield.

"Jenny?"

Elizabeth spun around at the sound of her childhood name. With a soft cry of recognition, she threw open her arms. "Grandma!"

Alice dropped her suitcase and moved into Elizabeth's embrace. They held each other, an island in the river of disembarking passengers.

Alice was the first to let go. "Let me look at you," she said. She stared at the younger woman as if refamiliarizing herself with every inch. "My goodness, you are a wondrous feast for these hungry eyes. I didn't think it was possible, but you just keep getting more and more beautiful."

Elizabeth grinned. "I can always count on you for an unbiased opinion."

Alice continued to stare at her granddaughter. "Can it be? Are we really seeing each other under such happy circumstances?"

"We are indeed."

Alice slipped her arm around Elizabeth's waist. "God, how I've missed you, Jenny. I'm sorry— *Elizabeth*. I've practiced saying 'Elizabeth' all the way out here, and the minute I lay eyes on you, it pops right out of my head."

"It's okay. I told Amado that Jenny was your nickname for me."

"You think of everything."

"It's almost behind us, Grandma. In two and a half weeks Elizabeth Preston is no more. You'll be able to come to California anytime you want. There's a guest cottage not two hundred yards from Amado's house where you can stay. It's surrounded by oaks and completely private."

"And have you come up with a reason I'm going to give everyone back home for these visits?"

"Between the two of us, we'll think of something convincing." They'd gone through so much to get where they were that Elizabeth refused to believe they couldn't have it all.

When they were inside the Mercedes sports car Amado had given Elizabeth for an engagement present and were headed for the Golden Gate Bridge, Alice turned to Elizabeth. "I saw George before I left. He told me to say hello and to give you his best wishes."

"How is Mr. Benson?" Even as old as she was, she didn't feel comfortable calling him by his first name.

"Word is that he's going to be offered the principal's job when Mr. Moore retires next year."

"I'm glad. He deserves it."

"He's very proud of you."

"I wonder if he's ever had any second thoughts about sticking his neck out for me the way he did."

"Not for a minute. He told me so himself."

"It bothers me sometimes that I didn't do something more worthy with my life—something equal to the chances you and Mr. Benson took. There's been a lot of times I thought I should have gone into politics or something. Somewhere I could have made a difference."

Alice wrinkled her nose. "Politics?"

"All right, so that was a little farfetched."

"The way those tabloids go after people nowadays they would have been on you like fresh-hatched mosquitoes."

They passed through the Presidio and were on the Golden Gate Bridge. "It's just that advertising isn't high on anyone's list of worthwhile or honorable professions."

"What's gotten into you? Why bring all this up now?"

Up until then she'd been careful not to let her grandmother see the doubts that had plagued her since leaving Farmingham. "Maybe I'm just nervous about the wedding."

"As soon as you become Mrs. Amado Montoya, you can put Elizabeth Preston behind you."

"Sometimes that's all I can think about."

"I hope it isn't the only reason you're getting married."

Elizabeth smiled. "I wondered about that myself at first. But as I've come to know him better, I decided I would marry Amado even if he told me I had to keep my own name."

They ate lunch at a restaurant in Sausalito that provided a sweeping view of San Francisco across the bay, but they were so caught up in being together again, neither paid attention to the sights.

Alice waited until they were on the road once more before she said, "I've changed my mind about your decision not to tell Amado about your past. You were right when you said the truth would only hurt your relationship, not help it. From all you've told me, it would be difficult for him to understand why you had to do what you did. His life has been too different."

Elizabeth hadn't told Alice everything. She'd left out the part about Amado telling her how he loved her strength of character and her integrity. "Maybe someday the time will be right and I'll be able to confide in him."

"Before you do, remember what happened to you when you told Bobbie Sue."

Dementia wouldn't let her forget Bobbie Sue Elroy. They had been inseparable from the day Jenny had started school in Farmingham.

As best friends, they'd told each other everything. Even then, it took a year before Jenny felt secure enough to share her deepest secret—who her parents really were.

What she hadn't realized was that their private, intimate circle also included Bobbie Sue's mother. By the next day the entire town knew that Jenny Cavanaugh was the daughter of hippies who traveled around the country blowing things up.

In the space of a day, with the simple sharing of a secret, Jenny had gone from Alice Taylor's lovely little granddaughter to a dangerous influence for every child who might come in contact with her.

Two months later, when Jenny graduated from sixth grade, not even the daughter of the town drunk was allowed to have anything to do with her. No one could see that underneath she was the same person she'd been before she'd shared her secret.

How could she, even for a minute, have forgotten the lesson she'd learned back then?

Even more to the point, why did she spend time wondering about such things when she'd devoted almost her entire adult life to promoting the idea that to the vast majority of people it wasn't substance that counted, it was image? As long as she kept her secret for only a few more days and Amado and everyone else in the Napa Valley continued to see her as the squeaky-clean Miss Elizabeth Preston, that was who she would be. After the wedding the slate would be wiped clean and she would begin anew.

10

A fly buzzed by Elizabeth's head. She brushed it away and turned a page in the book she was reading on the Australian wine industry. The crash course she'd designed for herself in preparation for the two weeks she and Amado would be spending "down under" on their honeymoon wouldn't be enough to convince anyone that she had more than a smattering of knowledge on the subject, but at least she'd be able to fill small gaps in the conversation.

Amado had hesitated asking her to combine business with pleasure, afraid she might feel offended or slighted. Elizabeth had been amused at the glimpse into her future life. With her own work for the winery taking on an ever-increasing importance, it was good to know Amado was pragmatic enough that he wasn't going to feel she was shunting him aside when she was too busy to accompany him on one of his frequent trips.

She glanced over at Alice, who was stretched out on a reclining lawn chair. The pages of the magazine on her lap fluttered in the breeze while she sat with her head back, her eyes closed. After two weeks of frantic activity in final preparation for the wedding that would take place in two days, Elizabeth had insisted Alice take the afternoon off. She'd agreed, but only on the condition Elizabeth join her. With lunch behind them, they'd settled under the shade of the valley oak that stood between the cottage and the main house.

Elizabeth had had no idea how many last minute details were involved in putting on a wedding. She didn't know what she would have done without Alice's and Consuela's calm and competent hands at the reigns. Especially when filming for the commercials that would air in the fall began to consume Elizabeth's every waking moment.

Just as she'd known they would, Alice and Amado had slipped into friendship as effortlessly as the grapes surrounding them were ripening in the hot August sun. If Alice harbored any doubt or concern over Elizabeth's choice for a husband, she'd kept it to herself. To Elizabeth she expressed only joy that her granddaughter was marrying a man so obviously and completely devoted to her.

Elizabeth looked up from her book when she heard a car pull into the driveway. She tilted her head to peer through the privet hedge that separated her from the main house and saw Elana's red BMW. Footsteps on the gravel walkway followed the slam of car doors.

Instead of receding, which would have indicated they were headed for the house, the sounds grew louder. Elizabeth wondered if Elana had somehow spotted her and Alice and had decided to join them.

In an effort to prepare Elizabeth for the inevitable meeting with his daughters, Amado had forewarned her that they had been less than enthusiastic about the wedding. She'd questioned him about their objections, whether it was the age or financial differences that had bothered Elana and Felicia the most. His only comment was that they were good girls and would come around once they met Elizabeth and saw how happy he was.

With that in mind, Elizabeth had made arrangements to meet Elana for breakfast one morning when she had to be in San Francisco on business. While their meeting had been short and more formal than friendly, Elizabeth had left with the feeling Elana was at least willing to give her a chance.

Felicia, however, remained an enigma. She'd arrived today, been picked up at the airport and brought to the house by Elana and her husband, Edgar, and had been off to visit friends before she and Elizabeth had done more than greet each other.

Elizabeth closed her book and had started to get up when she overheard something Elana was saying.

". . . go in the house yet. I swear Consuela can hear through walls and . . . know she tells Daddy everything."

"Stop worrying, Elana . . . we can't stop the wedding . . . marriage will never last. It's obvious she's only after . . ."

Soon their voices grew loud enough for Elizabeth to hear all the words.

"The whole thing turns my stomach. Christ, he's making such a fool out of himself. What could he possibly see in her?"

Elana laughed. "Edgar said that when a man goes without a woman as long as Daddy did, a hole in a board starts to look good."

"That's disgusting. Besides, what makes you think he's been doing without?"

"Have you ever seen a woman around here?"

"How would I know?" Felicia said. "It makes my skin crawl to think of him making it with anyone. As far as I'm concerned, he has no right to any happiness. Not even as artificial as this plainly is. Not after what he did to Mother. . . ."

The footsteps were getting closer as the two women ambled along the walkway. Elizabeth eased down on her chair, making herself as inconspicuous as possible. Under normal circumstances she would consider eavesdropping on a par with petty theft, but this time it seemed more like self-defense. They stopped almost directly behind Elizabeth. All they had to do was look, and they would see the two women on lawn chairs on the other side of the hedge.

"I told you about the breakfast we had together," Elana said. "What a joke. I might have bought the 'Amado and I love each other and want you to be a part of our lives' routine if she'd answered my questions about signing a prenuptial agreement."

There was a pause, then Felicia asked, "Who is that woman I saw wandering around the house when I got here this morning?"

"Alice something or other."

"Don't be obtuse."

"I'm not sure what her connection is to Elizabeth. Daddy told me, but I didn't care enough to pay attention."

"She's obviously not our kind of people. But then, if you looked past the surface, I'll bet you'd find Elizabeth isn't either."

"What can you expect? If Daddy had an ounce of sense about such things, would he have chosen Michael as his best man? Having the hired help stand up for you, for God's sake? I'm surprised he didn't ask Tony to be an usher."

The comment brought laughter.

There were sounds of another car pulling into the driveway. Elizabeth didn't chance looking to see who it was.

"Damn, there's Daddy now," Elana said.

"Has he said anything to you about his will?"

"I've tried to bring it up every time he's called. He hasn't been pleased with my persistence."

"We can't just let it drop," Felicia said. "There's too much at stake."

"I talked to Edgar's attorney, and he said without a prenuptial agreement, all she has to do is outlive Daddy and she'll end up with the bulk of his money."

"I don't give a damn about the money," Felicia said. They started moving again.

At first Elizabeth couldn't tell which way they were going, but then she decided they were headed back to the house.

"It's the . . ." The rest of Felicia's comment was lost in the sounds of a car door slamming.

"Oh, Felicia, he would die if he could hear you say that."

"Don't I wish."

Even when the chance she would be discovered had passed, Elizabeth didn't move. She wasn't as surprised at what she'd overheard as disappointed.

"That's quite a pair," Alice said, opening her eyes and turning her head to look at Elizabeth. "Just goes to prove it isn't only small towns that breed small minds."

Elizabeth set the book she'd been reading on the ground and ran her hands across her face as if she could wipe away the ugliness she had just overheard. "I was hoping you were asleep."

"No such luck."

"I can't believe how naive I've been. I thought they would be happy their father had finally found someone to love after all his years of being alone."

"You used to be smarter than that, Jenny . . . damn it all, *Elizabeth*."

"But I have been known to indulge in a little wishful thinking now and then."

Alice swung her legs over the side of the recliner and sat up. "I think you'll be able to handle Elana without too much trouble, but that Felicia is something else. What did she mean—after what Amado did to their mother?"

"Sophia committed suicide. It happened when Felicia was visiting. Amado said she left a long, rambling note blaming him for her unhappiness. Felicia has never forgiven him."

"That's a terrible thing to do to your own child."

"Felicia has never let Amado see the note, but every once in a while she throws one of Sophia's accusations at him. Of course she won't allow him to defend himself."

Alice gave a small shudder. "As far as I can see, the only good thing about Felicia is that she lives three thousand miles away. Imagine the two of them talking about their own father that way. They should be ashamed of themselves."

"Amado would be crushed if he knew."

"Are you sure he doesn't? He may indulge in a little wishful thinking himself where those two are concerned, but he isn't blind."

Elizabeth reached down to take an oak leaf out of her sandal. "I'm sure he would have said something to me."

"Like what? 'Look out for my daughters, they're immature little witches who will make your life miserable if you give them the slightest opportunity'? Amado loves you, Elizabeth, but Elana and Felicia are his children. My guess is that for a man like Amado, children are everything." Alice pulled her skirt over her knees in preparation to getting up. "Having a child of your own will tilt the scales," she said. "Especially if it turns out to be a son."

The thought of using a child as a pawn repulsed Elizabeth. "I don't want *a* son," she said. "I want at least five. And five daughters, too. Someday that great big empty house over there is going to echo with the sounds of playing children."

Elizabeth's heartbeat thundered in her ears as she waited in the foyer of the winery for the "Wedding

March" to begin. She took a deep breath and then another and another.

"Keep that up and you're going to pass out," Alice said. "And then just think how funny it's going to look when I have to drag you down the aisle."

"I can't believe how nervous I am," Elizabeth admitted.

"You're entitled—even though there isn't any reason for it."

"Consuela's a wonder, isn't she? I don't know what I would have done without her."

Alice chuckled.

"What was that for?"

"I was just thinking how traumatized your parents would be if they could see you now."

"You mean the petty bourgeois life-style their little girl so readily embraced?" Only minutes away from the safety of a new life, Elizabeth still felt the old fear at what people would think if they knew who her parents had been. Would Amado's friends think her unworthy of him? Would they question her motives for marrying him?

Would she never be free from the insanity of wondering?

"Did I tell you that Amado's friends have made me feel as if I've always been a part of their world?" she asked Alice. Having something valuable to lose gave credence and strength to her fears.

"Yes," Alice answered gently.

Consuela opened the door and motioned for Elizabeth to come forward. "You look like a princess," she whispered when Elizabeth was beside her. "Amado is such a lucky man."

Elizabeth felt as if she'd been given a gift. "Thank you, Consuela. Your kindness means the world to me."

She glanced from Elizabeth to Alice and back again to Elizabeth. "I will always be here for you."

The opening notes of the "Wedding March" sounded. Elizabeth put her hand on Alice's arm. "I love you, Grandma," she said.

"Now don't go getting all sloppy and sentimental on me," Alice said, blinking to clear the tears shimmering in her eyes. "I just might decide not to give you away after all."

11

Elizabeth slipped into the role of Amado's wife even more easily than she had anticipated. The two weeks they spent in Australia sped by far too fast. The days had been filled with stimulating new friends and ideas, the nights with erotic hours of discovery. As she'd suspected, Amado was a gentle lover who took as much joy in giving as he did in receiving. What she hadn't anticipated was his stamina and inventiveness.

Their return to St. Helena was marked with preparation for the upcoming harvest and a social life that was fuller than Elizabeth would have liked. If they weren't attending a party to celebrate the end of the growing season, they were at one being given in their honor. The growers and vintners in the Napa Valley maintained a competitive spirit, but it was always within the boundaries of a family.

She spent two to three days each week in San Francisco, making sure the launch of the television portion of the advertising campaign—which was set to hit the first of November—went off smoothly and that the ads that were set to run in the major magazines in the spring were nearing completion.

With only one exception, Amado's friends had welcomed her into their circle, making her feel as comfortable as if she'd always been a member. With Michael Logan it didn't seem to matter what she did or how she did it; he could not be swayed. When she entered a room, he left. If he was with Amado at the winery and she tried to join them, he remembered something else he had to do or somewhere else he had to be. With him living on the grounds, and with his office at the winery in the same complex as hers, it was impossible to avoid him. They ran into each other several times a day, each of their meetings as uncomfortable as the last.

Earlier that morning Amado had invited her to accompany him on a trip to Modesto, several hours' drive away. Elizabeth had begged off. It was the first day she'd had free in over a month, and she not only wanted, she needed some down time. When she'd gotten up that morning, her plans had involved nothing more strenuous or thought-provoking than a stroll through the hills or a day of sitting by the fireplace, immersed in a book.

It was almost noon, and so far she'd done neither. Instead she was standing on the deck, her elbows on the railing, Alice's latest letter propped up in front of her. After she finished reading the letter, she let her gaze swing lazily across the valley until it settled on a section of vines covered in brilliant red leaves. A year ago she would have seen only the beauty; now she realized that in order for a Zinfandel vine to produce such spectacular foliage, it had to be diseased.

Her attention was drawn to a movement in the vineyard to her right. There she saw a man dressed in a green plaid shirt and jeans walking slowly along a recently tilled row, stopping occasionally to examine something that caught his eye and then moving on. She watched the man for several seconds before she realized it was Michael Logan.

Most of the time that she looked at him, it was through a veil of growing anger. He stubbornly refused to give an inch after the mile she'd traveled to meet him, her goal to please Amado. In an effort to understand Michael better, she'd watched him at the frequent parties they attended. As far as she could tell, she was the only person he disliked.

If Michael's feelings toward her hadn't been of ongoing concern for Amado, she would have ignored him. More likely she would have told him to go to hell. But since Amado obviously cared so much, she felt obliged to continue making an effort.

With a resigned sigh over what she was about to do, she went into the house, put Alice's letter in a drawer, and took a jacket out of the hall closet.

Two hundred yards down the hill, Michael saw Elizabeth go back inside the house and drew a sigh of relief. He had been aware of her standing on the deck watching him and was angry with himself for allowing her to taint what had been a beautiful fall morning.

Without the frantic activity of the crush to keep him occupied, it was going to be damn near impossible to keep from running into her all of the time. He either had to find a way to come to terms with his feelings or find another job.

He started down the hill, then stopped to pluck and examine a bunch of grapes that had been left behind at harvest. They had raisined on the vine, their previous dark red color now nearly black. Come spring they would be tilled into the soil along with the decaying leaves, food for the next generation—a cycle that brought continuity and meaning to a world that sometimes lacked both.

Michael felt another presence in the vineyard long before he heard the rustling of vines that marked the person's passage. Tossing the grapes on the ground, he looked toward the sound and saw Elizabeth heading his way.

"Goddammit," he muttered, making no effort to hide his displeasure.

Elizabeth stopped and stared at him, a challenging look on her face. "I want to talk to you."

"Can it wait? There are some things I have to do at the winery."

"Fine. I'll go with you. We can talk on the way."

He shifted his weight from one foot to the other. The last thing he wanted was to be confined in a car with her. "You don't have to do that. I have a few minutes."

She closed the thirty feet that separated them before

she spoke again. "I think it's time you told me just what in the hell it is that you're holding against me."

"I take it this isn't going to be a lesson in diplomacy?"

"We're long past that, don't you think? I wouldn't be here at all if it weren't for Amado. He has this crazy idea we should be friends."

He shoved his hands in the back pockets of his jeans. "I'm afraid he set his hopes too high. There's no way—"

"Don't get the idea that I care, but would you mind telling me what I did that so offended you?"

He was reluctant to get into it with her but couldn't help responding to the challenge. "I have this thing about trophy hunters. They turn my stomach. Especially when the trophy they bag happens to be a friend of mine."

"I see. So you think I married Amado because of his money."

"Are you saying you didn't?"

"How is it you and his daughters are the only ones who believe that?" She shoved her jacket aside and propped her hands on her hips. "What is it, Michael? Do you think Amado has so little to offer that the only reason any woman would marry him is to get her hands on his fortune?"

"Amado knows lots of women who would have been better-suited—"

"Oh, so it's not a general thing, it's just me. Is it the way I look?" She glared at him. "Let's see, maybe it's the length of my hair? Or could it be the color of my eyes? No, I have it. I couldn't possibly love Amado because he's so old. That's it, isn't it?"

"He could be your father."

"Not *my* father," she said. "They don't have the first thing in common."

Her answer startled him. The fire in her eyes told him there was a lot more to her anger than the obvious. "Look, I have work to do, and this conversation isn't getting us anywhere."

"I just want you to know I'm here for the duration, Michael. That's a long time for two people to be at each other's throats."

"You're right," he said. He took his hands out of his pockets and started to leave.

She moved to block him. When he tried to step around her, she grabbed his arm. "This isn't meant to be a showdown. It doesn't have to be you or me."

"What do you want from me, Elizabeth?"

"An open mind."

He considered her request. "Fair enough. But what happens if I discover I was right?"

"You won't."

"Can you honestly say Amado's money had nothing to do with your decision to marry him?"

"Yes."

Her answer was no more than he expected; what surprised him was that he wanted to believe her. Still, he couldn't accept Elizabeth didn't have a hidden agenda. He loved Amado, but it was without blinders. Any man who had maintained a near celibate life for over twenty years couldn't possibly have the libido it would take to satisfy a woman like Elizabeth.

She was so goddammed beautiful—the kind of woman who, at the end of the day, could make a man forget he had muscles that ached or bills that needed to be paid. He was too well aware how long someone who looked like Elizabeth could haunt a man's dreams. She could have crooked her finger and had her pick of half of San Francisco. Why Amado?

"Is it a deal?" she prodded.

"For now."

She let go of his arm and offered her hand. "At least we're farther along than we were an hour ago."

Elizabeth was in the bedroom combing her hair when Amado came home that night. When she saw him standing at the door watching her, she crossed the room and gave him a kiss. "I thought maybe you'd decided to stay over in Modesto."

"I considered it, but then I pictured you doing what you're doing, dressed the way you are, and the next thing I knew, I was on the freeway headed north." He put his hands on her shoulders and dipped his head to kiss her throat.

"How did your meeting go?"

"I'll tell you about it in the morning."

"You must be exhausted."

"I was—right up to the moment I saw you." He hooked his thumb under the strap of her silk nightgown, pulled it down, and pressed his lips to the top of her breast.

"Mmmmm." She arched her back and caught her breath when he moved lower to let his tongue stroke her nipple. "I get the feeling you missed me today."

"Clever woman." He shrugged out of his jacket, led Elizabeth over to the bed, and lay down beside her.

"I have news, too, but it can wait."

Amado moved to look at her. "Are you sure?"

The edge of excitement in his voice left no doubt what he was thinking. His eagerness to give her the child she wanted superseded reason at times. She grabbed his tie and brought him to her for a kiss.

"It's not that," she said.

The flicker of disappointment that crossed his face was gone almost as soon as it appeared, in its place a look of dusky passion. "Then I think it is our duty to keep trying. I wouldn't want it on my conscience that we hadn't given ourselves every opportunity."

It was over breakfast the next morning that Amado told Elizabeth what he'd been doing in Modesto. "So there it is, the wedding present I promised." He looked incredibly pleased with himself as he picked up a carafe and refilled her coffee cup. "Tell me, how does it feel to be the owner of your own vineyards and winery?"

She was too surprised to feel much of anything else. The implications of what he'd done were far-reaching and complicated. "I don't know," she answered truthfully. "And besides, I thought the Mercedes was—"

He went on, oblivious of her confusion. "Modesto will be the backbone of our table wines. The vines are strong and healthy, and Michael believes the winery itself to be first rate. We'll begin expanding right away, of course, and that will mean updating the existing—"

"Michael knows about this?"

"I would never make a purchase like this without consulting him." He broke off a piece of toast and added a healthy scoop of Consuela's homemade strawberry jam.

"Will he be a part of the operation?"

Amado frowned. "Of course. He's wanted to experiment with making quality table wines as long as he's worked for me. Does it bother you that he will be fulfilling his dreams with your vineyards and your winery?"

"Of course not . . . well, yes, in a way. Have you told him that you want me to take an active interest?"

"I'm sure he has figured that out for himself. How could he not? He knows how important it is to me that the two of you find a way to work together. What better way than this?"

"Some things can't be forced, Amado."

"You must believe me when I tell you that this is not one of them. You and Michael are destined to become friends." He chuckled. "You have much in common. Me, for one—and a stubbornness that would make a mule proud."

"I hope you're right."

"Now tell me your news."

She thought about the fragile truce she'd established with Michael only the day before and how inconsequential it seemed now. "It's nothing," she said, hoping the words weren't as prophetic as they sounded.

12

The phone rang, jerking Elizabeth out of a sound sleep. She reached for the receiver, blinked, and tried to focus on the digital alarm. "Hello?"

"Oh, dear, I've called too early, haven't I?" Alice said.

It was six-thirty. "It's all right," Elizabeth said. "The alarm was just about to go off."

"Why don't I call you back in a couple of hours? I don't really have anything important to say."

Elizabeth propped her pillow against the headboard and sat up. "I'll forgive you—if you've called to tell me you changed your mind about coming for a visit."

"That's one of the reasons I called." She paused. "Now I don't want you blowing a fuse about this. I thought about it a long time before I agreed, and it's what I want to do."

"I don't like the sound of this already. Just what is it you've agreed to do?"

"Arnie lost another waitress—"

"You didn't," Elizabeth groaned.

"It's only part-time. I told him I didn't want to miss my bridge club or choir practice, so he didn't schedule me for Tuesdays or Thursdays. And he agreed to keep my hours down so I wouldn't lose any of my Social Security."

"If it's the money you need, I could—"

"Don't you dare send me another check. I told you I'm getting along just fine. Money has nothing to do with my going back to work. It just feels good to have something to do again."

Amado moaned sleepily, rolled over, and laid his head on Elizabeth's lap.

Elizabeth's disappointment went deeper than missing out on showing Alice the Napa Valley in spring. For the past month she'd felt an almost compulsive need to see her grandmother. She'd even entertained thoughts of again trying to talk her into moving to California. "I suppose it's too early to ask for a couple of weeks vacation?"

"Is there a special reason you want me to come out there now instead of this summer?"

On the surface the question seemed simple enough. It was the part left unsaid that created a quick stab to Elizabeth's heart. "No, not really. . . ." There, it was out in the open. She wasn't pregnant. Seven months of trying and still no baby. She would have told Alice about the appointment she had in two weeks with a fertility specialist in San Francisco, but she didn't want Amado to know.

With her free hand, Elizabeth brushed the hair from Amado's forehead. He let out a soft murmur of pleasure and burrowed deeper into her lap. "The holiday ad campaign had the wholesalers beating down the door at the winery. A couple of them tried to get Amado to sign exclusive contracts." She smiled at the memory. "But he wisely declined."

"Thanks to you and Michael," Amado murmured.

"I really liked the one you did for Valentine's Day," Alice said. "Showing all the indoor places you could have a picnic and all the wines that would go with them. It was so simple, it was brilliant. I especially liked the way you ended it with the couple in the bathtub."

"We weren't sure the censors were going to let us get away with that one, but it sailed right through. I guess they were so busy with the sitcoms that day, they didn't have time for us."

"How's it going with you and Michael?"

"Better. But that's probably because he's been spending so much time at the new winery in Modesto, we rarely see each other."

"Nonsense. I knew once he took his blinders off, he would love you as much as the rest of us do."

"You're jumping to conclusions." Just because she and Michael weren't openly hostile to each other didn't mean they were friends. Their relationship was more that of citizens of two countries that had suddenly stopped warring with each other—suspicious and wary.

"And it's work I need to be jumping to."

There was an unmistakable excitement in Alice's voice. "Don't overdo things, Grandma. I love you."

"I love you, too, sweetheart."

Elizabeth hung up the phone. At the same time Amado rolled to his side and took her in his arms. "You couldn't talk Alice into coming out?"

"Huh-uh. I'm beginning to think I'll never see her again."

"You know there isn't a reason in the world why you couldn't get on a plane and fly out there."

She was getting entirely too careless around Amado. "I just may take you up on that as soon as I feel comfortable with the new layout for the fall ads."

She and Alice had already discussed how they would handle her supposed visits home. As long as she planned them for times when it was impossible for Amado to come along, it would be a simple matter of getting on a plane and disappearing for a week. Alice would stay in Farmingham and handle any incoming calls. After a couple of trips Elizabeth would make a point of telling Amado how much she hated being away from him, and with a little luck, that would be the end of it.

Amado shifted his weight, then grimaced in pain and moved to his back. Elizabeth propped herself up on her elbow and looked down at him. "What's wrong?"

"Just a kink." He ran his hand over his chest. "I must have pulled a muscle yesterday when I was in the fields with Tony."

"Do you want me to rub it?"

He gave her a lecherous grin. "I would be an idiot to refuse such an offer."

She playfully hit him on the arm. "Roll over."

"It isn't my back." He drew an imaginary line across his chest. "It's here."

Elizabeth came up on her knees and began massaging the muscles that ran along his rib cage.

"Ahhhh," he sighed. "That's it." And then a minute later, "A little lower, I think." She moved to his waist. Another minute passed. "Your fingers are magic. Now if you could move just a bit lower?"

She laughed. "And here I was about to give you a lecture on doing too much."

He pulled her over to straddle him. "On the contrary. I will be sure to do even more strenuous work from now on. I had no idea what a good nurse you are."

She pulled off her nightgown and began to rock her hips slowly, moving rhythmically against his erection. He cupped her breasts with his hands and massaged the nipples with his thumbs. When he reached between them and guided himself inside of her, she put her head back and sighed in contentment.

Several minutes later Amado quickened his movements, and she could see that he was nearing climax. She said a silent, fervent prayer that this would be the time they made a baby together—a baby that would make them a real family.

A month later Elizabeth sat in the doctor's private office where the nurse had left her half an hour earlier with the out-and-out lie, "Doctor will be with you in just a minute."

She took the pamphlet *Infertility and Its Solutions* out of her purse and started going through it again. She'd had no idea there were so many things that could go wrong with a woman's body. Elizabeth couldn't remember ever hearing about any childless couples in Farmingham. But then that wasn't the kind of thing people openly talked about to their neighbors.

Dr. Steele came into the room, his gaze fixed on her file. "How are you feeling, Mrs. Montoya?" he asked.

His question seemed a little peculiar considering the reason she was there, but she answered anyway. "Fine."

He patted her on the shoulder as he moved to sit at his desk. He still hadn't actually looked at her. "As I'm sure my nurse told you, we have the results from X ray."

The time she'd put in waiting for this moment had seemed interminable. Her hands closed over the arms of the chair, her fingers dug into the plush material as if she were hanging on for her life. If Dr. Steele hadn't decided at the last minute to take an impromptu minivacation, she would have received the results a week ago. But everyone from the lab technicians to the radiologist had refused to tell her anything, insisting she should hear the "news" from her own doctor.

"I'm afraid it's even worse than I first thought." He flipped through the papers in her file. "Both tubes are completely blocked. Of course we won't know how badly until we do a laparoscopy, but I strongly suspect we aren't going to like what we find."

Elizabeth swallowed in an attempt to clear the lump from her throat. "Let's go with the worst scenario. Say the tubes are beyond repair—what are my options then?"

He tossed her file on the desk. "I don't like to cross those kinds of bridges until we've come to them. I find it's easier to keep an optimistic outlook if we take the process one step at a time."

A rage began to build in Elizabeth. If Dr. Steele charged for his clichés at the same rate he charged for his clinical skills, he could double his income. How could a man who made his living off women be so goddamned condescending toward them? "Screw the optimistic outlook, Dr. Steele. I want to know what the realistic chances are that I will ever be able to conceive a child."

He glared at her. "From what I've seen so far, it would take a medical miracle to get you pregnant. But even then I would be surprised if you could carry a fetus to term."

"And why is that?"

"Your uterus is extremely—"

"So what is the point of doing more tests?" She didn't need the details, the facts were enough to keep her awake at night.

"What can I say? Miracles happen."

It took concentrated effort, but Elizabeth managed to gather her purse and to get out of her chair without letting him see how devastated she was. "I don't believe in miracles, Dr. Steele."

"In time you'll think differently. When you do, I'll be here."

She hesitated and considered what one of her professors had once said in class—that in Japan, the first person to raise his voice lost the argument. "I hope you brought your skates," she said sweetly.

"I beg your pardon?"

She was mildly disappointed that with his expertise in the medium he hadn't made the jump himself. "You know . . . to use when hell freezes over."

°   °   °

When Elizabeth arrived home that afternoon, Consuela told her that Amado had gone to Modesto to check on some problems they were having with the installation of the new stainless-steel fermentation tanks and that he wanted her to know he would likely be spending the night. She wandered around the house for an hour and then went for a walk in the vineyards, hoping the beauty of the emerging mustard flowers and the promise of renewed life in the vines would distract her. But it was useless. All she could think about was the child she would never hold in her arms.

If only a baby hadn't represented Amado's hope for the future.

She forced herself to open her eyes and release the thought. The weight of it and the death of a dream were stealing her ability to function. If she didn't do something soon, she would be mired in her sorrow. There was only one place to turn—her old standby, work. If she could bury herself in the mundane, she could get through the rest of the day without breaking down. After telling Consuela where she was going in case Amado called, she headed for her office at the winery.

Elizabeth had lost all track of time when she heard a knock on her door, looked up, and saw that it was dark outside. "Come in."

Michael stuck his head inside. "I thought you were Amado," he said.

"He's in Modesto."

"Yeah, I know, but when I saw the light, I figured

he'd decided to come home tonight after all." He made a move to leave. "Sorry I disturbed you."

"Wait," she said, startled by her own request. She understood her need to be with someone, just not her choice. "I'd like to talk to you if you've got a minute."

"What about?"

Good question. "The winery."

He glanced at the clock on the wall behind her. "Can you make it fast? I have to be somewhere at seven-thirty."

She should have guessed as much for herself. Winery gossip had it that Michael was rarely without a date on the weekends. She twisted around on her seat to see how much time that gave her. It was already seven. "We can make it another day."

He frowned. "If it's important, I can—"

"No . . . that's all right. It'll keep."

He came into the room anyway. With an uncharacteristic gentleness where she was concerned, he said, "Let me be the judge of that, okay?"

God, did she look that bad? "I don't need your pity," she snapped. "Now why don't you just get out of here and do whatever it is you have to do."

He pulled a chair over to where she was sitting, turned it backward, and straddled the seat. "Me pity you?" He shook his head. "Not if you were covered in honey and tied to an anthill."

"Forget I said anything, okay? I can find out what I needed to know from Amado." She swung around so that she was facing her desk.

He grabbed the arm of her chair and swung her back to face him again. "Look, you know and I know things haven't improved so much between us that you would make a point of talking to me if you didn't consider it important. So why don't you just say whatever it is that's on your mind?"

"I talk to you all the time."

"Oh, now and then there's been a 'Good morning, Michael' thrown out, or, 'Have you seen Amado?' There've even been one or two times you've said good night as you were leaving. That's hardly what I would consider talking to someone."

"I suppose you think you've gone out of your way to encourage anything more?"

"Why should I? You're the one who thinks we should be friends."

"Get out of here. I've got too much on my mind to play these kinds of stupid games with you."

"Now you've really piqued my interest." He laid his arms across the back of the chair and propped his chin on them. "Is there a problem with one of the wholesalers?"

Several weeks earlier, when there had been a lull in the work on the ad campaign, Amado had asked her to familiarize herself with their distribution system. It was a not-too-gentle nudge toward what he hoped would be her eventual participation in the business end of the winery's operation. He'd also told her that he'd informed Michael she would be coming to him with questions. But it was too early. She didn't know enough yet to ask anything that sounded halfway intelligent. Reaching for something to say, she grabbed the first thing that popped into her mind. "I was just wondering how you felt about Amado's plan to buy the vineyard he found in Healdsburg last week."

"What possible difference could my feelings make?"

"He listens to you."

"I see." He tilted his head to one side and made a point of studying her. "Could this mean you don't like the idea and were hoping I didn't either so you could get me to talk him into changing his mind?"

"I'm worried about him." It was the first time she'd put words to feelings. "He's like a kid who's suddenly found himself with a limitless supply of building blocks. He just keeps adding more and more to the top and forgets if he doesn't expand the foundation, the whole thing is going to collapse."

"And I'm supposed to believe this bothers you, even though he's put the Modesto operation in your name?"

She shot him a disgusted look. "Don't you ever get tired of thinking the worst of me?"

"Not at all. It's as easy as breathing."

"I'm sorry I wasted your time."

He made no move to leave. "Now you want to tell me what's really bothering you?"

The pointed and astute observation caught her off guard. "No."

"Why not? You couldn't ask for a more neutral listener."

Grief filled her until she thought she would explode with the need to share it with someone. But not Michael. Anyone but him. "It's personal."

Hearing the distress in her voice, the taunting spark left his eyes. "I have a feeling I owe you an apology. There's obviously something bothering you. I had no right to bait you like that."

She could take his abuse, but not his kindness.

Moisture welled in her eyes. "If you don't get out of here right now, you're going to be late."

"It won't be the first time."

Her throat hurt from trying to hold back her tears. "I don't want to do this. Please . . . just leave."

"All right. If you're sure." He got up and walked to the door. With his back to her he said, "You know you've made it damn near impossible for us to go on the way we were."

"Why's that?"

He turned to look at her. "I think I might actually be starting to like you."

"You'll recover. Give it a couple of days."

Michael glanced at the clock on the dashboard of the truck as he pulled to a stop in front of his house. There was no way he was going to make the party on time. Normally it wouldn't matter if he was a little late, but this was one of those mystery things where everyone was supposed to come in character and then spend the evening trying to figure out which one of them had committed a murder.

Somewhere in the past hour he'd lost his party mood and would have stayed home that night if it wouldn't ruin the evening for everyone else. After all, what if he was the murderer?

Fifteen minutes later he was back in his truck, dressed in his version of a crusty old sea captain, no more excited about the evening than he had been before donning the pea jacket and yachting cap.

He saw Elizabeth's Mercedes coming toward him on the road into St. Helena. He waved, but they passed so quickly, he wasn't sure whether she saw him or not. An unexpected, powerful urge to turn around and follow her back to the house came over him. There was an unfinished feel to the conversation they'd had earlier that night.

With the sudden realization that his feelings toward Elizabeth had gone through a dramatic change in the past month, Michael frowned and tried to reason it out. When, and why, had his opinion changed?

And then it hit him. He no longer saw Susan when he looked at Elizabeth. Now, in hindsight, it was hard to imagine that he ever had. They were nothing alike, at least not where it counted. Michael found that once he came to know someone, he became blinded to how they looked. While Elizabeth's hair and eyes and build would always be similar to Susan's, they were superficial similarities.

He'd always prided himself on his ability to accept people for who and not what they were. It brought him up short to discover how quick he'd rushed to judgment where Elizabeth was concerned.

And all because she reminded him of Susan.

Would he never be free of her influence?

13

A week passed before Elizabeth found the right moment to tell Amado they would not be having a child of their own. He listened quietly and, when she was through, held her until her tears were spent.

Although she was never certain how he felt, they didn't talk about it again. It was as if the episode had been nothing more than a bump in the road of their life together; once crossed, all was smooth going again, at least on the surface. Only Elizabeth was aware how often her smiles were forced or how sensitive she'd become to the words so liberally used to describe the emerging season in the vineyards. Fruitful, rebirth, infancy—words sprinkled carelessly into daily conversation about the burgeoning vines, as if only she were aware of their power to hurt.

Elizabeth became fixated with a pair of nesting house finches, anticipating the eggs they would lay, the babies that would follow. Michael found her intently watching the birds one afternoon.

He came up to her where she was sitting on the front steps of the guest cottage. "Something wrong?" he asked.

She offered her binoculars and pointed him in the right direction. "They just hatched yesterday." She smiled. "Ugly, huh?"

"They're not so bad." He sat down beside her. "Have you ever seen an eagle chick?"

"Never in person."

He gave her a questioning look.

"I'm hooked on the nature shows on PBS."

"Someday I'm going to break down and get a television. I keep hearing about all these great shows I'm missing."

"I take it you saw your eagle chick firsthand, then?"

"When I was a kid, I spent a couple of summers working the canneries in Alaska."

Elizabeth chanced a sideways glance in his direction. Was this the real Michael Logan? Was it possible they were having a normal conversation? "That surprises me. I had you pictured as the nose-to-the-grindstone, get-out-of-school-as-soon-as-possible type."

He chuckled. "Running off to Alaska was my attempt at a rebellious youth."

She had her mouth open to question him further when she remembered how tightly Amado was tied to Michael's college years. Had Michael been rebelling against Amado when he took off for Alaska? Was it possible their history was not as trouble free as it appeared?

As if he could read her thoughts, Michael stood abruptly and announced he had work to do. Almost before she could acknowledge his leaving, he was gone. She watched him walk across the yard and get into his truck, pleased that another step toward friendship, however tentative, was behind them.

A week later Michael stopped by her office and stood in the doorway until she broke off what she was doing and looked up at him. "Busy?"

"Give me a second and I won't be." She finished the sentence she'd been writing and pushed her chair back from the computer. "What can I do for you?"

"Amado said you might be interested in tagging along with me today."

"He did?" She couldn't imagine a more awkward scenario. "Where are you going?"

"To Davis. I'm meeting with Charles Pinkley about the results of a fermentation experiment."

"I don't suppose Amado happened to mention *why* he thought I would be interested?" She had barely made it through college chemistry, immediately forgetting everything she'd learned the day the semester ended.

"Just that you wanted to learn every aspect of the business."

Amado came up behind Michael. "I see you have already spoken to Elizabeth about the meeting." A guilty grin crossed his face. "I was hoping to prepare her."

"Sorry, I thought I'd leave a little early and see if I could find something for Patty's birthday," Michael said.

"Who is this Patty person?" Amado asked. "Didn't you tell me you were seeing a woman named Faith just last week?"

"Patty is Faith's daughter. And I'm not seeing Faith in the sense you mean. We've been friends since high school."

Amado focused his attention on Elizabeth. "I will call Consuela and have her hold dinner until you return."

It was on the tip of her tongue to tell him she wasn't going, that she had a stack of correspondence she had to get through, but then she saw the determined set of his jaw and knew it would be easier to give in than to argue. As much as she enjoyed her increasing work load in the office, she was lost when it came to the gritty end of winemaking. "Don't do that," Elizabeth told him. "If I'm hungry, I'll fix something for myself when I get back."

Michael looked at his watch pointedly. "If we're going to miss the traffic, we should get going."

Elizabeth grabbed her purse, put the strap over her shoulder, then linked her arm though Amado's. "Walk me out to the car?"

He removed her arm gently. "I cannot. I'm expecting a call any minute now."

The subtle rebuff blindsided her. She sent a questioning look to Amado, but he either didn't understand or purposely ignored her.

"Give my best wishes to Charles," he told Michael. "And tell him I am looking forward to his visit next month." Almost as if it were an afterthought, he gave Elizabeth a kiss on the cheek.

Less than an hour later, Michael pulled into the parking lot of the Nut Tree, a combination gift shop and restaurant east of Fairfield. It was a favorite stopping place whenever he traveled that section of Interstate 80. He had a weakness for the specialty of the house, gingerbread cookies, especially when he could get them fresh out of the oven. They were closer to the ones his mother used to make than he had found anywhere else. "I'll just be a couple of minutes," he said to Elizabeth.

Behind the main gift shop was one devoted exclusively to children. "Want to give me a hand picking something out?" he asked as he turned off the engine.

"I don't think so," she said.

"What if I offered to buy you a banana milk shake as a bribe?"

"How do you know I like banana milk shakes? And besides, even if I did, do I look like the kind of woman who could be bribed with one? Never mind. I already know your answer."

He twisted on his seat to get a better look at her. "Am I that transparent?"

"About certain things you are."

"Come on," he prompted. "Give me a hand. I don't have the first idea what three-year-old girls like."

She bristled. "And what makes you think I do?"

"Because you used to be one."

Elizabeth threw up her hands. "What logic. Now I see why Amado thinks you have such a brilliant mind."

Michael grinned. "Now there's the Elizabeth I know. I was beginning to think you'd been kidnapped and that a sweet, timid clone had been left in your place." He got out of the car and came around to open her door.

"I really don't want to go into a toy store," she said.

It wasn't so much what she said as the way she said it that warned Michael it was time to back off. "Okay, why don't you get the milk shakes while I'm inside buying something completely inappropriate?"

"My treat, I suppose?"

He had to give her credit, whatever was bothering her, she managed to put up a credible front. He dug into his pocket for his wallet and handed her two dollars.

"This isn't enough," she protested.

"It is for mine. You didn't say I had to pay for yours, too."

When she smiled, he realized how long it had been since he'd heard her laughter around the winery. How could what had once been so much a part of her that he'd reached the point of taking it for granted disappear abruptly? What in the hell was going on between her and Amado?

It was dark by the time they were finally headed back to St. Helena. They'd traveled several miles in a comfortable silence, and Michael was beginning to think Elizabeth had finally run out of the questions sparked by their meeting with Charles. He should have known better.

"I heard you tell Charles you were trying to talk Amado into planting more varietals. Why?"

"I think it's a mistake to concentrate too heavily on Zinfandel and Chardonnay and Cabernet Sauvignon. Tastes change. We've got to anticipate the market, not follow it."

"You sound like a professor I had in college. He was one of those teachers who makes a real difference in your life. Before I took his course I thought advertising was a dirty word."

"Where did you go to school?"

"Safford Hill."

"I have a couple of friends who went there."

She gave him a sidelong glance. "Female, no doubt."

"I see you've been listening to the town gossips." At times his grossly inflated reputation for womanizing amused him; at other times, especially when it got in the way of a developing friendship, it was a nuisance.

"Amado says you could have any single woman in the valley, and quite a few of the married ones, too."

"I leave the married ones alone."

"All those women you date—what are you running from?"

He turned and pinned her with a disgusted look. "Come on. In today's world I'd either have to be stupid or have a death wish to be doing what everyone thinks I'm doing." He turned back to the road. "Why do people have so much trouble accepting the fact that a man can be friends with a woman?" He let several seconds pass before he added, "Besides, what gives you the idea I'm running from anything?"

She ran her hands through her hair and leaned against the headrest. "It was a dumb question. Forget I asked."

"You make me sound like a candidate for a psychiatrist's couch and then tell me to forget it?" He took his hand from the steering wheel and snapped his fingers. "Just like that." He hated pop psychologists almost as much as he hated people who judged a man's worth by his bank account.

"It's been such a good day. Let's not end it with an argument."

His anger was out of proportion. Why, all of a sudden, did he care what she thought? Let her believe whatever she wanted.

"I only asked because I see so much of myself in you," she said several minutes later. "I've spent half of my life running from commitment."

"That's you."

"True. I had no right to—"

"What were *you* afraid of?"

"Getting too close, letting someone see the real me, saying good-bye. There have been lots of reasons."

A warning bell sounded in Michael's mind that he didn't understand. "I'm not like that."

"I guess I was wrong, then. Obviously you just haven't met the right woman yet. When you do, you'll settle down."

"That's assuming I'll recognize her when I see her."

"Oh, I'm sure you will."

"How's that?"

She offered him a smile. "With you there will probably be bells going off. I can't imagine anything less."

"Is that how it was when you met Amado?"

She shook her head. "For me, it was more a matter of timing and circumstance."

"That doesn't sound very romantic."

"The romance came later, when I realized how much I loved him." She adjusted the shoulder strap of her seat belt, giving it more play. "At times I can be like the proverbial mule who needs to be hit in the head with a two-by-four to get its attention."

Michael left the interstate and turned onto Highway 12, the narrow, two-lane road that would take them to Highway 29 and home. "Amado's changed since he met you—for the better," he admitted reluctantly. "I've never seen him this happy."

"That's quite an observation."

"What you really mean is, coming from me."

"Am I to take it you've changed your mind about my motives for marrying Amado?"

"I might be stubborn, and I can be thick-headed when it suits my purpose, but I'm not stupid. Amado's crazy about you. And you're . . ."

"Yes?"

"Well, it's plain you're crazy about him."

"Thanks for noticing."

"What about you? Has the marriage changed you, too?"

"I don't know. It isn't something I spend a lot of time thinking about."

In subtle, invasive ways, the barrier that had kept them from becoming friends had been breached. It lay in ruins all around them, like shattered glass.

"Why didn't you want to go into the toy store with me?" He'd told himself he wouldn't bring it up again. If she'd wanted him to know, she would have told him when it happened. But an inner voice demanded he ask, not because the answer mattered to him, but because he sensed somehow that whatever was bothering her needed to be shared, and he wanted to do this for her.

She turned to look out the side window, even though it was too dark to see anything. Several minutes passed before she answered. "I recently found out that I can't have children, and I guess I'm still a little sensitive about it."

The pain he heard in her voice made him doubt his decision to encourage her to talk. There were some wounds only time could heal. And there were some that simply became a part of you. "I didn't know you and Amado were planning to—"

She turned to look at him. "I shouldn't have told you that."

"Why?"

"Because it's personal and doesn't concern you."

He didn't buy her explanation. She'd known that before she ever opened her mouth. But it hadn't stopped her. "If you're worried I'm going to say something, I'm not. Whatever you tell me stays between us."

"I'm usually more circumspect."

"Everyone needs a friendly ear now and then." She must have been fresh from receiving the news the night he'd run into her in her office. All the strange behavior was beginning to fall into place—the tears, the sadness in her eyes, Amado's rebuff. What better way for Amado to be able to turn his back on Elana and Felicia and the grief they had put him through than with a new son? He must have been devastated.

"And you won't say anything?"

"I promise." On impulse he reached for her hand. Her fingers closed around his. For a moment—before the contact became awkward in its intimacy—it seemed as if they had always been friends.

Elizabeth let go first. "How much longer before we get home?" she asked.

"Half hour, more or less—depending on the traffic through Napa."

"Suddenly I'm famished."

"There's a couple of apples in the backseat. You're welcome to them. Or we could stop someplace and get something. It's up to you." He was grateful for the change of direction in their conversation. It was as if the coin that represented their relationship had abruptly flipped from tails to heads. He wasn't used to being proven wrong in his initial reaction to people. Elizabeth was an exception, and he didn't know what to think about it yet.

"The apple sounds perfect." She took off her seat belt, got up on her knees, and reached behind Michael. "You want one?"

"I eat mine cut and cored."

She brought the sack with her anyway. "My, aren't we the picky one?"

"It's necessity, not choice. My front teeth were sacrificed to a blocked field goal attempt."

"But you won the game."

"Damn straight."

"Well, mine were lost to vanity, but I don't let it slow me down." She bit into the apple, pulled off a large chunk, and handed it to him. The gesture was natural and spontaneous and gave him the same sense of belonging that winning the football game had.

"Do you peel grapes, too?" he said.

"We have a saying about people like you where I come from."

"Something tells me I'm better off not asking."

"Be wary the neighbor who eats his fill of beans, then wants to sit a spell and visit."

Michael laughed out loud, almost choking on his apple.

"Boy, you're easy," she said.

The rest of the way home, they tried topping each other with the worst jokes they'd ever heard.

Elizabeth won hands down.

Amado must have heard them approaching because he was on the step to greet Elizabeth when she arrived. After a quick rundown on the results of the meeting and a promise for greater detail in the morning, Michael took off for Patty's house and Faith's birthday dinner.

"Have a good time?" Amado asked as they walked inside.

"As a matter of fact, I did."

"You sound surprised."

"I'm pleased to report that your plan to throw Michael and me together until we became friends or killed each other in the attempt is finally working."

"What plan? I had no plan."

"You can cut the innocent act." She dropped her purse on the hall table and slipped her arms around his neck. "When are you going to accept the fact that I can't be fooled? I know what that devious mind of yours is up to almost before you do."

He pressed his lips to her forehead. "In that case, my dear Elizabeth, why don't you tell me what I am thinking of at this precise moment?"

She tilted her head and gave him a seductive smile. "That you want to have your way with me."

"Remarkable. I shall have to be more careful with my thoughts from now on."

"It won't do any good." She snuggled closer. "I have a magic potion that can penetrate a lead shield."

"The magic you work has nothing to do with potions."

"Too much talk." She took his hand and led him down the hall toward the bedroom. "Time for action."

Half an hour later Elizabeth and Amado were lying side by side, a sheet tossed carelessly over their nakedness, the room so quiet they could hear the gentle pulsing of the clock radio.

"I'm sorry," Amado said.

"Please don't." Elizabeth rolled to her side and nestled her head against his chest. "Sometimes I'm not in the mood either. It's no big deal."

"You wanted to make love."

"I wanted to feel close to you. And I do."

"It is not the same."

"Not to a man, maybe. But to a woman, it's the touching and the tenderness that matter most."

"I promise you it will never happen again."

"You can't make a promise like that. You aren't a machine, Amado. No one can perform on command."

"Perhaps it is the . . ."

She waited. When he didn't finish, she propped herself up and looked at him. "The what?"

"Nothing."

"Don't shut me out. Not now."

He turned his face away from her. "There has been

so much to do this spring. There are times I wish I had another pair of hands."

He was lying, but she didn't know what to do about it. Realizing she was making him uncomfortable looming over him like an inquisitor, she lay back down. "Would it help if I told you how much I love you?"

He pressed a kiss to the top of her head. "They are the words I live to hear."

"Then I shall repeat them to you every waking hour from now on."

"I would like that," he said. "Now I think we have talked about this enough. I would like to hear about my friend Charles. How did you find him?"

Elizabeth felt as though something were slipping away from her, but she had no idea what or how. "I found him short and bald and remarkably nearsighted."

"Charles Pinkley? Are you sure—" He chuckled and brought her to him for a hug. "I do not know what I would do without you."

"Good thing, because I'm not about to go anywhere."

He gave her another kiss. "Now will you tell me about Charles?"

She allowed herself to relax a little. They would get through this. "He's a astonishingly tall man. And those sideburns . . ."

14

Elizabeth stared at the front page of the newspaper that blocked her view of Amado. He was seated across the dining room table from her, indulging his recently adopted habit, reading instead of talking to her over breakfast. She'd already tried unsuccessfully to get his attention several times that morning. She tried again.

"I forgot to tell you the camera crew will be here at five instead of seven tomorrow morning," she said. "They want to set up for a couple of backlit shots in the vineyards."

Amado answered without lowering the paper. "When do they want me to be there?"

"Jerry said if you could be finished with makeup by six, that should give them plenty of time."

The barrier came down. "That shouldn't be a problem." With meticulous care, he refolded and returned the section of paper he'd been reading. He looked at his half-eaten grapefruit and then at the wall behind Elizabeth. He seemed ill at ease, almost nervous. Several more seconds passed before he spoke again. "We must talk." He paused. "I have put off telling you something, Elizabeth, because I knew it would cause you unnecessary concern."

She sat up straighter on her chair, fighting the urge to come to attention. She had no idea what would come next, just a feeling she wasn't going to like it.

"I have asked Consuela to move my things to the guest room this morning after we have left for work." Finally he brought his gaze up and looked at her. "Please . . . Elizabeth. Try to understand. . . . The move is only temporary. You know I have not been sleeping well, and I worry that my restlessness is disturbing you. As soon as everything is normal again, I will have Consuela move my things back into your room with you."

She didn't have to ask what he meant by normal. That would be the day he could put aside his disappointment in her inability to have his children long enough to make love to her again. "My room?" She fought to keep her voice steady. "When did it stop being 'our' room, Amado?"

"It was an unfortunate choice of words. Nothing more."

She left her seat and came around the table. When she was beside him, she sank to her knees and put her hands on his arm. "If you leave, the distance that's already developing between us will only continue to grow. We'll never be able to work this out."

He touched the side of her face with infinite gentleness. "You are making far too much of this."

"The way I feel, I could be lying in the middle of the floor kicking and screaming and it wouldn't begin to express how terrified I am. I love you, Amado. I know how disappointed you are—"

His hand moved to lightly cover her mouth. "My love for you has nothing to do with whether or not we have children together. I told you we would never speak of it again. It is behind us and of no more consequence."

If only she could believe him. "Then why are you doing this?"

"I have decisions I must make, and I need time to think about them."

Elizabeth went cold inside. "What kinds of decisions?"

"I will tell you about them later."

If she had learned nothing else about Amado in the ten months they had been married, it was that he could not be pushed. "Does this new room of yours come with visiting privileges?"

"I think it would be best if you waited a while."

"I see," she said softly. Her heart felt as if it were slowly, inexorably breaking.

He took her hand and held it tightly. "The sadness I see in your eyes is like a knife in my chest. You must believe I love you, my beautiful Elizabeth. You are everything to me, the very air I breathe."

"Then stay. I promise you we can work it out."

"I will not be far away, just down the hall."

His mind was made up. He would not be swayed. She nodded, defeated.

"Now I must be going. I am supposed to meet Michael at the winery in less than ten minutes."

Elizabeth moved to let him pass.

He started to leave and then, as if it were a last-minute thought, came back to give her a kiss. The meeting of their lips was almost perfunctory, without passion or even hope.

"Are you free for lunch?" she asked.

He frowned. "I thought I told you I am having lunch with Elana this afternoon. She is meeting me in Santa Rosa."

He hadn't told her, and she could only guess why. "Be sure to say hello to her for me."

"Would you like to join us?"

The invitation was so insincere, it was almost laughable. "I don't think so."

A look of relief flickered in his eyes. "I have already told Consuela not to hold dinner for me."

If Elizabeth didn't like Consuela so much, there were times she could hate her. "You're planning on being home late, then?"

"I have no idea how long my meeting with Elana will take."

"I thought you were just having lunch with her. When did it become a meeting?"

He looked uncomfortable. "With Elana you can never tell how long anything will take. We see each other so seldom, I hate to put a limit on our time together."

Something snapped in Elizabeth. "All you had to do was ask, and I could have disappeared for the day, for the weekend, even. After all, this is your home. You shouldn't have to sneak off to Santa Rosa to visit your daughter. God forbid I should stand in the way of family. How does that old saying go? Something about blood being thicker than—"

Amado grabbed her arms, stopping just short of actually shaking her. "I won't listen to you talk that way. Elana mentioned to me she was driving to Portland to meet Edgar. I asked if she would let me buy her lunch. It was a simple thing. Why do you want to make it complicated?"

She twisted free, her anger unabated. "Michael is waiting for you."

"He can wait. What is happening here is more important."

"You can see that and still do nothing to change it? Amado, we can't ignore what's going on between us and hope it will go away." At that moment their future seemed as fragile as a piece of fine porcelain in the hands of a two-year-old. "You could see a doctor." She'd promised herself she wouldn't do that to him. "Maybe there's something medically wrong."

He seemed to grow smaller as she watched. "I saw Dr. Murdock last week," he said, betraying no emotion. "There is nothing he can do."

Then Amado's impotence was her fault. Or, more to the point, it was caused by Amado's feelings toward her. Her stomach convulsed. She felt as though she were going to be sick. "He was sure?"

"Yes."

"Maybe in time . . ."

"Anything is possible."

She had to get away, to be by herself, to think. "If I go to Modesto for a couple of days, can you handle the film crew tomorrow without me?"

"If there is a problem, I will call."

"Then you don't mind if I go?"

"Not at all. Michael will enjoy the company."

Goddammit. Michael was the last person she wanted to be around. "I thought you said you had a meeting with him this morning."

"In preparation for his trip. He will be gone several days, and there are some things we need to discuss before he goes."

"Don't say anything to him about my going. I just remembered there are some reports I have to finish before I leave, and I'm not sure how long they will take. Besides, if we ride down together, I'll be stuck there until he's ready to come back. I'm not sure I want to stay away that long."

Amado nodded. "As you wish."

"Then again, I may not go to Modesto after all," she said breezily. "It seems like forever since I've been to the city to see Joyce."

Amado was quiet for a long time. "Perhaps what you really need is some time with Alice."

"So I can dump my problems on her?"

He winced. "I know this is difficult for you. . . ."

"*Difficult?* My husband is so disappointed in me that he—"

Amado pulled her into his arms. He held her tightly, as if afraid of what she might do if he let her go. "I will not listen to such things. You must not even think them." He pressed his cheek into her hair. "If I feel disappointment, it is only with myself. I have failed you in a way no husband has a right to fail his wife."

Elizabeth laid her forehead against his shoulder. "Please don't leave me," she said.

"You must trust me with this," he said. "What I am doing is for the best."

Elizabeth stayed in Amado's arms until she was sure she could look at him with clear eyes. "I'll probably stay in the city over the weekend," she said.

His face was a mask. It was his hands that gave him away. They trembled noticeably when he let her go. "Elana tells me there is a wonderful new play at the Curran."

"How nice." It was everything she could do not to question Elana's newfound interest in her father. Could he have told her there would be no more Montoya children after all? How could she warn Amado about his daughter without sounding like a jealous, grasping wife? "Would you like me to get tickets for us?"

"I thought you and Joyce might enjoy—"

"Of course. I should have known better."

"Perhaps in a couple of weeks we could . . ." He gestured helplessly.

"We could what?"

"Nothing. Michael is waiting. And you have packing to do."

She walked him to the door. Their life together had been devastatingly altered, and it had happened without tears or shouts of protest or an angry word being exchanged.

Was it the pain of her heart breaking that made her behave in such an accommodating way?

Or was it her instinct for survival?

°   °   °

It was almost one o'clock when Elizabeth pulled into the parking lot of the apartment Amado kept in the city. She was annoyed to find another car in their reserved space, but not surprised. The other residents had undoubtedly noticed how rarely the space was used and were disinclined to let anything so valuable go to waste.

She circled the area for half an hour before a meter finally opened up. By then she wasn't annoyed anymore, she was out-and-out angry. She fed the emotion, letting it grow until it crowded the pain. When she discovered the manager wasn't home and that she would have to wait to find out who owned the offending car, she almost welcomed the fuel it added to her fire.

She was so caught up in a rehearsal of what she would say to the manager when he came home that she got off the elevator on the wrong floor and had to take the stairs up another flight. Finally she reached the right apartment, went inside, and stopped in midstride.

There were dirty dishes on the coffee table. And the drapes were tightly drawn. She distinctly remembered leaving them partially open the last time she and Amado had been there. Stale cigarette smoke permeated the air, along with a faint hint of perfume.

Elizabeth crossed the room and peered in the kitchen. There she found more dishes and an empty champagne bottle. Damn it all, anyway, Amado could have told her he was letting Michael use the apartment for his weekend trysts. She tried to ignore the niggling little fact that she was every bit as disappointed in Michael as she was angry with Amado.

If the mess was this bad in the living room and kitchen, what would she find in the bedroom? How could Amado expect her to sleep in the same bed he loaned out to Michael?

She headed down the hallway, her stride quick and determined. What she found stole the shelter of her anger and left her feeling almost as exposed as the two people fumbling at each other on the bed.

"Edgar?" Elizabeth said.

"What the hell?" He pushed away the blond woman who had been straddling him and made a grab for the bedspread. "Elizabeth? What the hell are you doing here?"

"Me? What about you? Aren't you supposed to be in Portland?"

"I'm flying up there tonight."

"But Elana thinks . . ." Despite herself, Elizabeth smiled at Edgar's frantic efforts to cover the woman beside him, as if he were a magician and with the wave of a hand he could make her disappear.

"This isn't what it looks like, Elizabeth. I don't want you going off half-cocked and spreading rumors about what you think you saw."

"Me go off half-cocked?" She leaned her shoulder into the door frame, perversely, enjoying herself for the first time in weeks. "Now why would I do that?"

"I know you don't like me. And Elana certainly isn't your favorite person."

A muffled voice came from under the bedspread. "Edgar, I can't breathe."

He put a hand on the mound next to him. "Shut up, Gloria."

"What are you doing here, Edgar?" Elizabeth asked. But before he could answer, the ludicrousness of the situation struck her and she laughed out loud. "Never mind. It was a stupid question. What I really want to know is, who gave you a key?"

"I have my own."

"Since when?"

"I had a copy made when Amado had Elana check on the maid service." A guilty look came with the admission.

She frowned. "I don't remember him doing that."

"It was before he met you."

"I see. So this isn't a spur-of-the-moment, first-time-you've-ever-strayed kind of thing?"

"That's none of your business."

A slow smile spread across her face. "It is now."

"You bitch."

"Don't worry, Edgar. I'm not going to tell on you."

"In exchange for what?"

The woman under the bedspread began to squirm again. "Goddammit, Edgar, let go of the fuckin' covers. I told you I can't breathe."

"I want a new bed in here by tomorrow," Elizabeth told him.

"That's it?"

"You don't have anything I want, Edgar."

A sneer passed over his face. "You're not even going to make me promise never to do it again?"

"Unless you're good at breaking and entering, or have a locksmith on the payroll, you're not going to get the chance. At least not here, you aren't."

"You can't keep Amado's daughter from having a key to her own father's apartment."

"Wanna bet?"

"You've got a lot to learn about how he really feels about his daughters. They come before anything, or anyone. Always have, always will."

Elizabeth turned to leave, then paused, turned back, and looked him directly in the eye. "If that's really the way it is between them, seems to me Amado would go to any lengths to see Elana isn't shackled to a philandering husband."

"You said—"

"Just don't push me, Edgar." She had no intention of ever telling anyone what she'd seen, but it wouldn't hurt to leave a little doubt in his mind. "I don't mind sharing the neighborhood with a skunk, just as long as it doesn't stick its tail up and start backing toward me."

She didn't wait for a reply.

15

Elizabeth rolled the windows down in the Mercedes as she left Sacramento, headed for Modesto. It was unseasonably warm for the first week of May, the air heavy with the sensuous feel of summer. She pulled the pins from her hair and let the wind take the heavy mass from her grasp.

It would have been good to see Joyce again, but Elizabeth didn't regret her decision not to stay in San Francisco. She didn't have the energy it would have taken to keep up the pretense that everything between her and Amado was as it should be.

On the unlikely chance Amado might try to contact her, she'd called Consuela and left a message that her plans had changed and she was going to Modesto after all. An inner voice insisted she was trying to run away from her problem, but until that same voice came up with a solution, she refused to listen to it. Whatever it took to get through this new crisis she would do, even if it involved a little denial.

Because he'd left her no choice, she would give Amado the time he said he needed. Eventually he would overcome his disappointment and see that even without a child they could still have a full, rich life together.

And with any luck, someday she might even believe it herself.

Michael Logan swung his leg over the rafter he'd been straddling and gazed at the rust-colored sky to the west. At his back the Sierras formed a deep purple monolith in the setting sun, a border that defined the eastern edge of the valley. The air was still and fiery, the only sounds those of crickets, birds, and an occasional frog.

In less than an hour the sky would be black and blanketed with stars. They would shimmer in the heat rising from the baked earth. The night would draw men spoiling for a fight and lovers seeking to escape the stifling confines of houses and apartments. When the lovers came together, their coupling would be primitive and urgent. For the men seeking battle, all it would take was a challenging look or a careless word.

An old and familiar yearning swept through Michael, one that had grown stronger over the years but had steadfastly refused definition. There were times the feeling was so overpowering that he could do nothing but give in to it. For days he would be consumed with a pervasive emptiness that neither work nor friends could fill. And then the hunger would leave him and he would be all right again. But even in the calm between the storms he knew there would be a next time.

To keep his thoughts from taking him places he didn't want to go, Michael concentrated on the reason he'd come to the winery. He was pleased with the progress made on the showroom in the two weeks he'd been gone. Three weeks ago the crew he'd hired had been setting the foundation forms. Today the building wore a full skeleton, waiting to be skinned in plywood.

With the stainless-steel tanks installed in the winery, the new crushers due to be finished in a week, and the bottling plant scheduled to come into operation that winter, they could be ready to go to market months sooner than planned.

Michael had spent the afternoon interviewing applicants for the wine masters who would be doing the actual hands-on work once the expanded plant was in operation. As soon as the winery was up and going again, Amado wanted Michael's full attention back on the Napa Valley operation.

Elizabeth's advertising campaign had already succeeded beyond even her expectations. The demand for Montoya Wines had stripped the shelves in a dozen of the country's top markets. Wherever Amado went, even on the streets of St. Helena, he was stopped by passersby. They sought his advice on wine or asked for his autograph on a scrap of paper they dug out of pockets or purses. At the winery they would ask the tour guides if he could be found to sign the bottles of wine they purchased in the gift shop.

The surge in business had added even more fuel to Amado's ongoing expansion plans. He had started looking north again, concentrating on the Dry Creek Valley area. Michael said a silent prayer of thanks every time Amado came back disappointed.

While it was exciting to see and be part of the explosive growth happening at Montoya Wines, Michael still harbored doubts. Instead of the cool and calculated business decisions he'd come to expect from Amado, it seemed as though there were a frantic edge to everything he did lately. He was quicker to lose his temper with the workers and slower to apologize. That past week, when Michael brought up their old argument that control would be sacrificed if they continued to grow as rapidly as they had, Amado had uncharacteristically snapped that he hadn't asked for and didn't want his advice.

Michael's gaze swept the horizon again, settling on a cloud of dust and its slow skyward swirl. The winery was several miles from the interstate, the last two still unpaved. With the tons of heavy equipment that had traveled down those roads the past months, the earth had turned into a brown talcum that took flight at the slightest provocation. This time it was a car that created the stir—a white Mercedes.

Elizabeth's white Mercedes.

Michael braced his hands on the wide beam and shifted his weight to a more comfortable position while he waited to see what she would do. If she was looking for him, she would see his truck and stop. If she was headed for the office, she would simply drive by.

She did neither. She took the cutoff that led to the back of the winery, where the on-site guard and his dog lived in a trailer. He listened and heard her car door slam. A few minutes later he saw her walking toward the half-finished showroom. His mouth was open to call to her when it occurred to him a voice coming out of the shadows would likely scare the hell out of her. He'd wait until she spotted his truck and figured out for herself she wasn't alone.

But she didn't circle the building as he'd expected. She crawled over the piles of lumber, sawhorses, and ladders and came inside through the opening in the framed wall. When she finally stopped, she was almost directly under him.

In the rapidly diminishing light, her features were difficult for him to distinguish. Still, it was obvious something was wrong. It was more than the curve of her normally squared shoulders or the tilt of her head or even the way she walked, slow and mechanical rather than her usual sure stride.

And then he saw her hands come up to cover her face and heard her catch her breath in what sounded like a sob.

His first thought was of Amado. Something terrible must have happened, and Elizabeth had come here to tell him. It didn't matter that the thought lacked logic; fear was the antithesis of rational thinking. He moved his weight to his hip, grabbed the beam, and swung down.

Startled by his sudden appearance, Elizabeth screamed and bolted. Afraid she would trip on one of the loose boards that lay scattered over the subfloor, he reached out to grab her arm. She swung wildly, her hand connecting with his chest and then his face.

"It's Michael," he said, holding his arms open to show he meant her no harm. "I'm sorry. I didn't mean to scare you."

"You bastard." She swung at him again, and the blow glanced off his hand as he jerked backward. "Why didn't you tell me you were here?"

"I figured you would see my truck." He took a step toward her.

She backed up an equal distance. "Get away from me."

"Gladly, as soon as you tell me what's wrong."

"Nothing."

"Right."

"It doesn't concern you."

"Has something happened to Amado?"

"No . . . Amado is fine." She turned her back to him. "Please, Michael, just leave me alone."

"Hey, everyone needs a friend now and then. Even you."

"I don't dump my problems on other people."

He went to her and took her in his arms, offering the comfort of a shoulder to cry on. After all, wasn't that what friends did for each other? She held herself stiffly but didn't try to pull away.

"This isn't going to help," she said.

Her voice was little more than a whisper, and he bent his head to hear her better, breathing in the perfume of her hair. His lips accidentally touched her forehead. She tilted her head to move away, and he felt her breath on his cheek.

And then she stopped moving. Her face was only inches from his. He could see the remnants of her tears and was shaken by the sorrow in her eyes. A compelling need to share her pain, to take it into himself and to gift her with peace, came over him.

Without thought to the consequences, he gave in to his instincts and kissed her. At first contact, her lips were unyielding. Then, as it began to hit him what he'd so foolishly started, her mouth opened and she kissed him back, deep and long and hard, unleashing a need that shattered the last of his sensibilities.

Her arms went around his neck; his encircled her waist. She clung to him with a quiet desperation. Her heat penetrated his clothing as potently as her need penetrated his mind. He had no more defense against one than he had the other. His hands moved up her sides and then down to her hips. No matter how or where he touched her, his skin burned at the contact.

As quickly as it had started, it was over. She pressed her palms against his chest and pushed herself away. "My God, Michael," she said, "what are we doing?"

It was everything he could do not to reach for her. "I don't know," he admitted. He didn't want to think about who she was or what had just happened to them. Most of all, he didn't want to think about Amado and what it would do to him if he ever found out.

She took another step backward. "This was my fault. I should never have—"

"Don't do that." He couldn't let her accept the blame for something he now realized he had wanted to do for months. He'd believed it was Susan who'd returned to haunt his dreams at night, but he'd been wrong. The realization left him feeling sick to his stomach.

She nervously tucked her hair behind her ear, then crossed her arms over her chest. "We have to forget this happened." Panic made her voice sound brittle. "It was a terrible mistake."

He had no choice but to agree with her. To believe anything else was not only foolhardy, it was dangerous. "I can pretend it never happened, I don't know about forgetting."

"Amado can never find out."

"For Christ's sake, Elizabeth. I don't want to hurt him any more than you do."

"Then promise me."

He didn't understand what was going on inside of him. Why this wrenching urge to fight for something that wasn't his? How could he feel loss over something he'd never had? "I promise."

She nodded. "I think you should leave now. No, that's not fair. You shouldn't have to leave. I'll go."

He couldn't let her just walk away. Not yet. If they were to have any hope of getting past this moment, they needed time to ground their relationship so that when they saw each other again they would remember the words that had passed between them, not the action. "Why are you here?" There was accusation in his voice. He lowered and softened the tone. "Why didn't you go to San Francisco?"

"I did, but it didn't work out. And I didn't go home because I wanted some time alone, to think."

"About what?"

"It's not important."

"Are you and Amado—" What was the matter with him? Did he really want to know all was not as it should be between them?

"Having problems?"

"It's just that I've never seen you like this."

"There are a lot of ways you haven't seen me, thanks to your pigheaded behavior."

He almost smiled at the waspish reply. This was the Elizabeth he knew. "It's the baby thing, isn't it?"

"Jesus, the *baby* thing? I'll bet no one has ever accused you of being overly sensitive."

"I'm sorry. It's just that I find it hard to believe Amado would put such a high priority on starting another family that he would jeopardize what the two of you have now."

"Maybe you don't know him as well as you think you do."

So that was it. "What did he say when you told him?"

She hesitated. "That it didn't matter."

"But you didn't believe him."

Again she hesitated. "He can't make love to me anymore."

That was not something he wanted to hear. "Can't or won't?"

"What difference does it make?"

"From a man's point of view, a hell of a big one."

"Can't."

A peculiar mixture of disappointment and relief swept through him. "Maybe there's something physically wrong. Something that has nothing to do with you."

"He saw a doctor."

"And?"

"It wasn't medical. If there was anything that could have been done, Amado would have done it." She moved to what would one day be the front entrance to the showroom and leaned her head against the two-by-four that framed the doorway.

Michael followed her. "What happened?"

"I just told you."

"No, I mean what happened that triggered this trip?"

"Amado told me he was moving out of our bedroom."

Michael almost groaned aloud. "None of this makes any sense. I've never seen Amado happier than he's been this past year. He married you because he loved you, not because he wanted a brood mare."

"Then give me another explanation."

He didn't have one.

"Another favor?" she asked.

"Two in one night?" he teased gently. "I don't know, that's going to leave you pretty deep in my debt."

"Forget we ever had this conversation."

"I can promise never to bring it up again, if that's what you want."

"You're a good friend, Michael."

He'd been an idiot to allow himself to believe, even for a second, that it could be any other way between them. "If you ever change your mind and want to talk . . ."

"I won't."

There wasn't anything else to say. He held his hand out to her. "Come on. Let's get something to eat."

"You go ahead. I'm not hungry."

"When was the last time you ate anything?"

Several seconds passed before she answered. "I stopped for lunch at the Nut Tree."

"You're lying."

"What difference does it make?"

"I hope to hell you don't think starving yourself is the way to get Amado back to your bed."

"I'm not starving myself."

"When I was holding you I could feel every one of your ribs."

"You're not my keeper, Michael."

"But I'm your friend."

"Then be a friend and leave me alone."

"I will. As soon you've eaten."

"Goddammit, what do I have to do—" She stopped and let out a resigned sigh. "All right, I'll go out to dinner with you, but no fast-food restaurants."

"It's a deal."

She lowered herself to her haunches and prepared to jump the six feet to the ground. Michael put his hand on her shoulder to stop her.

"Let me go first," he said. When she looked up at him he saw there were fresh tears in her eyes.

"Thank you," she said. "For caring."

She was telling him something that went far deeper. "Have there been so few people in your life who did?" he asked on a hunch.

A sad smiled passed over her face. "Mostly it's been by choice, Michael. What you don't have, you can't lose."

Nothing she could have said would have surprised him more. "What happened to you that made you think that way?"

"It's a long story. Maybe someday . . ."

"You'll tell me about it? Somehow I doubt that."

"You know, I think I may be a little hungry after all."

She'd closed him out again. In a way he was relieved. He swung over the wooden threshold and reached up for her. "I happen to know a terrific Mexican restaurant. The chips are fresh, the salsa's hot, and the beer's the coldest in town."

"My treat," she said.

"I hope you don't think I'm going to argue."

She laughed. "I know better."

They were back on safe ground.

16

Elizabeth pulled the Mercedes into the driveway, parked under the oak that shaded the side of the house, and rolled down the windows. With a little luck and an occasional breeze, the car wouldn't turn into an oven before she made the return trip to the winery. With neither, the shower she'd come there to take would turn out to be a waste of time.

She glanced at her watch as she climbed out of the car. In seven hours she and Amado would be hosting three hundred distributors, wholesalers, and their guests at a gourmet picnic on the expansive lawn at the winery. By now the tents were up, the tables and chairs were in place, and the caterers were busy at work in their mobile kitchen.

At least that was the plan.

God forbid there had been a hitch in the process;

she'd never seen Amado more anxious about a party. She must have heard him tell Consuela a dozen times how important it was that everything be perfect.

It took less than twenty minutes for her to shower and put on fresh clothes. Best of all, she felt as if she could make it through the rest of the day without turning into a shrew. She was headed for the front door when her stomach made a loud rumbling noise, reminding her she'd skipped breakfast. She went into the study and tried calling Amado's private line at the winery to tell him she would be a few minutes longer than anticipated, but there was no answer. She finished tucking her blouse into her cotton skirt as she made a detour into the kitchen and nearly ran into Michael. He was rummaging through Consuela's junk drawer.

"What are you doing in here?" she questioned artlessly. In the three months since their chance meeting in Modesto, it had become a toss-up as to which of them worked harder to avoid being alone with the other. She was confident the awkwardness would disappear in time. At least that was what she told herself. Even though she'd vowed she would make a greater effort to socialize when she moved to St. Helena, Michael was the only real friend she'd made. And with Amado making himself less and less accessible, she missed having someone to talk to. Too many times lately she'd had her hand on the phone to call Alice, but an almost overwhelming guilt stopped her. She didn't want to be the one who told her grandmother that the prince and princess in her imagined fairy tale were not living happily ever after.

"I rang the bell, but no one answered."

"That's not what I meant. Why aren't you at the winery helping out with the party? I was under the impression no one had escaped being assigned a job."

"It's a long story." He went back to the drawer. "Do you know if there's an eyedropper in here? I forgot to ask for one."

"Why are you looking for an eyedropper?"

"Kittens. Five of them. They're over at my place howling their heads off to be fed, and they won't have anything to do with the bottle the vet gave me."

"What's wrong with their mother?"

"She had a run-in with a tractor this morning." He slammed the drawer in frustration.

Elizabeth no longer felt like eating. "How old are they?"

"No one seems to know for sure. Tony said the mother showed up at the barn about a week ago. She looked starved, so the guys started feeding her scraps from their lunches." He opened another drawer, saw it was filled with kitchen towels, and closed it again. "The vet put the kittens at two, two and a half weeks. He doesn't think they'll make it, but he gave me some special canned milk and said I could try feeding them if I wanted."

"Are their eyes open?"

"Barely."

She tried to remember where she'd seen a dropper, and then it hit her. When Amado's allergies were bothering him he used eyedrops. "Why don't you go back and try the bottle on them again," she said. "If I can't find something around here, I'll drive down to the store."

A funny feeling came over her when she went into Amado's bedroom. It was only the third time she'd actually gone inside since he'd moved in. The other two times had been in the middle of the night when a feeling of overwhelming loneliness had driven her from her own bed. She had wandered around the house, ending up in his room. With the stealth of a burglar she had lain on top of the covers, careful not to touch him but close enough to hear his every breath. By morning she was gone.

Amado's eye medicine wasn't in the bathroom cabinet, but then neither were the pills he took for his allergies. She looked in his dresser and then the nightstand. She was ready to give up when she spotted a box at the back of the closet shelf. Inside were several bottles of medicine, along with an extra dropper still in its sealed container.

She'd known Amado was fanatic about not leaving anything dangerous within eyesight of his granddaughters, but she couldn't help thinking he'd carried things a little far this time. Especially considering Elana's children lived less than a hundred miles away and he was lucky if they came to see him twice a year.

After shoving the package in the pocket of her skirt, she put the box back where she'd found it and told herself to be sure to remember to tell Amado that she'd been the one rummaging through his room.

She knocked on Michael's front door. When he didn't answer she assumed he was busy with the kittens and let herself in. It was the first time she'd been inside his home. As she glanced around the unpretentious living room, taking in the overloaded bookshelves and heavy masculine furniture, she smiled. So it was a love of books that kept him up nights. It was something—another thing—they had in common.

She liked that he was neat without being obsessive about it. The throw pillows on the sofa weren't put there for effect; they were the kind you used to prop up your head when you were curled up with a book. There were lots of lamps for light, none of them matching. The fireplace looked well used and the pictures on the wall were original, most of them watercolors of ocean scenes.

"I found one," Elizabeth called out, asking Michael his whereabouts as much as announcing her presence.

"In here," he called back.

There were three doors leading off the hallway that stretched out in front of her. "I need a bigger hint."

Seconds later he walked through the door opposite the stairs. His hands were cupped in front of him as he came toward her; an insistent mewing preceded him. "Boy, am I glad to see that," he said, spotting the package. "I was about to cut the finger off one of my gloves."

She laughed. "That's what you do for baby cows, Michael. If I didn't know better, I'd think you'd been raised in the city."

He handed her the kitten and took the eyedropper. "My father was a farmer, not a rancher. He didn't believe in pets."

She brought the squirming ball of orange-striped fur up to her cheek. "How can you not believe in pets?"

"He said he worked as hard as he did to feed his family, not animals."

The kitten pressed its nose against Elizabeth's earlobe and tried to suckle. "Where's the milk the vet gave you?"

"In the bedroom. I was trying to get them to lick it off my finger."

"They aren't old enough for that yet." Frustrated at his failed attempt to nurse, the kitten began to howl again. Elizabeth tucked it under her chin and started down the hall. "It's okay," she said softly. "Just a few more minutes . . . shhh . . . I know you're hungry . . . it's okay."

"You act as if you've done this kind of thing before," Michael said.

There was no mistaking the hope in his voice. "My grandmother was the real expert. Before my grandfather died and she had to sell the farm, everyone in the county used to bring her their orphaned animals. By the time I came along she was already living in town, so all I ever got to help her with were kittens and puppies."

She moved into Michael's bedroom, spotted a box sitting in the middle of his bed, and peered inside. Exhausted, the remaining kittens had fallen asleep, huddled in a corner, one on top of the other. "With five of them, it's going to go a lot faster if we both do the feeding. I'll stop by the pharmacy later and pick up some extra droppers."

Michael filled the one they had with milk. "Now what?"

She sat on the edge of the bed and held the kitten's head. "Put the tip in his mouth and gently squeeze the bulb."

The kitten responded by wrapping his tongue around

the tube and swallowing greedily. "Well, I'll be damned," Michael exclaimed softly.

He sounded so pleased with himself, Elizabeth couldn't help but smile. "Not too fast."

"This is going to be a lot easier than I thought."

"When they're through eating, they need to be stroked for several minutes."

He stopped to refill the dropper. "Why's that?"

"According to my grandmother, the mother isn't just cleaning them when she licks them, she's making sure that what went in comes out. Personally, I think the attention is what makes them grow up to be lap cats, too. The ones who like to be petted seem to come from attentive mothers."

It took several more trips to the milk bowl before their first charge was satisfied and could be exchanged for another. When they'd established their rhythm again, Michael looked up at Elizabeth and asked, "How old were you when your parents died?"

"I moved in with Alice when I was ten." When she could, she sidestepped questions rather then tell an outright lie, especially to someone she cared about. It was a minor thing, one that undoubtedly mattered only to her, but at the time it had been all she'd had to give.

"Was it a single car crash?"

"What?"

"The accident."

"Oh . . . yes, it was late at night." When she left for college, George Benson and her grandmother got together and decided it would be easier and safer if she adopted Elizabeth Preston's background as well as her name.

"It must have turned your life upside down, losing your parents and then all your friends when you went to live with Alice."

The bits and pieces he knew were too scattered for her to keep strictly to one story. Her mind demanded she tell him about Elizabeth; her heart chose to tell him as much as she could about Jenny. "We moved around a lot when I was growing up, so I didn't have any real friends. By the time I started living with my grandmother, the pattern must have been set. It seems as though I've been a loner all my life."

"Kind of like the kitten that didn't get stroked enough?"

She didn't want him to try to figure her out. Not that she was afraid of what he would do with the information, it was more that if he were to find out who and what she was, a compelling bond would be established. No matter how sweet the temptation to have someone close she could talk to freely and openly, she couldn't take the chance. Not with Michael. "I suppose you could say that."

"There's more to it, isn't there?"

"Yes," she admitted. She waited; it was almost as if deep inside her she expected something to happen. But nothing did. There wasn't any lightning, no thunderclaps, not even a damning look from Michael at the revelation.

"But you don't want to tell me what it is."

She took the hem of her cotton skirt and wiped the milk from the gray kitten's mouth before returning it to the box and removing the next one, another gray, only with longer hair. Her actions became her answer.

"You're estranged from your father's family, I take it?"

Elizabeth laughed and, despite her resolve, gave in and answered his question. What frightened her was how easily and readily she gave in. "Estranged, such a fancy word."

"I didn't mean for it to be. It's just that I find it hard to believe you'd get married and not invite any relatives other than Alice. There must be at least one or two of them you still see."

"My father's family disowned him before I was born. When I was in high school and going through one of those curious stages, Alice made it her summer project to find them for me. When she finally made contact with them, they told her they weren't interested in seeing or hearing from me." At least this much was the truth.

Michael stopped feeding the kitten. "That's really shitty. I should have let it go. I'm sorry."

"You couldn't have known."

"But I sure as hell could have guessed. You really had me confused when you found out you couldn't have kids and reacted as though it were the end of the world. I thought the baby thing was something you were doing for Amado. But it wasn't, was it?"

"When your own parents abandon you, you grow up thinking you can be Superparent to your own children. Dreams die hard."

"I never thought about it before, but I guess to a child death would be a form of abandonment."

She needed a graceful way out of their conversation before she told him even more. Above everything else, she didn't ever want to look back and regret this day. "When you're a kid you think you're the center of the universe," she said dismissively.

He responded to her attempt to lighten the tone of their conversation by saying, "I'll bet you wore a lot of ribbons and lace when you were a little girl. I can just picture you with curls down to your waist, pinning uppity little boys like me to the wall with those big blue eyes of yours."

"You missed by a mile." She concentrated on the kitten in her lap.

He scrunched down lower so that he was in her line of vision and she was forced to look at him. "So tell me what you were like."

Before she could answer she was stopped by the sound of Amado's voice. "Elizabeth? Michael? Are you in here?"

Michael rose from his haunches. "We're in the bedroom."

Seconds later Amado filled the doorway. He smiled at Elizabeth, then looked at Michael. "I knocked, but I guess you didn't hear me. When Tony told me about the kittens I had a feeling I would find you here."

"I tried calling to let you know I was going to be a little late," Elizabeth said. "But then I got so busy with the feeding, I forgot to try again."

"I understand. I only came looking for you because I was worried you might be stuck somewhere." He gave her a teasing smile. "If you would let me have a phone installed in your car . . ."

She'd steadfastly refused to be convinced that she was so important that anyone, even Amado, needed twenty-four-hour access to her. "We just have one more kitten to feed."

"How are they doing?"

She smiled. "Come and see for yourself."

He held up his hand. "Even at this distance I can feel—"

Her heart sank. "You're allergic to cats, too?"

"They are the worst for me."

"I'm sorry, Amado," Michael said. "You never mentioned anything about it before. I had no idea."

"There is no problem having them out here with you. But I do think it best that I leave you to your work and get back to my own."

"Where should I look for you when I'm finished here?" Elizabeth asked.

He seemed uncertain how to answer her. "It is not necessary that you look for me at all. I was in a hurry to get everything done this morning because I have an appointment in Santa Rosa this afternoon."

"Is there something you want me to do while you're gone?" She already knew what his answer would be but felt she should ask anyway. After a decade of organizing parties for Amado, Consuela was the pro. It was a job Elizabeth gladly yielded to her.

"Conseula tells me she has everything under control. If you find you have time, however, I would appreciate it if you would make sure the cottage is ready for guests."

"You didn't tell me someone would be staying the night."

"Elana and Edgar have found they will be able to come after all."

She hadn't seen either of them since her run-in with Edgar at the apartment. "I'll go over as soon as I'm finished here."

Amado nodded. "Until later, then."

Michael walked Amado to the door while Elizabeth got up to trade kittens. The remaining four were huddled in the corner again. She sorted through until she found the one that still needed to be fed. Lifting the littlest of the five out of the box, she caught her breath in surprise.

"*Howard.*" She held him up and studied his face. Seeking denial more than confirmation, she ran her fingers down his tail, looking for but not really expecting to find a bump on the end. It was there. She brought him to her cheek and closed her eyes. "You've come back to haunt me, haven't you?" She stroked him with the tip of her finger. "I hate to tell you this, Howard, but you really screwed up this time. I can't take you home with me."

Michael came back in the room. He sat down beside Elizabeth and picked up the eyedropper. "Ready?"

Just as she'd expected, the reincarnated Howard didn't eat as eagerly as the others and turned away after only two droppers full of milk.

"Do you think he's sick?" Michael asked.

"He's probably just worn out from crying." She didn't think it wise to try to explain that Howard had always been a light eater.

Michael ran his finger down the kitten's back and then under its chin. "I hate to say this, especially where he can hear me, but there's no sense trying to make it better than it is." His voice became an exaggerated whisper. "This is one incredibly ugly cat we've got on our hands. He looks like an anorexic bat. We may be a long time finding him a home."

"He'll improve," she said.

For the first time since coming back in the room, Michael actually looked at Elizabeth. "Are you upset about something?"

"Of course not. Why would I be upset?"

"I don't know." He studied her more closely.

"It's the kitten," she finally admitted. "He reminds me of a cat I used to own. Actually, it would probably be more truthful to say a cat that owned me."

"Want to talk about it?"

Elizabeth groaned. "You and Lucy. You ought to see if Charles Schulz would let the two of you go into business together."

"Never work. She gives advice to anyone who'll pay her a nickel. I'm more selective."

Her heart did a funny little dance when she looked into Michael's eyes. Unbidden, the memory of what it felt like to have his arms around her returned. She shifted her body away from him, pretending it was in an effort to get more comfortable. "I'm going to show you what to do with Howard, and then you can take care of the others while I drive down to get another eyedropper."

"I take it Howard was the name of your cat?"

"It's what I called him, not that he ever acknowledged me when I used it."

When they were finished with Howard's rubdown, Michael put him back into the box and walked Elizabeth to the front door.

"Are you sure you're going to be able to handle them alone tonight?" she asked.

"Are you questioning my abilities or my maternal instincts?"

"I was just thinking you're not going to get much sleep feeding them every two hours."

Michael made a face. "The vet didn't say anything about every—"

"That's what I thought." She stepped out onto the porch. "I was going to offer to take them off your hands tonight, but with Amado's allergies and Elana and Edgar in the cottage, there isn't anywhere for me to keep them. Once everything is back to normal, we can switch nights. Until then—"

"We'll be fine. How much trouble can they be?"

She smiled knowingly. "We'll talk about it in the morning."

Amado arrived home earlier that afternoon than he'd expected. They still had half an hour before he'd told Elizabeth he wanted to leave for the winery when he came to her bedroom and stood in the doorway.

"Come in," she said.

He smiled when he saw her. "You are breathtaking, as always."

"Thank you." The gown she'd chosen to wear that night was a Bob Mackie original, buttercup yellow, knee length, and simply but beautifully cut. She'd loved the way it moved when she walked, as if it were a part of her. "Alice helped me pick it out. She was sure the color would please you."

"She was right." He put his hand to his chin and studied her. "But I believe there is something missing," he added mysteriously. "Don't go away. I will be right back."

When he returned he was carrying a package the size of a small cereal box. It was wrapped in gold foil and had a fresh orchid attached to the bow on top. He handed the package to her. "Happy anniversary."

The blood drained from Elizabeth's face as she scrambled to remember the date. "But it isn't." Good God, could she have forgotten? "Not yet."

"I knew the only way to surprise you would be to have the celebration early."

"The party we're having tonight is for our anniversary?"

He looked immensely pleased with himself. "I can see that I succeeded."

"Beyond your wildest dreams," she admitted.

"Open your present."

Slipping her finger under the paper, she released the tape. She saw immediately that a jewelry box was inside. Knowing what she was sure to find made her uncomfortable. She couldn't wear the earrings Amado had given her for Christmas, or the bracelet he'd sent in a box of roses on Valentine's Day, or the cocktail ring he'd hidden in the cake on her birthday without feeling like an advertisement for De Beers. "Amado, this wasn't necessary. I would have been happy with—"

He could hardly contain his grin of anticipation. "Look inside before you say anything more, Elizabeth."

Reluctantly she opened the lid. It was even worse than she'd imagined. A lot worse. She tried to think of something to say as she stared at the center stone. There were Third World countries with yearly budgets less than what Amado must have paid for an emerald the size of this one, not to mention the diamonds that were setting it off and those that formed the actual necklace itself. "I'm speechless," she told him. At least that much was the truth.

"May I put it on you?"

"Please. I don't think I could manage it myself." He slipped the necklace around her neck. The stones were cool against her skin. And heavy.

"Now let me look at you," he said as he turned her around.

Her hand went to her throat to touch the emerald. This was the kind of thing movie stars wore, not the daughter of Bill and Anne Cavanaugh. And then she thought about the remark Elana had made at Christmas when she saw Elizabeth wearing the earrings Amado had given her. In a stage whisper timed to catch Elizabeth as she walked by, Elana had said to Edgar, "It's a cliché, but true, I'm afraid. The only thing that separates men from boys is the price of their toys. Too bad Daddy couldn't have picked something we could all use, like a yacht or an airplane."

A smile tugged at Elizabeth's mouth when she considered what Elana's reaction to her father's latest gift would be. "Well?" she prompted Amado.

He shook his head as if disappointed, but there was a spark of mischief in his eyes. "You overshadow the piece. It is nothing compared to you. I think we should take it back."

In that instant, with breath-stealing poignancy, Elizabeth was reminded of the man Amado had been when they were married. Could it have only been a year? She would gladly trade every gem in the necklace to have him back, for just one night. Responding to his playfulness, she gave him a challenging look. "You just try to get this necklace off of me. I know all that legal stuff about possession being nine-tenths of the law."

He came toward her, and for a moment she actually thought he was going to take her in his arms and kiss her. For a glorious heartbeat she believed the nightmare they'd been living the past three months might actually be over.

She was half-right. He did kiss her. But his lips were pressed to her cheek, not her mouth. She struggled to hide her disappointment. "Thank you, Amado," she said. The only words that came to mind were the obvious. "It's the nicest present anyone has ever given me."

"You're welcome, Elizabeth."

Before he could turn away, she was convinced she saw a sadness in his eyes that matched her own. She started to question him about it, but when he turned back, the defensive veil had dropped back into place and she was closed out again.

"Shall we go?" he asked.

"We have to talk about what's happened to us." It was the wrong time. She knew it before the words were even spoken. Still, she couldn't stop herself.

"Yes," he said. "But not tonight."

"Do you mean that?"

He stared at her for a long time and then, as if surrendering the battle that raged inside of him, too, bent to kiss her. This time their lips met. There was no holding back, no question that he wanted her as much as she wanted him. Fire raced through her veins. She opened her mouth and deepened their kiss as she pressed herself hard against him. But then as quickly as it had begun, it was over.

"No one would miss us if we were a few minutes late," she suggested.

He smiled and held her tightly in his arms. "Sometime, somewhere, I must have done something wonderful to deserve you. Your patience and understanding are what sustain me."

It was appreciation for something entirely different that she wanted from him. "I've missed you, Amado."

"I will always be here for you. For as long as you want me."

"Then you will be here forever."

He pressed a kiss to her forehead. "From your lips to God's ear, my darling."

17

Without a moon, it was difficult to make out the horizon, to determine where the stars ended and the lights in the valley began. Elizabeth shoved the sleeves of her sweatshirt back to her elbows and let the fanciful thought take her on its short ride, grateful for any distraction from the questions that haunted her. She left the railing and crossed the deck, thinking that a walk might tire her enough that she would feel like going back to bed. Then she remembered there were "guests" in the cottage. At two-thirty in the morning they were undoubtedly asleep already, but she didn't want to take the chance that insomnia could have struck either Elana or Edgar and that they might see her wandering around the grounds. Instead she sat on one of the deck chairs and listened to the crickets. After a while she brought her knees up and laid her head against them.

Everyone had agreed, the party was the best that season. Amado had spared no expense—beluga caviar, Alaska salmon, Nebraska steaks, a pastry chef from Stanford Court, and a string quartet from the San Francisco Symphony. She shuddered to think what the cost per guest had been. And then to multiply that by three hundred.

It wasn't so much the cost that bothered her as the appalling waste. In their social circle, how much someone weighed was more important than how well he or she was fed. As usual, more food had been thrown away that night than eaten. Half of the world went to bed hungry every night while the other half worried about their landfill problems.

And to what point?

If the party had been given solely to please her, she would have been far happier with a private, candlelit dinner. A hint that she would be welcome in Amado's bed that night would have excited her far more than his promise of two weeks in France.

When they arrived home, after an evening of doting on her, of looking at her with undisguised hunger, Amado had walked her to her bedroom, kissed her chastely, and bade her good night. In an attempt to keep him there longer, she'd reminded him of the talk they were supposed to have. But he'd begged off, saying he had a meeting in the morning and that it was important he be at his best.

She was confused and hurt, and it had taken every ounce of her self-control not to make a scene. Not that she wouldn't have staged the granddaddy of all scenes, if she'd thought it would do any good. It was the fear that an emotional outburst would only drive him farther away that had kept her in check.

But her behavior that night went beyond fear. Somehow, without her being aware it was happening, her pride had become involved. What if she went farther, telling him how she actually felt? What if she even went so far as to beg him to make love to her? And then, Amado being the compassionate man he was, what if he relented and tried and failed yet again? The fantasy they harbored that, given enough time, they would work things out between them would suffer a fatal blow.

She got up and returned to the railing, her body taut with nervous energy. Instead of looking out at the valley, she turned and stared at the house.

What had gone wrong? There had to be something more than his inability to have children. She'd done everything to fit into his world, his life. He decorated her like a Christmas tree. He said he loved her; at times, like tonight, he even acted as if he still loved her; but he couldn't or wouldn't make love to her.

She missed the intimacy more than she'd believed possible.

She felt so alone.

Michael slowly became aware of something nudging his chin. He groaned and rolled his head to the other side. The kitten followed. "I just fed you," he grumbled. "Go back to sleep."

"It isn't food he's looking for," Elizabeth said.

His eyes flew open. The black kitten was standing with its front paws on his cheek, its belly stretched across his mouth. He blinked and tried to focus as he shifted the furry bundle off to the pillow. "Elizabeth?"

"I'm over here," she said.

And then he saw her. She was standing by the door, dressed in an old pair of gray sweats several sizes too large. She had the box with the kittens tucked under her arm. "What are you doing here?"

"I was up and saw your light and thought maybe it was feeding time and you could use my help." She shrugged. "When you didn't answer my knock, I figured you were tied up with one of the kittens. You know, you really should think about having a doorbell installed." She set the box back in the corner, waited a second to see if the movement had disturbed any of the kittens, then turned her attention back to Michael. "I'm sorry about just barging in the way I did."

He yawned and blinked several more times, then rubbed his eyes. It was tempting to put off what was happening to a particularly vivid dream—which, when he thought about it, made a hell of a lot more sense than actually having Elizabeth standing in his bedroom in the middle of the night. "How long have you been here?"

"I don't know for sure. About half an hour, I'd guess. The way you were sleeping I decided you were so out of it you wouldn't wake up if I took the kittens in the other room and fed them for you. I was going to leave a note."

Howard moved across the pillow and climbed back up on Michael; when he reached the soft mat of hair covering his chest, he lowered his head and made an eager, rooting sound. "That's not going to do you a bit of good."

"Want me to take him?"

Michael caught the kitten to him, sat up, and leaned his back against the headboard, careful to keep the sheet pulled across his hips. "He's okay," he said. "We've already been through this a couple of times tonight." He put Howard on his shoulder. Within seconds the tiny bit of fur had nestled into the hollow behind Michael's collarbone and adjusted himself so that his head was tucked under Michael's chin.

She smiled. "So I see."

"What are you really doing here?"

The question erased her smile. "I told you. I saw your light and—"

"I know—you thought you could help."

"Look, if you don't want me coming here, just say so."

For all the defiance he heard in her voice, there was a peculiar vulnerability, too. Something was going on. But what? It was on the tip of his tongue to ask when it hit him that if he pushed her any more, she would simply walk away and not come back. He didn't want that to happen. "You caught me by surprise, that's all. I can't imagine anyone willingly getting up in the middle of the night if they don't have to."

She seemed to accept his explanation. "I couldn't sleep."

"Too much excitement?" He wanted to give her an easy way out.

The look she gave him acknowledged she knew what he was doing and that she was grateful. She leaned her shoulder into the door frame. "The party was incredible, wasn't it?"

"The best I've seen around here in years."

"So, do you want me to feed Howard for you before I go?"

"That's okay. I'll take care of him." When she made a move to leave, he added, "It's amazing how fast they all caught on to this eyedropper thing. As soon as they get a whiff of milk, they go crazy." What was he doing trying to keep her there? It was insane, but he couldn't stop himself. "I don't have to hold them down anymore, I have to try to keep them from chasing the dropper back to the bowl."

Several seconds passed before she said anything. When she did, she had a peculiar, faraway look in her eyes. "I just remembered something I haven't thought about in a long, long time," she said in awe. "There was a kitten I found at a house we were staying in when I was a little girl." Surprise and wonder filled her voice as the memory came back to her. "It was a black-and-orange-and-white calico with four white paws. My father told me I couldn't keep it, but I didn't listen. I'd sneak food out to it whenever I thought no one was watching. Then one night it was so cold . . . I was afraid the kitten would freeze if I left it out there. I waited until everyone went to bed and then brought him inside to sleep with me."

She shivered and brought her arms up to hold herself. "It was just for that one night. I was never going to do it again."

Michael was hesitant to say anything, afraid he might break the spell. Finally, when it seemed she'd become lost in her thoughts, he prompted, "And what happened?"

She shook her head several times, as if trying to rid herself of something. "The kitten started crying. I tried to make it stop, but it must have been hungry. My father came in and caught us." Several seconds passed before she continued, her voice flat and distant. "He yelled at me and said if the bad guys found us, and all of our friends got killed, it would be my fault."

Bad guys who killed their friends? What kind of father would tell his child something like that? Michael looked at Elizabeth. It was almost as if she'd actually become that child again. "Did he make you give the kitten away?"

Instead of answering, she reached for a strand of hair and began twisting it around her finger. As if her legs would no longer hold her, she slowly sank to the floor. She stayed there, unmoving, her knees drawn tightly to her body.

Michael had a gut feeling he didn't want to hear what would come next. When Elizabeth finally did begin to speak again, he had to strain to hear her.

"He said I had to learn a lesson . . . that it was a really important one. I had to know that when I was given rules, terrible things would happen if I broke them. Then he made me put my pillow on top of the kitten. I had to keep the pillow there until it stopped crying. He said I was making the kitten go to sleep. I must not have believed him because he had to hold my hands down on the pillow."

Every part of Michael recoiled at the cruelty. "How old were you when this happened?"

She frowned. "I don't know. Four or five, I guess. I think it was when we were living in Boston." She sat perfectly still, her gaze fixed on the opposite wall. "Or it could have been when we were in New York. All those years ago. How could I have forgotten something like that?"

She'd disappeared into a world closed to Michael. "I've read that kids have a built-in defense mechanism that kicks in to protect them when things get too bad."

"My God, I wonder what else I've forgotten."

"Are you sure you really want to know?" he asked gently.

"Probably not," she admitted.

"Was your father sick?" This was not the childhood he had pictured her living.

"I don't think so. . . . Oh, you mean did he act the way he did because he had a mental problem?"

"That would explain his behavior."

"He and my mother took drugs, but then everyone we ever stayed with did, too. They couldn't have all been crazy."

Now Michael was really confused. None of what she was telling him fit the woman Amado had described. "You moved around a lot, I take it."

"Every couple of months. There was one time we changed houses every day for a week."

He sensed if he wasn't careful with the questions he asked, she would stop talking entirely. What he really wanted to know was what or who was after her father that had put him on the run. Instead he asked, "You moved around like that even after you started school?"

"I didn't go to school until I moved in with my grandmother."

"How did you—"

"My mother, or one of the other women we lived with, taught me."

"Was your father a salesman?" He almost groaned aloud at the lack of subtlety and the sheer stupidity of the question.

She gave him a blank stare. "A salesman?"

"I just wondered why you moved so often."

She ran her hand across her forehead several times. "Why am I doing this? I never talk about my family. I don't understand what made me tell you these things."

"Friends tell each other about themselves," he suggested.

"You aren't listening to me, Michael." There was an almost desperate quality to her voice. "When I said I never talk about my family, I meant *never*."

"Maybe it was the kittens."

She hugged herself, curling her body into an even tighter ball. "Is it all right?"

"Is what all right?"

"That I told you. God, I'm so confused. What's happening to me?"

"What are you afraid of, Elizabeth?"

She hesitated, as if caught up in a fierce mental battle. "Truthfully?"

"Of course."

"If you find out who I really am, we'll stop being friends."

"That's crazy."

"I know what I'm talking about. It's happened before. Lots of times."

He lifted Howard from his shoulder and settled him on the pillow, then reached for his jeans, slipped them on, and joined her on the floor. At first he was afraid to touch her, afraid of the power of his own need to be the one who gave her comfort. But when he looked at her, what he needed, what he wanted, didn't matter anymore. He put his arm around her and drew her into his side.

"There isn't anything you could tell me that would make me stop liking you," he said.

"What if I said I was a serial killer?"

"Are you?"

"No."

"We could argue the point all night. But until you have enough confidence in me to actually tell me what you're hiding, there's no way either one of us is going to prove we're right." And then something else occurred to him. "Or could it be you're afraid that if you tell me, I might not keep your secret?"

She didn't answer him.

"The next move is yours, Elizabeth. I'm not going to try to push you into something you don't want to do."

More to herself than to him, she said, "There's so much to lose and so little to gain."

"Then don't tell me. We'll go on like we've always been and forget tonight ever happened."

"Could you really do that?"

It scared him to think what he could and would do for her. "Yes," he answered without hesitation.

Long minutes passed without either of them saying anything. Finally Elizabeth asked, "Have you ever heard of Anne and Bill Cavanaugh?"

The names were familiar, but he wasn't sure why. "I think so, but I'm not sure."

"They were part of a radical group that bombed military bases and robbed banks back in the seventies."

"I remember now. Weren't several people killed at one of the bases when a bomb went off before it was supposed to?"

She nodded.

"Are you saying Anne and Bill Cavanaugh are your parents?"

"Biologically. They left me with my grandmother when I was ten. Other than a couple of birthday cards sent months after my birthday, I never heard from them again. I had no idea they were even in California until they were caught."

He pressed his cheek to the top of her head and closed his eyes against the pain he heard in her voice. "Your parents must have been the biggest thing that ever happened to the town of Farmingham, Kansas."

"It wasn't just the people in Farmingham. After the news hit the wire service that there was a local angle, reporters came from all over the state. They followed me everywhere I went. And then when they finally went home and the town gossips moved on to someone else, my parents were shot trying to escape, and it started all over again."

"I can see why you would want to change your name."

"It wasn't the only thing I changed."

"Whatever it was, it's over now. It doesn't matter anymore. Hell, if we were all held accountable for what we did when we were kids, we'd all be behind bars." And then he remembered Amado's version of Elizabeth's background. "Does Amado know about this? Is that why—"

"I've never said anything to him. And you can't either. Promise me, Michael."

"I promise."

It seemed to satisfy her. She moved to stand up. "As soon as Elana and Edgar are gone, I'll move into the cottage so that we can switch nights on the feedings. I haven't been sleeping all that well lately anyway."

They had moved back on safe ground again, as if the past half hour had never happened. "And have Amado mad at me for taking you away from him? Thanks, but no thanks. I'd rather struggle through on my own."

"Amado won't even know I'm gone."

It took a second for what she'd said to sink in. When it did, he felt as if he'd had the air knocked out of him. "He still isn't sleeping with you? Not even tonight?"

"Michael, this is one thing I won't talk to you about. It isn't fair to Amado."

"But he was all over you at the party. Jesus Christ, what does he do when you get home, kiss you good night at the door to your room and take off for his?"

She made a move to get up. He blocked her. When she tried to get around him, he grabbed her arms. Her anger was swift and explosive. "What business is it of yours what Amado and I do or don't do? Why do you care?"

There it was. He could say something insipid about being her friend, but she would only believe him because it was what she wanted to hear. She had trusted him enough to tell him hard truths. Could he do any less? "Come on, Elizabeth. You're a smart woman. Surely you can figure it out for yourself."

"I don't know what you're talking about."

He was dangerously close to the edge of an emotional precipice. The ground crumbled beneath him in warning.

If he fell, there would be no rescue, no way back. "I think . . . no, I *know* . . . I love you."

She flushed and turned her face from him as if warding off a blow. "No, you can't. I won't let you."

"It's done. And there's not a damn thing you can do about it." The fire left him. "There's not a damn thing I can do about it, either."

"But you don't understand. . . ."

And then, with breath-stealing sureness, he did. "When did you know?"

"I didn't, not until now. I never would have come here tonight if I had."

He released her and leaned heavily against the wall. All of his life he had waited to hear the woman he loved tell him that she loved him, too. This should have been the sweetest moment he would ever know. Instead it was the worst. How could he ever celebrate or forgive himself for falling in love with his best friend's wife? Surely there was a special place in hell reserved for anyone who acted on that kind of betrayal.

18

Elizabeth lay awake the rest of the night, watching for the sky to change from black to deep purple. At first sign of dawn she got out of bed and took a shower. She was at the table waiting for Amado when he came to breakfast.

Determined to put some normalcy back into their relationship, she got up and greeted him with a kiss. When he tried to turn his cheek to her, she took his chin and forced him to meet her lips. He was plainly surprised and not quite sure how he should react to her enforced intimacy.

She held his chair for him. "How did you sleep?"

"Like a baby," he told her. "And you?"

"Not very well," she admitted.

"Is there something wrong?"

She marveled at his ability to continue the pretense

that their lives were as they should be. "My mind wouldn't shut down. I couldn't stop thinking about what's going on with us."

Amado glanced toward the kitchen where Consuela was noisily preparing their breakfast. "I don't think this is the time or place for us to go into—"

"I won't be put off anymore, Amado. Our marriage, our life together, is too important." She started to move around the table to her normal chair, the one opposite him, but changed her mind and sat down next to him, scooting her chair even closer. "I want us to go away together this weekend."

He frowned and reached for the newspaper. "That's not possible, Elizabeth. There are some—"

"Don't do that, Amado. There's nothing you have to do that's as important as us."

"I am sorry. Normally I would agree with you, but the gentlemen coming to see me on Saturday are old friends I met on one of my trips to France. It would be impossibly rude if I were not here to greet them."

"You didn't tell me you were expecting guests. How long will they be staying?"

"Only the day. It is business."

"Then next weekend."

He reached for her hand and gave it a gentle squeeze. "You know how busy this time of year is for us."

"I won't take no for an answer, Amado."

When he met her gaze there was a sadness in his eyes. "I am afraid this time you will have to," he told her.

"Please?" She hated that he had reduced her to begging.

Consuela entered the room, carrying a tray. Amado let go of Elizabeth's hand. "We will talk about this another time," he said to Elizabeth.

"Like we talked about you moving out of our room?"

He gave her a stern, disapproving look. "I said, another time."

"Good morning," Consuela said brightly. "From the looks of it, we're in for another hot one today." She set the tray on the table and began serving.

Elizabeth pushed her chair back. The thought of trying to eat made her stomach convulse. "Thank you, Consuela, but I'm not hungry this morning."

"But you must eat something."

"Later, maybe."

Consuela looked at Amado. "And are you not hungry, either?"

Amado opened the paper and laid it beside his plate. "On the contrary. My appetite is especially sharp this morning."

Elizabeth felt as if he'd hit her.

August slipped into September, and Elizabeth welcomed the ensuing preparation and anticipation of the harvest season as if it were an answer to her prayer for something to help her forget that she was in love with her husband's best, and most trusted, friend. She filled her days with work, whenever possible spending them in San Francisco when Michael was in St. Helena, at the winery in St. Helena when he was in Modesto. Every morning she awoke with the thought that it was as possible to fall out of love as it was to fall in. Somehow she would find a way to put her feelings for Michael behind her. All she needed was time—and a little cooperation from Amado.

After deciding the advertising campaign was more than she wanted to continue directing alone, she conducted interviews with agencies as far away as Los Angeles and Portland. In the end she settled on one closer to home, Smith & Noble's chief northern California rival, J. P. Hawkins and Associates of San Francisco.

The transition from the several specialists Elizabeth had been working with to the single agency took longer than she had anticipated because of her almost obsessive need to be sure everything was up and running smoothly before she let go of the reigns. Whether it was guilt or interest that prodded her into spending more time with Amado didn't matter; she was determined to make their marriage work.

She and Michael continued to share the responsibility of raising the kittens, switching nights when both were in town, one or the other taking over completely when one of them was away. They communicated by cryptic notes whenever it was necessary to pass along information. It was through one of those notes that Elizabeth learned Michael had found homes for the kittens and that their new owners would be picking them up the last week in September.

Intellectually she'd known the day would come when she would have to give them up; emotionally she reeled with the prospective loss. She tried to protect herself by scheduling a series of meetings in San Francisco that would keep her out of town the week they left. After two days she realized her efforts were useless and headed home.

The afternoon she returned, she ran into Michael as he was pulling out of the driveway. She motioned to him to stop. He swung his pickup beside her car and rolled down the window.

There was a lump in Elizabeth's throat when she asked, "Are they gone?"

"You just missed the last one." He laid his arm along the open window, his gaze focused on something in the distance. "There was a problem with Howard," he said after several seconds. "He bit the woman who came to get him."

She wasn't surprised. Howard was not the kind of cat who would bond easily with a new owner. He needed someone with the patience of a rock climber and the understanding of a Little League umpire. "How . . . why . . ."

Michael greeted the inquiry with a short, disparaging laugh. "She actually had the audacity to try to pet him."

"Was he sleeping?"

He turned his head to look at her. "No, Elizabeth, he was sitting on the arm of the sofa."

She didn't want to know what happened then but couldn't keep herself from asking. "Was she understanding?"

"Would you be?"

"She won't be mean to him?"

"If you had hung around instead of running off to San Francisco, you wouldn't have to ask." He raked his hand through his hair and then wrapped it around the steering wheel. "I'm sorry. You didn't deserve that. I promise you the woman won't be mean to Howard."

"How can you be sure?"

"Because I talked her out of taking him. We waited too long with him, Elizabeth. As far as Howard's concerned, he has a home." Michael was quiet for several seconds. "Everything considered, I decided what the hell, I might as well keep him myself."

Instant tears of gratitude stung her eyes. "What's the real reason, Michael?" she asked. It was a stupid question; it didn't matter why he'd kept Howard, only that he had.

"Because I'm an idiot." His gaze dropped, and he let out a pent-up sigh. Finally he looked at her and said, "Because I knew how attached you were to him."

She was afraid to trust her voice to thank him.

"I also knew you wouldn't mind staying out in the cottage with him when I'm gone. Of course you can have him other times, too, whenever you want. Just let me know."

She wished she could tell Michael that after the loss of his friendship, Howard had become her lifeline. Even knowing the kitten would be gone in a matter of weeks and her heart would be broken all over again, she had not protected herself emotionally. She was aware that she had been using Howard to fill some of the loneliness that never seemed to lessen and that it was stopgap at best, but he was all she had. But she couldn't tell Michael something like that. It wasn't the kind of thing you said to someone you were trying to put out of your life. So, instead, she said a simple, "Thank you."

He put the truck in gear and let it roll forward. "You're welcome."

o   o   o

September eased into October. The winery and those who worked there were caught up with long hours and frantic activity. By the end of the month, preparations for winter had begun and relative quiet reigned again. Tractors moved through the fields, opening the earth for a final application of fertilizer and the coming rains. When the job was completed, the vineyards were finished for the year. Equipment was stored and barbecues were held for the workers. Elizabeth and Amado moved through their lives in an almost scripted attempt at normalcy. The same words, or close approximations, were exchanged at breakfast and dinner. They were unfailingly polite to each other both in private and in front of others, and they were the perfect, loving couple at parties.

Inside the winery itself, the final week of fermentation continued in the stainless-steel tanks while casks and barrels were prepared to receive the wine as soon as it was ready. The barrels were made up of a broad variety of woods, a continuation of Michael's experiments to seek subtleties Elizabeth would never be able to discern but which would determine the future and ongoing reputation of Montoya's Premium Wines.

The rains came in November.

Two weeks before Thanksgiving, Amado abruptly announced his desire to have his entire family with him for the upcoming holiday. When Felicia told him it was impossible for her to get away, he left for New York the following morning to convince her otherwise.

His plane touched down seconds before the first

major snowstorm of the season. The limo he'd arranged to have meet him was late arriving and hours getting back to town. It was almost ten o'clock when he finally knocked on Felicia's front door.

She was not happy to see him.

"What are you doing here?" she asked by way of greeting.

"The mountain would not come to Mohammed, so . . ." He shifted his suitcase from one hand to the other. "May I come in?"

"You intend to stay here? With me?"

"Just for this one night, Felicia. I thought it would be easier that way."

Reluctantly she moved aside and let him enter her apartment. "If you're here to try to talk me into going to your house for Thanksgiving, you can save your breath. I told you I've already made plans, and I'm not going to change them."

While his back was still to Felicia, Amado took a look around the rooms he could see. The furniture was spartan and had a heavy Spanish feel to it. The portrait he had had painted of Sophia to celebrate their first wedding anniversary hung over the fireplace. A long, narrow table stood against one wall in the wide hallway. Candles were set up altar fashion on either side of a row of photographs of Sophia.

Amado felt the blood drain from his face. He'd always know Felicia felt close to her mother, but he'd had no idea how deep the attachment had run. How could he hope to compete with a woman whose continued existence was in the mind of a loving daughter? What chance did he have to tell his side of the stories

Felicia had heard about him when to do so meant calling her mother a liar?

He set his suitcase next to the doorway to the living room and walked over to the fireplace to study the painting more closely. A wash of memories swept through him. He and Sophia had been happy then, or at least what had passed for happy between them.

After several seconds he went to the black leather sofa and sat down. He'd hoped to ease into what he'd traveled so far to say, but Felicia had made it clear that any attempt at small talk would only add to her irritation over having him there. "Your mother was a beautiful woman. You favor her in many ways."

Felicia went to the painting and touched one corner, making a minute and unnecessary adjustment while laying a proprietary claim. "I'm grateful her father had the foresight to have this painted while she was still in Spain." She turned and gave her father a penetrating stare. "Otherwise Elana and I would never have known what she looked like when she was truly happy."

"José had nothing to do with that painting," Amado said.

"Oh? And just who do—"

"Look at the background, Felicia—the window, the picture on the wall—that's the guest house at the winery."

Her eyes widened in disbelief as she swung around to look at the painting again. "It's a coincidence," she insisted.

"Who told you José had the picture painted?"

"My mother."

Hope flared in Amado. Maybe he had a chance to

convince his daughter he was not the monster Sophia had portrayed after all. "I had the painting done as a gift to José to mark his daughter's and my first wedding anniversary. If you look closely, you can see her wedding ring on her—"

"She told me about that. The ring is a family heirloom."

"And how did she explain the rest?"

"I never asked," Felicia admitted. "But I'm sure there's a logical—"

"Of course there is, the truth."

Her eyes narrowed in cold fury. "No one comes into my home and says anything bad about my mother, especially not you."

Amado recoiled at the hatred in her voice but wouldn't back off. He had done so too many times in the past. "Why especially me?"

"After what you did to her, you lost all rights where she's concerned. Even the right to talk about her."

There it was again, the same accusation she'd hurled at him for years. "Just exactly what is it I'm supposed to have done to Sophia?"

"She killed herself because of you."

The venom in her accusation so surprised him, he didn't have an immediate reply.

His hesitation brought a triumphant look to Felicia's eyes. "You knew she didn't have any money of her own and that if you stopped the alimony checks when Elana and I were grown, she would be destitute. But did you care?" The question was punctuated with a bitter laugh. "You didn't even bother calling or writing to see how she was doing when you stopped—"

"Sophia and I were never divorced. There never were any alimony checks. I sent her enough money every month to take care of herself and half her family." He got up and came toward her. "Who do you think paid for the funeral?"

Felicia backed away from him. "It was your guilty conscience."

"I had nothing to feel guilty about. It was your mother who left me."

"Because you forced her to."

"And how did I do that?"

"You promised to love and take care of her and then brought her to California and ignored her. You knew she couldn't speak English and that she would feel isolated in this country, but you didn't care. You probably even liked it. All you were interested in was having someone to clean your house and have your babies while you took care of that goddamned winery of yours. It must have driven you crazy when she left before you got your son."

"Did you never wonder why, if having a son was so important to me, I didn't marry someone else long ago? Especially if I'd divorced your mother as she told you I had?"

"You're Catholic. You couldn't."

She had an answer for everything. Sophia had taught her well. "If I can show you that there was a check from me countersigned by your mother and cashed only days before she died, would you at least listen to my side of this story?"

Felicia waited several seconds before she answered. "There isn't anything you could show me that would change my mind."

"If that's true, then it won't hurt you to listen."

"You've known how I felt about you for years. Why the sudden interest in patching things up now?"

It was the one question he'd known she would ask, and he'd come prepared. "When a man turns sixty, he can no longer pretend time is his friend. There are many things I want to do with whatever time I have left, none more important than this."

She caught her lower lip between her teeth as she studied him. "All right," she said at last. "I'll come back with you, but only if Elana is there, too."

Amado didn't believe for a minute he had convinced her out of any reason but her own greed. With Elizabeth in the picture, the pie was no longer cut in such generous portions. If Felicia was nothing else, she was pragmatic. Whatever her remaining share of his estate, it was far more enticing than nothing.

19

the Monday before
Thanksgiving
Elizabeth

A fierce storm blew in the Monday before
Thanksgiving, ripping branches from trees and causing
widespread, minor flooding. Because there was no reason to go home, Elizabeth stayed at the winery long
after everyone else had left for the night. Finally, at nine
o'clock a nagging hunger prompted her to call it quits.

Halfway home she rounded a curve and nearly
slammed into a tree that had been uprooted by the
gusting wind. She jammed on her brakes, and for an
exaggerated second it seemed as if she would avoid the
tree and stay on the road. But then the rear tires hit a
slick spot and broke loose. The car began a slow, arcing
spin; the headlights sliced the scrub oaks lining the side
of the road as the asphalt yielded to gravel and then to
mud.

She waited for her heart to stop racing before she

tried moving back onto the road. It was useless. With each effort the car only settled deeper.

An hour later she arrived back at the office. She entered the reception area and frowned when she saw a light reflecting into the hallway from the direction of the lab. "Who's there?" she called out on the off chance she hadn't left the light on by accident and someone had come in.

Seconds later Michael appeared at the doorway. "What happened to you?"

"There was a tree in the road—"

"My God, are you all right?"

"I didn't hit it, but my car is stuck in the mud." She looked down at herself. She was soaked to the skin, and her jacket and heavy wool sweater felt like cloaks of lead. "I had to walk back." She looked up at him again.

A draft of cold air swept past her. She shivered convulsively. "I'm going to need a tow truck for the car."

"And some dry clothes." He started toward her and then stopped as if unsure of his welcome.

"I suppose I should report the tree that's down, too," she said.

Michael closed the distance that had separated them and slipped out of his jacket. "Here, put this on." He waited while she took off her coat, hesitated, and then pulled off her sweater, too. Seconds later she was burrowed deeply into his jacket. "What in the hell were you doing running around on a night like this?"

She bristled at the attack. "I wasn't 'running around.' I was on my way home from here."

"If you had left when you were supposed to, this wouldn't have happened."

The tension created by their enforced closeness found release in a sudden explosion of anger. "When I'm *supposed* to? I wasn't aware—"

"Skip it," he said. "There isn't any sense arguing." He turned and went to the receptionist's desk. With his back to her he flipped through the telephone pad and picked up the phone.

After relaying the necessary information and verifying with Elizabeth the precise location of her car, he hung up. "The dispatcher said she'd have someone here as soon as possible, but that it might not be right away. The storm is keeping them pretty busy."

"You don't have to wait with me." She tried to make the statement seem casual, all the while knowing it was wasted effort.

"Where's Amado?"

"He left for New York this morning."

"For all the good it's going to do." Michael walked to the window and made a show of looking into the blackness. "I'm betting that before the trip is over, Felicia is going to make Amado wish he'd never heard of Thanksgiving."

Amazingly, they were back to the ordinary, as if no angry words had been exchanged, as if the tension had been created by the storm raging outside and not the one between them. "There was no talking to him about it."

"It's a waste of time to try to talk to him when he's made up his mind about something."

He turned to look at her. She met his gaze, and the air between them grew heavy with expectation. She purposely broke eye contact and went to the desk. "I'm going to call someone else. If we don't get a tow truck out here soon, I'm . . . I'm liable to wind up spending the night," she finished feebly.

"I'll take care of it."

"That isn't necessary. I can—"

"For Christ's sake, Elizabeth, it isn't personal. I'd do the same thing for anybody."

She forced herself not to respond to his anger. "I didn't mean it like that. I just thought you might have plans. You usually do when you're in town."

"How would you know that?"

"I see you leaving—"

"And do you wait up to see when I come home, too?"

"If you think I'm spying on you, you're wrong. It's just that I—"

"What? That you care?" He came toward her, not stopping until he had pointedly invaded her protective space. She took a step backward. "Or is what you're really saying that you can't sleep at night wondering who I'm with and what I'm doing with them?"

"So what if it is?" she shot back. "Now that you've heard me say it, does it make you feel better?"

"*Nothing* I hear or do or say or pretend to believe makes me feel better."

His anguish was like a knife in her chest. "I know," she admitted.

"I've tried being with other women, but then I only imagine they're you. You've never been in my bed, and it feels empty when I wake up and you're not there. I've told you everything about myself, from the time I was a kid and stepped on a rusty nail and wound up in the hospital to what it feels like to watch my brother farm the land I wanted for myself—and you haven't heard a word."

"Tell me now."

"What's the use?"

The fight drained from her. "I love you, Michael."

He reacted as if she'd hit him. "Why are you telling me that now? Nothing's changed."

"Because it's true, and it hurts too much to keep it inside anymore."

She reached up to touch the side of his face, and he caught her hand. For an instant she thought he was going to push her away. But then he slowly turned his head and, with infinite longing, pressed his lips to her palm.

"I've used up all of my todays hoping tomorrow will be better," she said. "They're spent, gone forever."

"And nothing's changed," he repeated. "We can't go on like this, Elizabeth."

"What other choice do we have?"

He drew her into his arms. "I wish to hell I knew."

She laid her head against his chest; his heartbeat thundered in her ear. "I want you to tell me what you were like when you were growing up." She tilted her head back to look at him. "I want you to tell me about your brother." There was a catch in her voice. "I want you to tell me what you dream about at night."

"I dream about you . . . always you."

Headlights flashed across the window. Elizabeth tightened her arms around Michael. She didn't want to let him go.

"It's the tow truck," he said.

"I thought he couldn't come right away."

"They probably put you in front of someone else." His arms dropped to his sides. "Being Amado's wife has its privileges."

Reluctantly she let him go. Without his support she felt empty, exhausted.

He leaned forward and brushed her temple with his lips. "Take my truck. If you cut through the Hendersons', it should get you past the downed tree. I'll go with the tow truck to get your car."

The door opened, and a tall man with a full beard came in. "Someone here call for a tow?"

"Be right with you," Michael said. He exchanged keys with Elizabeth. "Are you going to be all right?"

She almost laughed out loud at the question. *No*, she wanted to scream, *I'm not going to be all right. Not now. Not ever again.* "I'll be fine," she told him.

20

The rain had stopped and started again by the time the tow truck reached the house and dropped off Michael and Elizabeth's Mercedes. He started toward the house to tell Elizabeth she had her car back, but when his foot hit the front step, he pulled up short and considered whether he really wanted to see her again that night. The answer became cloudy when he tried to balance his need to see her with his desire and the fact that with Amado in New York, the barrier that had effectively kept them apart was gone. In the end he decided it would be better for them both if he went home and called her from there.

He headed back across the driveway, his head tucked low against the powerful gusts of wind and driving rain. When he came around the oak in his front yard, he saw that the lights were on in his living room.

His stomach knotted at the thought Elizabeth might be inside waiting for him.

But what if she wasn't? What if she'd come to take care of Howard and simply left the lights on so he wouldn't have to come home to a dark house?

Then, goddammit, he would find her.

For once in his life he would do the wrong thing for the right reasons. He was weary of fighting a battle that he lay awake nights aching to lose.

He stepped on the porch and quickly shed the rain gear he'd taken from the winery. When he looked down and saw that his boots were caked with mud, he cursed the added delay. Finally, there was nothing standing in his way but his fear and his desperate need to discover Elizabeth inside waiting for him.

He opened the door and saw her immediately. She was sitting on the chair by the fireplace, her feet curled under her, Howard on her lap. She was wearing the baggy gray sweatsuit she'd worn the first night she'd come to his house.

When she looked up at him there was a vulnerable shimmer in her eyes. Before he could see more, her gaze dropped to her lap. "I'm sorry. I didn't mean to be here when you came back. I'll get my coat and be on my—"

"No, I don't want you to leave. Not yet." He closed the door. He had fantasized seeing her there waiting for him so many times, he wanted a moment to savor the reality, to hold it against the consequences and regrets that would inevitably follow.

Elizabeth shifted Howard from her lap and stood. She nervously brushed her hair from her shoulder. It was still damp from the rain.

A band tightened around Michael's chest, and he struggled to draw in a breath. He crossed the room and stopped inches from her. Slowly he brought his hand up and touched her cheek.

She started to pull away and then let go of a resigned sigh and swayed toward him. "Kiss me," she whispered. "Please, just once."

And he did, tenderly at first and then with a fierce hunger. She met his tongue and matched its thrust. There was no subtlety in her desire, no holding back.

He kissed the soft skin at the base of her throat. Heat emanated from her, enveloping him in a sensuous, invisible cloud.

He dug his fingers into her hair and forced her to look at him. "I want more than this," he told her.

She met his gaze unflinchingly. "We've already gone too far, more will only make everything harder than it is now."

"I don't care."

"You will tomorrow."

"Damn tomorrow."

"Just loving me has already cost you that special bond you had with Amado. What will happen if—"

He stopped her with a deep, almost brutal kiss. "Not tonight, Elizabeth," he murmured against her lips. "Tonight is ours."

She answered with a soft moan of surrender. "I love you," she said. And then, as if this would be the only time she would ever be able to tell him freely, she said it again and again.

Michael had promised himself that after Susan he would never again allow a woman to become his reason for living. But as hard as he'd tried to shield himself, Elizabeth had found a way past his defenses.

How was he to have known? How was he supposed to recognize what Elizabeth would come to mean to him when she'd arrived in his life on the arm of his best friend, the man who treated him like the son he'd never had?

He grew desperate to escape the growing prison of his thoughts. He looked at Elizabeth. It was as if she could read his mind.

"We can't do this, can we?" The regret, the sorrow, was heavy in her voice, but there was also acceptance.

"Not and go on as if nothing had happened. We'd never be able to pull it off."

"I can't leave him, Michael."

"I know."

"Amado has done nothing to—"

"Do you remember that conversation we had in the car coming back from Modesto when you told me I would recognize the woman I fell in love with when bells went off in my head?"

"Yes."

"I never told you, but they went off that day, when you gave me the piece of apple. If I hadn't had the radio on so loud, I would have recognized what I was hearing. But I didn't want to know."

She became quiet, thoughtful, and then with a pained sigh said, "I remember something else we talked about, Michael—you and married women."

He pulled her closer and pressed a kiss to her temple. His mind rebelled at the necessity to ground their actions in reality. "Not now, Elizabeth."

"Will there ever be a right time?"

It was then that he realized she was crying. In an attempt to protect herself from what lay ahead, she was already turning her back on what had just happened between them. They could pretend for another hour or two, but there was no escape. "I can't have an affair, Elizabeth. Not with you. With you I want it all."

"What other choice do we have?"

He wasn't sure whether she was testing him or if she simply couldn't see the obvious. "You could leave Amado."

"Yes." She lifted her head to look at him. "But could you?"

He was taken aback by her question. She had cut through the hypothetical and laid him open, something he had been unable to do himself. Amado might survive the loss of his wife or his best friend, but to lose them both? And to each other? Could they do that to a man they both loved?

"I didn't think so," she said.

"There has to be an answer."

She stepped away from him. "This isn't it."

Every part of his being demanded he tell her she was wrong. His mind cried out at the injustice. His heart swelled with the pain. He reached for her and brought her back into his arms. "If we can't have tomorrow, we could at least have tonight."

"If I stay, there will only be more memories. You will say things to me I won't be able to get out of my head and do things that will keep me from sleeping at night."

"You can't protect yourself. I'm here, Elizabeth. I'm a part of your life. You're going to have to find a way to deal with me." It wasn't fair to vent his own frustration and fear on her, but he was beyond fairness. He was desperate. He wanted her to find an answer to a question that didn't have one. Without that answer his life would be empty, devoid of even the hope that had sustained him before he'd found her.

She wiped the tears from her cheeks with the backs of her hands. "I love you, Michael, but I wish to hell I'd never laid eyes on you."

21

Elizabeth fingered the string of matched Mikimoto pearls Amado had given her that morning as a Christmas Eve present. She had acted surprised and pleased, drawing on the memory of how she'd felt when he'd given her other extravagant gifts.

Every morning she woke up with the hope that the day ahead of her would be a little easier than the one just past, that her guilt and sorrow would begin to lose some of its edge, that her heart would stop feeling as though it were in a dozen pieces.

She was exhausted from the constant vigilance it took to hide from Amado what she was going through. There were times when the occasion called for a smile, and she almost cried out at the effort it took. Worst of all was the haunted look she saw in Michael's eyes. He didn't whistle or hum or sing to himself anymore but walked through the winery in a thoughtful silence. Although it didn't appear he was avoiding Amado, when they were together there was a subtle difference in the way they interacted.

Amado was troubled by the change and in a private moment had confided to Elizabeth that he feared Michael was having trouble with a woman. She hadn't known whether to laugh or cry.

Which was the same reaction she'd had when he'd given her the pearls. He'd told her he was giving the necklace to her early because the pearls would set off the red dress she was planning to wear to the Hendersons' party that evening far better than the emerald he'd given her for their anniversary. She was convinced the real reason he'd given her the present early and in private had more to do with his concern over his daughters' reactions than with fashion.

After a final, assessing glance in the mirror, she had to agree, the pearls looked stunning against the red. Elizabeth left her bedroom to find Amado and tell him so. She ran into Felicia first.

"New necklace?" Felicia asked. She set her glass of sparkling water on the coffee table, slipped her hand under the pearls, and lifted them, as if measuring their weight. "My God, don't tell me they're real." She brought the pearls up higher before letting them drop. Picking up her water again, she said, "What does one have to do to earn a gift like that?"

Elizabeth almost smiled in gratitude over Felicia's wholly unintended but immensely welcome diversion. She let her gaze lazily sweep Amado's oldest daughter, from her severely straight hair worn in a chin-length bob to her size seven feet stuffed into size six shoes. "One has to give great"—now she did smile broadly and added a wink—"back rubs." She held her hand up and wiggled her fingers, making sure to turn her hand to show off the ring Amado had given her to celebrate that year's harvest. "It's all in the fingers."

Felicia was plainly unaccustomed to being bested at her own game. "You're cheap. And disgusting. For the life of me I can't understand what my father sees in you."

Elizabeth was worn out from trying to protect Amado from the hurt he would feel if he found out about her and Michael. In the mood she was in, she wasn't about to stand by and allow Felicia's attacks to go unchallenged. It was time someone took her on and let her know what a bitch she could be and how deeply she hurt her father by the comments she so easily let slip off her tongue. "Maybe Amado was lonely and I was someone he didn't have to drag home for a holiday."

Felicia ran her hand down the front of her dress, stopping to pick off an imagined piece of lint. "I have my own life to live. I can't be at my father's beck and call every time he feels nostalgic."

"Beck and call? Before your father and I were married, you hadn't spent a total of two weeks with him in five years."

She was instantly on the defensive. "He had no right to expect more. We have nothing in common. And this place—it's so backward"—she made a face—"so provincial."

"Whereas anything East Coast is the epitome of sophistication? Tell me, Felicia, do the natives think the way you do, or just the transplants?" Elizabeth had met women like Felicia when she'd worked for Smith & Noble. They were so caught up in their own world, they were oblivious of the laughter at their expense.

"Come on, Elizabeth, even you can see how benighted this place is."

Elizabeth smiled. "Even little old me? I think I've been insulted. But then maybe not. Could it be you were giving me credit for the years I lived in San Francisco? I realize it's not New York, but then Elana and Edgar live there, too, so it must have something going for it."

Felicia put her glass back on the table. "I should have known better than to try to talk to you."

"Why? Because I drink your father's wine and think it's good? Or is it because I hate escargots and think sparkling water is pretentious? Maybe it's because I buy my clothes from West Coast designers?"

"The best couturier in Paris couldn't hide your calico mentality. You aren't capable of recognizing the finer things in life, let alone appreciating them."

"Tsk, tsk—and I was so looking forward to having you teach me."

Felicia sneered. "I'd rather shovel shit for a living."

Elizabeth put her head back and laughed. "Felicia, that's wonderful. What a classy line. Maybe there's hope for us after all."

Amado came into the room. He was smiling. "I'm pleased to see the two of you getting on so well. This is what I had hoped would happen if you had an opportunity to spend some time together."

Elizabeth moved to his side, took his arm, and kissed his cheek. She couldn't bear to have him know the truth. "We're working on it, Amado." She shot a penetrating look at Felicia. "Aren't we?"

"Oh, indeed." Felicia picked up her glass and saluted her father. "I had no idea Christmas in the country could be such fun."

Amado put his hand over Elizabeth's. "Are we ready?"

"I just have to get my purse and coat."

"That will give me time to see if Michael is ready, also."

She felt the blood drain from her face. "You didn't tell me Michael was going." They took a chance every time they were together around Amado, knowing it would only take one look, one awkward pause in the conversation, one gesture, to alert him to the change in their feelings.

He gave her a puzzled look. "Why should that surprise you?"

"That's what I admire about this place," Felicia said, the sarcasm heavy in her voice. "There's no class distinction. The hired help is right up there with the owner."

Elizabeth focused her attention on Amado. "It's just that he so rarely attends these things anymore. He's usually busy doing something else."

"I asked him to come," Amado admitted. "I thought Felicia might enjoy his company."

Felicia groaned. "Does this mean I'm expected to baby-sit Michael Logan all night? I really wish you'd consulted me about this."

Amado stiffened. "Michael is capable of taking care

of himself, but that doesn't mean I will tolerate your being rude to him."

"Perhaps, if given the option, Michael would prefer to stay home," Elizabeth said.

"I would not suggest such a thing," Amado replied. "He is undoubtedly dressed and waiting for us right now."

"And we wouldn't want him to waste the money he spent renting a tux, now, would we?" Felicia said.

Visibly upset, Amado excused himself to make the call to Michael. When he was out of earshot, Elizabeth turned to Felicia. "I've got to hand it to you," she said. "I've never known anyone as courageously outspoken as you are. One would think you believed your father's child-producing years were behind him."

"You don't scare me. I'll always be his firstborn. And in case it's missed your notice, things like that are very important to a man like my father."

"Firstborn *daughter*," Elizabeth said. She waited for a twinge of guilt over the lie but felt only satisfaction that for the first time since she'd met Felicia, she actually seemed speechless.

The Hendersons held their annual Christmas Eve party in the hundred-year-old Victorian mansion they had converted into a combination wine tasting room and showroom for their winery. The guest list read like a *Who's Who* of California vintners.

Elizabeth took Amado's arm as they entered what had once been the ballroom. A holly garland with red velvet bows and gold beads had been draped around the perimeter of the room. The musicians hired for the evening played a mixture of pop and country, providing a constant but constantly changing group of dancers.

Throughout the evening Elizabeth had tried but had been unable to talk Amado into dancing with her. Finally he'd told her that his reluctance to join her had nothing to do with the admittedly lively music but stemmed from a catch in his hip. She'd kept an eye on him from then on, and although she hadn't seen him favor one side over the other when he walked, she had noticed that he'd seemed unusually tired.

Now she leaned in close to Amado and in a low voice asked, "What is this thing I'm eating?"

He studied the canapé she held up for his inspection. "It looks like the buffalo sausage Barbara served at her Christmas party a couple of years ago."

She made a face. "It hasn't aged well."

Amado laughed. "I was not implying it was the same sausage."

"I thought buffalo were protected. Aren't they on an endangered species list or something?" Out of the corner of her eye, Elizabeth saw Michael cross the dance floor and head toward them.

She chanced a longer glance in his direction. Her heart quickened. No one who had ever seen Michael wearing his tuxedo could think it was rented. The jacket fit too smoothly over his broad shoulders, the pants too snugly across his flat stomach.

"Excuse me for interrupting," Michael said to Amado. He studiously avoided eye contact with Elizabeth. "I just wanted you to know I won't be riding back with you."

"That doesn't surprise me," Amado said. "I saw the way Janet Williams looked at you when we came in."

"Not even close," Michael told him. "It's just that I haven't been in much of a party mood lately. I should have known better than to come tonight."

"How will you get home?"

"The Bickers."

An awkward moment passed before Amado asked, "Is it Felicia? Has she said something?"

Michael frowned, obviously confused by the question. "I've hardly seen her this evening."

"It was a mistake to make her come home again so soon. I should have been content to have her with me at Thanksgiving."

Michael finally looked at Elizabeth, plainly seeking an explanation.

"Felicia didn't want to come tonight," she said. "Amado is afraid she might have taken her anger out on you."

"I should find her and see if she is all right," Amado said. "If she is ready to leave, perhaps you wouldn't mind taking her home with you?"

"Of course." It was said politely, without much enthusiasm.

Amado turned to Elizabeth. "Would you mind keeping Michael company while I look for Felicia?"

"Why don't I help you?" Elizabeth said.

"It isn't necessary for Elizabeth to stay with me," Michael said at the same time.

"I would rather Elizabeth stay here with you than take the chance of being subjected to one of Felicia's tempers again." He put his hand on Michael's shoulder.

"Elizabeth has been longing to dance this evening. Perhaps you would stand in for me?"

"I'm not such a shrinking violet that I need you to find dance partners for me," she snapped at Amado. "I can take care of myself."

Amado appeared nonplussed by the attack. "Elizabeth, please, that is not what I meant at all. I was only thinking a dance with you might be just the thing Michael needs to put him in a party mood again."

Michael directed his gaze at Elizabeth. He held his hand out to her. "Who knows, he could be right."

Amado bestowed a pleased smile on them before he turned to leave.

Elizabeth waited until Amado was out of the room before she said, "I can't do this, Michael."

He ignored her protest and guided her onto the dance floor. When she placed her hand on his shoulder the tips of her fingers accidentally touched his neck. Her hand curled into a fist, as if she'd been stung. Her pulse sounded so loudly in her ears, she had trouble making out the music, but Michael was a skillful dancer and made it seem as though they moved together effortlessly.

"I've dreamed of holding you again."

"Don't tell me things like that."

"I thought the guilt would make being without you easier."

"Do you really believe it will ever get easier?" Her words were more a cry for help than a question. She felt on fire where their bodies touched. His cologne stung her eyes. When she blinked to clear them, a tear slid down her cheek. She laid her forehead against his chest, hiding her face, stifling the sob that rose in her throat.

She missed a step and almost tripped. Michael pulled her closer. His breath was warm and soft against her hair. Her feet refused to move. She wasn't going to make it to the end of the song. She, too, had dreamed of having Michael's arms around her again, but not like this, not where anyone who bothered to look could see their longing and guess their secret and pity Amado.

A terrible pain filled her. "Michael, I have to get out of here."

Wordlessly he led her to the hallway, waited until it was clear, and then opened a door that led outside. Elizabeth stepped into the cold air and pulled it deep into her lungs. They stood in the shadows, neither saying anything. After several seconds Michael reached up and touched her where the pearls lay against her breast. She put her hand over his. "If you keep touching me like that, I won't be able to go inside again without Amado knowing something is going on."

"I was just looking at your necklace," he said. "It's beautiful."

She knew what he was really saying. "And expensive, and something I didn't ask for or want."

"But it suits you. It's as if you were born to wear fancy jewelry and expensive party dresses."

"But you and I know that isn't true, don't we?"

What seemed like an eternity passed in silence. When he did speak, his voice was flat and calm, the words unmistakingly final. "I can't go on like this, Elizabeth."

The cold air seeped through her velvet dress, stealing what little heat remained. "I keep telling myself it will get easier. Maybe we haven't given it enough—"

"After what just happened, I can't go on believing our lives will ever get any easier. There's never going to be a time when I can look at you and not feel as if I were being eaten up inside with wanting you."

He was acting as though they'd suddenly been given options, as if there were answers to questions neither had the courage to voice. "Nothing's changed, Michael."

"And it never will. That's why I've decided to leave."

"Do you really think we would be any better off in Modesto?" As much as it hurt to see him every day, she couldn't bear the thought of his being gone.

He brought his hand up and started to touch her again, then let it fall back to his side. "I wasn't talking about going to Modesto."

A chill swept through her that had nothing to do with the night air. "Then where?"

"Some place far away. Maybe France, or Australia. I don't know yet."

"You can't mean that." She began to tremble. "What will I do without you?"

"I can't stay, Elizabeth. Living like this is killing me."

She searched for the words that would stop him, words filled with promise or even hope. But there were none. "When?" she asked.

"I haven't decided yet."

"Amado won't let you go."

"He won't have a choice."

"He loves you." *And so do I.* How could she face the future without him there?

"Why are you fighting me on this? You know as well as I do it's the only answer. You said yourself we can't keep living this way."

She could hardly draw a breath through the pain that filled her chest. "I could go with you," she whispered.

He leaned closer. "What did you say?"

She'd spoken out of impulse, out of the fear of losing him. The thought of going with him, of actually leaving Amado, of facing what it would do to him, was too new, too unsettling, to be repeated again so soon. "Give me some time, Michael."

"So you can get used to the idea of my leaving?" His pain had turned to anger. "I'm many things, Elizabeth, but a masochist isn't one of them."

"Please. Just a few more weeks." Somehow she'd find a way to tell Amado, a way that wouldn't destroy him.

22

The day after New Year's, Elizabeth rode to San Francisco with Amado to see Felicia off at the airport. She hoped the isolation of the trip home would provide the opportunity for her to begin the process of breaking away. But as they pulled back onto the freeway, he surprised her by suggesting they stay the night in the city and take in a play. She considered refusing but couldn't deny him this last favor. A glimmer of hope still existed in her mind that she could find a way to be with Michael that would leave Amado's pride intact.

They arrived home late Friday evening. Saturday morning Elizabeth ran into Michael at the winery. He had a troubled, sleepless look about him. "I can't wait much longer," he told her quietly. It wasn't a threat, it was a statement.

"I only need a little more time," she said.

"For what? How is a little more time going to change anything?"

"I'm not sure yet."

He dropped his gaze to the floor. "You're fooling yourself, Elizabeth. There isn't some miracle waiting to happen."

Later that night Elizabeth and Amado were in the living room watching the evening news when Consuela came in and told them good night. Elizabeth waited until she heard Consuela's car pulling out of the driveway before she said, "There's something I have to talk to you about, Amado."

He turned to look at her. A flicker of pain followed the motion. He absently ran his hand across his chest. "Would you like me to turn off the television?"

His actions drew her attention. "Is something wrong?"

He made a dismissive gesture. "I am either getting old and my constitution has become less tolerant, or Consuela is adding more spices to her casseroles than usual."

"I'll say something to her tomorrow." She immediately realized how inappropriate her offer would seem once she told him she was leaving, but there was no way to take it back. The lead-in she'd planned escaped her, and she floundered. How did one segue from spicy food to divorce?

"Excuse me a moment," he said, and got up. "I think I will take something for my stomach before it keeps me up all night again."

"How long have you been having stomach trouble?" When would she stop thinking of herself as his wife? Would there be an instant transformation or a prolonged, painful letting go? "Have you seen the doctor?"

"He said it was all a part of the aging process." A quick, sardonic smile lifted one corner of his mouth. "So far I have found nothing to recommend in getting old."

Alone, Elizabeth tried to concentrate on the weather report. Somehow it seemed right that rain was in the forecast. She couldn't picture leaving Amado when the sun was shining.

After the weather came the sports, and finally a piece on a man who was building a house out of aluminum cans he'd filled with concrete. Amado still hadn't returned. Concerned, she got up to look for him. She found him on his bed, propped up by several pillows.

"Amado? Are you all right?"

He opened his eyes and tried to get up. The effort proved too much, and he lay back down again.

She went to him. He looked gray; there was a thin layer of perspiration across his forehead and on his upper lip. A bubble of fear grew and then burst in her midsection. "What's wrong? What's happening to you?"

"It's nothing," he said.

"I have eyes. I can see—"

"It will pass. It always does." He reached for her hand to try to reassure her.

"What in the hell is that supposed to mean?" As she listened to his labored breathing, her fear gave way to panic.

"Sometimes the medicine works more slowly."

"Since when are you taking medicine?" Abruptly, with sickening clarity, she remembered the box where she'd found the eyedropper. She should have realized there were too many prescriptions for allergies alone.

"There is this trouble with my heart."

"This *trouble?*"

"I'm sorry. I didn't want you to find out this way."

It was as if the key piece to a puzzle had suddenly fallen into place. So many things made sense now—the shortness of breath he sometimes experienced and tried to pass off to lack of exercise, the chest pains, the extra pillows on the bed. Even the desperate attempts to bring his daughters closer to him.

"How long have you known there was something wrong?" she asked.

"Not until several months after we were married." He let go of her hand and motioned for her to sit on the bed beside him. "You must believe I would not have done this to you had I known."

Afraid she would make him more uncomfortable if she crowded him, she brought over a chair and sat on it instead. Almost as an afterthought, she put her hand back in his. Her emotions in turmoil, she took refuge in the clinical. "What do the doctors say?"

"You know how doctors are. It is their job to—"

"Don't do that to me, Amado. Not anymore. I have a right to know what's happening to you." A lump formed in her throat. "Goddammit, you're my husband."

"The technical terms will do you no good, Elizabeth. They are only words for the doctors to hide behind when they must tell you that you are dying. All it is necessary for either of us to know is that my heart is wearing out and there is nothing that can be done to stop it."

"You shouldn't have gone through this alone."

"How could I promise you that if you became my wife, all that was good in life would be yours and then, less than a year later, go back on that promise?"

"You didn't know." Her mind struggled to bring focus to her thoughts while her emotions ran through them unchecked. Amado dying? How could that be? He was so strong and vital, so full of life. She leaned forward and brought his hand up to her cheek.

"You are what keeps me alive, Elizabeth. Without you it would be meaningless for me to go on."

His words were like a band around her chest. She had to fight to draw a breath. "You give me too much credit. You have your daughters and granddaughters and—"

"And Michael and Consuela and a hundred friends who I know will be sad when I am no longer here," he finished. "But none of them are you." He arched his back as if trying to expand his chest to draw more air into his lungs. After several seconds he relaxed again. "I have had a good life, Elizabeth. My only regret is that there was not more time for us. Leaving you will be the hardest thing I have ever had to do."

"Don't talk like that." She wasn't ready to hear his calm acceptance of something so unthinkable.

"I should have told you what the medicine had done to me," he went on. "Instead I let you think you were somehow to blame when I moved from our bedroom."

"The medicine? What did that have to do with your leaving?"

"It was the reason I could no longer make love to you. On some men it is one of the side effects. Unfortunately, I was one of those men. I didn't tell you because I kept hoping there would be a new medicine I could try. Or, if I began to respond better, an adjustment could be made that would let me become your husband again."

She felt sick. If only he had told her. How different everything would be. "I wish you had trusted me."

"My silence had nothing to do with trust, Elizabeth. I have thought about it many times, and have finally faced the truth. I was afraid of losing you. I believed as long as there was hope, you would stay."

"Did you think I married you just for the good times?" The question and all that it implied gently but firmly closed the door that had led to her leaving with Michael. The knowledge brought her a strange sense of peace.

"They should not have been over so soon."

"Are you positive there is nothing that can be done? Have you seen a specialist?"

He smiled. "I have seen everyone there is to see. Surely you do not think I would leave you without a fight."

She thought about the times she'd been unable to reach him in Modesto, about the afternoons at the winery when no one had seen him and she'd assumed he was off somewhere talking to a farmer about his crop. "What did they say?"

He hesitated. "That a transplant was my only hope."

The idea terrified her. She was aware the success rate for transplants had improved dramatically over the past decade, but there was still no guarantee. "When will it happen?"

"I told them I wasn't interested."

"I don't understand. If it's your only—"

"I am sixty years old, Elizabeth. If I were healthy, I would still have many good and productive years ahead of me, but it is not only my heart that is wearing out. The disease has damaged my kidneys and my lungs. How can I, in good conscience, take a heart for myself when there are so many others in need?"

"Why do you automatically assume they are more worthy than you? Besides, if you had a heart that worked better, wouldn't it help your kidneys and lungs?"

He closed his eyes, as if exhausted. When he opened them again, his gaze fixed on the ceiling. "One day I was at the clinic for evaluation and met a young woman who was there for the same reason. She had three daughters and told me how she was preparing them to go on without her in case she should die before a heart became available. When I suggested she might be unnecessarily frightening her children, she told me about an eighteen-year-old boy she had met at the clinic the year before who had died waiting for his new heart. And there were others. So many others that I've lost count." He turned his head to look deeply into her eyes. "Now do you understand?"

She knew then that there was nothing she could say or do that would get him to change his mind. "I should," she told him. "Your selflessness was one of the reasons I fell in love with you."

"Then we can agree that the subject will never be brought up again?"

It was useless to argue with him. "If that's the way you want it."

He released the pressure on her hand, leaned his head back, and closed his eyes again. After several seconds he said in a soft voice, "Would it be all right if we finished our conversation in the morning?"

"Are you okay?" She thought about the number of times Amado had disappeared recently, the meetings he supposedly attended, the late lunches with other growers. He must have been resting somewhere, shoring up his strength to convince her everything was as it should be.

"I'm just a little tired. It has been a long day."

"Is there something I can get you before I leave?"

"No, I have everything I need."

She stood. Her throat constricted as she held back threatening tears. He would not want her to cry. "I'm sorry, Amado."

"Don't be. God has been good to me even in this. Before He let me find out I was dying, He gave me you."

She would do whatever it took to be sure Amado never found out she was not the bargain he believed her to be. It was all she had left to give him. She bent and touched her lips to his forehead. "I'll come in to check on you before I go to bed."

"I love you, Elizabeth."

"I love you, too, Amado." What did it matter that the love she had for her husband was not that of the poets? At least she was no longer faced with the need to make a choice—it had been done for her.

°   °   °

Midnight came and Elizabeth paced her bedroom, struggling with what she would and should tell Michael, thinking the right words would come to her if she only waited long enough. A part of her, the cowardly part, kept insisting she shouldn't be the one to tell Michael about Amado at all. But no matter how compelling her arguments, she couldn't convince herself that keeping Amado's secret was the right thing to do. Amado needed Michael's love as much as he relied on his skill.

Regardless of the mental path she took, she reached the same destination. There wasn't any more good or right way to tell Michael about Amado than there had been to tell Amado that she was leaving him.

Silently she slipped out the front door and into the fog that had moved down the hillside and settled thickly around the houses. Her foot was poised to step onto the porch when an inner voice stopped her from going any farther. She could give Michael so little, one more night's uninterrupted sleep suddenly seemed a wondrous gift. She retraced her steps through the fog and slipped quietly into the house, pausing at Amado's door to listen to his breathing before heading for her own room.

At six-thirty the next morning when Elizabeth walked past Michael's house on her way to pick up the newspaper, she saw that his truck was already gone. She thought it strange that he had left for work so early but was too caught up in what she would say to Amado when she saw him at the breakfast table five minutes from then to give Michael's absence more than a cursory notice. Given a choice, she undoubtedly would have sought escape in the ordinary, too. Instead she had to find a way to look at Amado without pity in her eyes, a way to talk to him without sorrow in her voice, and a way to live each day without wondering if it would be their last together.

Amado opened the door for her as she approached the house. "I see no reason for you to take over picking up the newspaper," he chided her.

"I was up and about and thought—"

"That you would save me the effort?"

She came up on tiptoe and kissed his cheek. "Something like that."

"This is precisely why I waited so long to say something to you, Elizabeth. I did not want you to begin treating me as though I am an invalid." There was an unmistakable thread of anger in his voice. "That time will come soon enough. Until then, let me live my life as I have always lived it. Give me that much."

Elizabeth stepped away from him. "I'm sorry. I just wanted—"

"I know." His voice softened. "I have had months to try to come to terms with what is happening, you have only had hours." He put his hand across the back of her neck. "Come inside. There is something I want to show you."

She followed him into his office and waited without saying anything as he pulled a folder out of the desk. When she saw that the samples of the new labels were inside, she was both surprised and relieved. She'd anticipated something to do with Amado's condition and was grateful that he was intent on forcing an air of normalcy no matter how artificial. She needed time to come to grips and to accept what was happening before the need to make decisions was thrust at her.

Most important, she had to find a way to tell Michael. And then find a way to leave him emotionally, knowing he would need her to be with him in his grief almost as much as Amado needed her to be with him in his dying.

When she arrived at work later that morning, she looked for Michael's truck in the parking lot, but it wasn't there. A flicker of concern went through her. She dismissed the feeling as a case of misplaced paranoia, telling herself there were a hundred logical places he could be.

Amado called at ten and told her he had decided to take the day off to catch up on personal business and to rest for the party they were to attend at the Robertsons' that night. She considered asking if he'd seen or heard from Michael but didn't want to draw attention to the fact that she was looking for him.

When noon had come and gone and Michael didn't show up at the winery for lunch or call in to tell Christine where he could be reached, she put her work aside and went to look for him. No one she ran into at the winery or the vineyards had seen or heard from him. On a hunch she called Modesto. No one there had seen him, either.

Finally she went home to see if he'd returned there. Even though his truck was still missing, she decided to try the house anyway. She was still several yards away when she spotted a piece of paper attached to the front door. A growing sense of unease gripped her as she stepped on the porch and saw that the envelope had her name written on it.

She opened the flap and took out the single sheet of paper.

Elizabeth,

I'm sorry, I honestly tried, but I couldn't stay any longer. We've both known all along that no matter how long we waited, nothing could change or make any difference.

Somehow, in falling in love with you, I allowed myself to become second best after I'd promised it would never happen again. If there is blame to be passed out, I accept it all. I knew better.

I've left a letter for Amado at the winery, filled with what I hope will seem logical and rational explanations for my leaving. I was going to tell him in person, but then realized I could never pull it off. As cruel as it may seem, this was the only way.

Michael

P.S. Howard is with me. He doesn't seem very enthusiastic about leaving, but then neither am I. We should make a hell of a pair, don't you think?

She leaned her head against the cool glass, closed her eyes, and let the pain come. It wrapped itself around her like an old friend, confident of its welcome. She cried out at the injustice of losing both Michael and Amado.

"Elizabeth?"

She turned at the sound of Amado's voice. He was crossing the driveway, heading her way. She took a deep breath and blinked the moisture from her eyes before stuffing the note into her pocket.

"I don't think Michael has come home yet," he said as she met him on the walkway. "At least I haven't seen him."

She couldn't concentrate. She didn't know what to say. So many hurts and sorrows hammered at her, those received and those she would give. "He's gone, Amado."

"Yes, I know." He said the words slowly, as if they were spoken in a foreign language. "Have you checked the winery?"

"He isn't there, either." She tried to smile to soften what would come next, but her lips refused to respond. "He's left us."

The coaxing look faded from Amado's eyes. "What are you talking about?"

She didn't want to be there. She wanted to escape, to hide, to run until she couldn't run anymore. "Michael decided it was time for him to move on." A gust of wind swept through the yard. She hugged herself, feeling as though she were about to be carried away. "I suppose we should begin looking for another wine master. As much trouble as we had getting someone for Modesto, there's no telling—"

Amado made a grab for her as if he were afraid she might fall. "Are you all right?"

"Of course. Why wouldn't I be?"

He hesitated. An inner turmoil showed on his face. Finally he let out a sigh and brought her close. "You don't have to pretend with me anymore. This is my fault. I knew what would happen. Hell, in a way, I suppose I planned for it to happen."

His words took a long time to penetrate. "What do you mean, you knew what would happen? That you planned it?"

"Come inside. There is much I have to tell you."

She moved out of his embrace. "No, Amado, I think you'd better tell me now."

He shifted from one foot to the other, clearly uncomfortable with what he was about to say. "You must understand how difficult this is for me."

"You knew what was going on between Michael and me, didn't you?" She didn't want to believe what she was saying, yet her mind raced with the possibilities. "My God, that's what all the trips to Modesto were about. You planned them so Michael and I would be alone together."

He held out his hands in a pleading gesture. "I didn't want you to be left without anyone when I was gone."

An ugly suspicion hit her as her mind skipped ahead of his words. She felt as though she were going to be sick. "Was it me you were concerned about, Amado, or your precious winery?"

"I never intended for you to be hurt by this. You know I have always thought of Michael as—"

She dug Michael's letter out of her pocket and threw it at Amado. "Do you have any idea the hell you put us through with your manipulations?"

"How was I to know you would fall in love with each other so quickly?"

"Perhaps if you'd let me in on your timetable in the

beginning, I could have delayed the actual moment to better fit your plans."

"You are making too much of my involvement. I admit I looked for ways to arrange to have you and Michael together and that I hoped that eventually you would"—as he spoke, he bent to pick up the piece of paper she had thrown at him—"find each other." He paled when he read what Michael had written. "My God, how could I have forgotten?"

The words drifted to Elizabeth on a silent gust of wind. "What is it, Amado?" He looked so lost, so alone, her anger turned to fear. "What did you forget?"

He raised his head and looked at her. "That he would feel second best. Please, Elizabeth, you must believe me. I never would have . . ." He let out a groan. "How could I have forgotten?"

"I don't know what you're talking about."

Amado turned from her and stared out across the valley. "He never told you about Susan and his brother?"

Even with Amado at her side, Elizabeth had never felt more alone. Someday she would ask him to tell her about Susan and Michael's brother, but not now, not today.

Now was too soon. Her own pain had filled her to capacity. In time there would be room for Michael's. But not yet.

For whatever the named reason—love or loyalty or duty—she and Amado would be together until death parted them. She reached for his hand. "You shouldn't be out here without a jacket," she said. A small part of her noted that despite everything, the tenderness and caring in her voice were real. "Let's get you inside where it's warm."

His fingers closed around hers. "It wasn't just the land and the winery I was worried about protecting, Elizabeth. I was thinking of your happiness, too."

A sorrow swept through her. All that she had to face would be far easier if only she didn't believe him. But she did. "I know, Amado."

23

"It just isn't fair," Alice said, "for either one of you. You just found each other."

"If I let myself get caught up in thinking about the fairness of what's happening to Amado, I'm not going to be able to do anything else." Elizabeth shifted the telephone receiver to her other shoulder and leaned back in her chair. When her gaze fell on the stack of correspondence she still had to go through that day, she turned to face the wall.

"Are you sure you don't want me to come out there to help? I could be packed and on a bus in an hour."

"I want to save you for later, Grandma."

"I'm not some fragile piece of China, Elizabeth. There isn't a reason in the world—"

"If you come out too early, it will be a constant

reminder. Amado will never have a moment when he can pretend he isn't sick, even on the good days."

"Of course. I should have thought of that myself. I just feel so helpless."

Elizabeth caught the telephone cord in her hand and fingered the coils absently. "Me too."

"When is he going to tell Felicia and Elana?"

"They're up at the house with him now. He almost had to threaten Felicia to get her out here."

"How do you think they'll take it?"

"I honestly don't know."

"Wouldn't it be nice if they used the time Amado has left as an opportunity to establish a real relationship with their father? I'd like to think something good could come from all this."

"I thought about that, but I don't know if it's even possible. With everything that's happened in the past, if Felicia and Elana did have a change of heart, how could Amado trust that it was real?"

Several seconds passed before Alice said, "He's going to believe whatever he wants to believe. And who's to say that isn't for the best?"

Elizabeth couldn't argue the point. There had been too many times in her own life when fantasy had buffered reality and made day-to-day living possible.

"Promise you'll tell me when things start getting bad," Alice went on. "And never forget there's always something given when something is taken away. It's hard to live each day knowing you're dying, but when you do, you get a chance to set things right—to tidy up, if you will. Look at it as a gift, Elizabeth."

"I love you, Grandma."

They talked a few more minutes and promised to talk again soon before they hung up. Unbidden tears welled in Elizabeth's eyes as she placed the receiver back in its cradle. She never knew from which direction she'd be ambushed in her daily battle with grief. Some days a problem at work would give her hours of freedom. And then an errant thought would hit, and the weight of the future would come crashing down around her.

A tear spilled from her eye. She sat very still and mentally marked its path down her cheek. A part of her mind disassociated itself from the pain that had triggered the tear and sent a gentle warning that there were many more to come.

Again, someone she loved was leaving her. She could rail and cry out at the injustice, she could swear and raise her fist to the heavens, she could hide in her work.

None of it would make any difference.

Amado was going to die. And when he did, a piece of her would die with him.

"How long do you have?" Felicia asked.

Amado adjusted himself on his chair, seeking a position that would allow his lungs easier expansion. Instead of being offended by the brusqueness of her question, he was relieved that she hadn't tried to fool him with an insincere show of sympathy. "It could be months, it could be a year, or even more. There are many variables."

Elana shot a nervous look at Felicia before she stammered, "Are—are you all right now? I mean, is there something we can do for you?"

"No," he told her. "Everything that can be done is being done."

Felicia stood and walked over to the window. She pushed back the curtain and stared outside. With her back still to her father, she asked, "Then why did you ask us to come here today? You could have told us about this over the phone."

"*Felicia*," Elana said, gasping. "How could you say something like that?"

She whipped around and glared at her sister. "If you'd be honest for once in your life, you'd admit you were thinking the same thing. Since when do we get together for family pronouncements?"

"This is different," Elana shot back.

"Why? Because Daddy is dying and he needs us?" She turned full on Elana. "Where was he when Mother needed him? For that matter, where were you?"

"Felicia, do not do that to your sister." Amado held out his hand in a pleading gesture. "You have to learn to let go of your mother. What she did—"

"Don't you talk to me about my mother!" Felicia shouted. "You have no right."

"Why won't you listen to him, Felicia?" Elana looked to Amado. "Can't you see he's dying? This is our last chance to be a family."

Felicia's head snapped back, almost as if Elana had hit her. She stared at her sister and then her father. Her eyes narrowed in thought as she swept her hair back with her hand. "I . . . I'm sorry. I don't know what came over me. It must have been the shock of . . . of hearing about your illness . . . Dad."

Amado wasn't sure what he'd hoped would be the

result of their meeting that day; he only knew this wasn't it. Felicia's smile had the regretful sincerity of an IRS agent throwing out a deduction. Amado suspected that the terrified look in Elana's eyes had more to do with the unpleasantness of someone dying than it did actually losing the man who was her father.

"I do not want to die with things left unsaid between us," Amado told them. "Surely there are questions you would like to ask me, things you would like to know about your childhood before you moved to Spain with your mother. When I am gone, there will be no one left to answer those questions for you."

"How would you know what we were like as children?" Felicia asked. "You were never around."

Amado nodded slowly, acknowledging her anger. Even when it was to her benefit to do so, she could not let go of her bitterness. "I worked very hard to grow the best grapes and make the best wines I could. My father expected this of me, as his father expected it of him. I did not know that my work would cost me my family. It was simply the way things were done then."

"Are you saying you would do things differently now?" Felicia asked.

"Yes, I would do whatever it took to keep you and your sister with me." He looked for something in her eyes that would tell him his answer mattered, but she had shifted her gaze to the window again, effectively and pointedly closing herself off from him.

Felicia brought up her arms and folded them across her chest, stating her position in every way possible to her. "And Mother?"

"I said I would do whatever it took," he repeated.

She turned to face him. "Does that mean you're sorry for the way you treated her?"

"More sorry than I can say." He left it up to her to interpret his meaning.

"How did you intend for us to go about becoming a family again?" While the words were conciliatory, the body language was tight and controlled.

Before his daughters arrived that morning, Amado had told himself not to expect too much. He'd felt Elizabeth's concern when she'd looked at him over breakfast and had heard it in her voice when she'd volunteered to stay with him instead of going to work that day. Nothing he or Elizabeth could have done would have prepared him for the disappointment he felt that not even the finality of his dying had managed to get through to Felicia. And without Felicia, he stood little chance with Elana. "I was hoping we could spend some time together, to get to know each other again."

Felicia shot a quick look at Elana. "I suppose we could manage to get together on a regular basis from now on, couldn't we, Elana?"

Elana was caught off guard by her sister's quick turnaround. "Of course. I would like that."

Where Amado should have felt a sense of triumph, there was only a hollow feeling.

The boat carrying Michael across the Pacific dipped in a sudden swell, forcing him to grab hold of the ropes holding the sail to stay upright. He sent a quick glance to where he'd left Howard preening himself. Howard met his gaze with a smug, superior look before he went back to licking his paw.

They were three weeks into the trip, and Michael still hadn't gotten his sea legs. Jeremy Andrews, the slightly off-center captain who'd agreed to take Michael on in exchange for food and transportation to Australia, had assured him the transition would take place. It was only a matter of time.

And, after all, wasn't time something Michael had in abundance?

Not many men could say there was nowhere they had to be and no one waiting for them when they got there. Never before had Michael known what it felt like to be truly free. Maybe someday, if he worked at it hard enough, he might even begin to like it.

Howard got up, stretched, and came across the deck. He planted his front feet on Michael's leg and let out a soft meow. Michael picked him up and set him on his shoulder, pressing his cheek into Howard's side, letting the soft black fur caress his skin.

"Hang in there, Howard," he murmured. "Nothing lasts forever." The last was more for himself than the cat.

The night Michael got in his truck and drove out of the Napa Valley for the last time, he'd had no idea where he was going, only that he had to get away. Originally he'd headed east, following some latent desire left over from childhood to see Yellowstone Park. At Winnemucca, Nevada, he'd arbitrarily turned north and then, in Idaho, west again, finally ending up in Seattle. A day spent wandering the docks, a willingness to pitch in and lend a hand loading supplies on the most beautiful sailboat Michael had ever seen, and a chance conversation over thick salmon steaks, and here he was, about to close in on the Hawaiian Islands.

He'd left California looking for a cure, all the while knowing there wasn't any.

Wandering might not be the answer, but it was a hell of a lot better than standing still. He couldn't shake the feeling that if he stopped, even for a minute, everything he'd left behind, everything he was running away from, would catch up to him. And he wasn't ready to deal with it yet.

Until he could find a way to live with what he'd lost, he'd keep moving.

If it took forever . . . what the hell.

24

St. Helena—March 1990

Elizabeth stood at the edge of the vineyard, dressed in the black suit she'd bought eight months earlier in readiness for the day she would say her final, public good-bye to Amado. Knowing how hard it would be to go shopping for something appropriate when the time came, she'd considered her decision not only perceptive, but practical. Instead the suit had become a mental burden, a constant added reminder that hung at the back of her closet, waiting to validate her decision to purchase it.

The months of waiting had been difficult on multiple levels, the days filled with urgent strategy meetings on ways to release Amado from his role as head of the winery and as spokesman for Montoya Wines, the nights filled with watching him slowly becoming a shadow of the man she'd met at Smith & Noble's Christmas party. In the end Elizabeth decided that rather than try to rush a new campaign, they would gradually ease back, running fewer and fewer ads with Amado until they simply disappeared. Then, after she'd had an opportunity to reassess their position, she would decide where she wanted to position Montoya Wines in the marketplace.

She knew she was taking a huge risk that she would ever be able to regain their market share, but that fell into the category of "tomorrow's problems." With Amado gradually laying claim to her every waking hour, it was all she could do to keep up with her work at the winery.

As she'd expected, Amado had not gone quietly into the night. Even as he'd neared the end, where it seemed every new breath took more energy than the last, he'd continued to fight for yet another day. There were times when she would stand outside his room and listen to his labored breathing, and in her mind she would silently beg him to let go, to put his trust in his often stated belief that after this lifetime they were destined to find each other again.

In the end, when his body could no longer respond to the will of his mind, he had awakened from a deep sleep to take his final leave of her—his eyes open, his mind clear, a raspy, whispered declaration of love on his lips.

When the funeral was over and everyone had gone home, she would say her own private farewell to Amado with the Merlot he had set aside on their wedding night to celebrate their tenth anniversary. She would build a fire in the fireplace and drink the wine from the Lalique glass he had used to toast their engagement. After the wine was gone, the glass would join the flames. The suit would be packed up, along with Amado's clothing, and sent to a halfway house somewhere, anywhere, far away from St. Helena.

Taking one last look around her before heading back to the house and the waiting limousine, she let her gaze sweep the gnarled stumps, careful to keep herself balanced on the balls of her feet and not let the spike heels sink into the soft ground. Had Amado been able to visit the fields that year, he would have approved of how well the pruners she'd hired had listened to the vines. Most of all he would have taken pride in her ability to judge the work they had done.

She looked down at the Rolex watch he had given her for her birthday that year. To the end he'd taken a childlike pleasure in surprising her with expensive, useless trinkets, never listening or giving credence to her protests. Amado had loved her without ever knowing her. She had been what he needed her to be, fulfilling every fantasy save one, the mother of his son.

In a half hour she would be standing in front of their friends at a church filled to overflowing, trying not to search the crowd for the one person she knew in her heart would not be there. Even if Michael had learned about Amado's death in time to make the funeral, instinct told her he wouldn't have come. Staying away, denying himself the right to say good-bye, was only proper punishment for the sin he believed he'd committed against his best friend.

But then Michael might be so far away that the news hadn't even reached him yet. If he hadn't remained in the wine industry, he might not find out about Amado for months. No matter when Michael discovered Amado was gone, a part of him would die, too.

Elizabeth turned and started up the hill. She glanced toward the house and saw Alice and Consuela waiting for her on the deck. Even from that distance she could see the worried looks on their faces. She would do what she could to reassure them she was all right. Eventually she would convince them and everyone else that she not only had the strength and tenacity to take up where Amado had left off, she had the capability. Of all the gifts Amado had given her the past year, the one that held the greatest value for her was his knowledge.

The gift she'd given in return was a promise to go on without him and to let his dream become hers.

Two weeks later Elizabeth was in Napa for the reading of Amado's will. Other than the attorney, Elana and Edgar were the only other principals in the mahogany-paneled office. The longtime employees Amado had wanted remembered had received handwritten notes of appreciation mailed the day of the funeral, each containing a personal check made out and signed by Amado. Felicia had designated Elana her liaison, declining to attend herself, telling her sister she had already spent too much time in California the past year and that expecting her to fly out twice in one month was simply asking too much.

The reading of the three typewritten pages brought no surprises. Everything was as Amado had carefully explained before his death. Elizabeth stood, eased the strap of her Bally purse over her shoulder and held out her hand to the attorney, James Webster. "Thank you, Jim," she said. "Amado wanted me to tell you how much the extra work you put in these past few months meant to him."

He took her hand with both of his and met her gaze with a look of compassion. "If I can be of any help to you in the future . . ."

Elana, with Edgar less than half a step behind, pressed forward to intercept Jim when he moved to come around the desk. "Excuse me for intruding," she said, her tone making it clear the apology was perfunctory. "But Edgar and I have another appointment in the city this afternoon, and I wanted you to know that I've hired an attorney to represent my sister and myself in this matter. His name is Sanders Mitchell—perhaps you've heard of him?" She let out a dismissive little laugh. "What am I saying? Of course you've heard of him. Anyway, he has instructed me to tell you his office will be in touch with you within the week."

Jim frowned. "Bringing another attorney on board is up to you, of course, but I hate to see you going to the expense. If you have any questions, I'd be happy to answer them for you. Your father's will is relatively straightforward. And I can assure you everything is in order."

"It wasn't my idea to hire Mr. Mitchell, not that I don't think it's a good one. Felicia was the one who insisted we have our own representation."

Jim seemed taken aback at the implied suggestion. "Your father was a fair and generous man, Mrs. Sullivan. I'm sorry you feel—" He stopped and took a second to compose himself. "Forgive me. You are certainly entitled to handle this in any manner you see fit. If you think it would be helpful, I'll have a copy of the will sent to Mr. Mitchell's office first thing tomorrow morning."

Felicia's behavior didn't surprise Elizabeth. If Amado hadn't been running out of time and desperate to believe what she told him, she would never have been able to convince him that she had undergone a change of heart. She'd been clever in her pursuit of her father's affection, knowing if she made an about-face too quickly, he would never have believed her sincerity. But the prize was worth the effort, and Felicia was as greedy as she was spiteful. What she obviously didn't know was how long and hard Amado and Jim had worked to set up the will. There were no loopholes. She and Elana were wasting their time and money looking for one.

"I'll talk to you later, Jim," Elizabeth told him.

"Don't leave yet," he said. "This won't take much longer."

"We'll have to make it another time," she said. "Alice is waiting for me to pick her up from shopping."

A light rain had started to fall when Elizabeth pulled into the shopping center parking lot and saw Alice wave to her from under the awning of a coffee shop.

"How did it go?" she asked as she tossed her package onto the backseat and climbed into the car.

"As expected," Elizabeth said. "There weren't any surprise codicils, if that's what you mean."

"Actually, I was wondering about Elana and Edgar. I hope they didn't make the morning any harder on you than it was already."

Elizabeth slipped her hand over her grandmother's and gave it a squeeze. "I like having you around. You make me feel loved." When Alice didn't respond immediately, Elizabeth glanced in her direction. "What's up?"

"I've been thinking . . . there really isn't anything to keep me in Farmingham."

"Oh?" Elizabeth had suspected something like this was coming. Alice hadn't been very good at hiding her concern over Elizabeth's decision to run the winery herself. "Finally decided to retire, huh? Well, you aren't going to get any arguments from me." She pulled up to a stoplight and turned to look at Alice. "But what about all your friends? Nothing's changed as far as they're concerned, Grandma. If you move out here, either you cut yourself off from them, or we take a chance someone will find out about me."

"There's nothing saying I couldn't go back for a visit now and then."

"And what happens if one of them wants to return the favor?"

"I would deal with it if and when that happened."

"I love you for caring, Grandma, but I'm not about to let you give up your life and all of your friends to move out here and take care of me."

They'd traveled several miles before Alice broke the silence that had grown between them. "I wish your grandfather could have known you."

"I do, too. But what made you bring it up now?"

"Oh, you know how you start thinking about one thing and it leads to another and then another."

Elizabeth knew her grandmother was comparing the burden of trying to run a farm alone with her taking over the operation of the winery. If she could put Alice's fears to rest, perhaps she would feel less pressured about making the decision to leave Farmingham. "How long did it take you to decide you didn't want to keep the farm after he died?"

Alice seemed startled by the question. "The decision was never mine to make. I thought you knew that. The bank took over right away. There was an auction, but it barely covered the debt. Surely you didn't think I took up waitressing because I enjoyed it."

"You never said anything."

"It isn't one of my better memories. You do what you have to do in this life. If complaining made the work go faster or easier, I'd be right in there giving Felicia a run for her money. But it doesn't, so I never bothered."

"You couldn't afford to take me in back then, could you? And yet you never said anything. Why?"

"The minute I laid eyes on you I knew you would put purpose in my life again. I didn't give a fig about the money."

Elizabeth had never been able to disassociate the pain of being abandoned by her mother and father from the joy of meeting her grandmother for the first time. The day continued to elicit feelings that confused her. Seemingly apropos of nothing, she asked, "Did you love Grandpa?"

Alice easily made the shift with Elizabeth. "Yes, but I

never knew how much until he was gone. Sometimes the regret of it is almost as powerful as the loneliness."

"Before I met Amado I had no idea there were so many ways to love someone." She could have added that she'd also had no idea it was possible to love two men at the same time, but she thought better of it. Alice would rest easier thinking her granddaughter had only one heartache that needed mending.

25

An *electricity permeated* the winery as everyone geared up for the initial crush of the season. A sense of excitement, tinged with more than a little relief that the transition of ownership had taken place and they still had a job, put a quickness in the steps of the workers. Elizabeth had been aware of wagers being made, both inside and outside the winery, on whether Montoya Wines would still be in private ownership when harvest season arrived. She took a perverse pride in the fact that the odds had been against her.

Winning hadn't come easy. For the past half year she had focused her thoughts, her energy, and her passion on the business, sometimes putting in fourteen- and fifteen-hour days and more often than not putting them in seven days a week. When she wasn't working she was reading, going over and over the technical details of wine production, picking up details Amado had missed or forgotten to tell her about, studying everything she could get her hands on until the vocabulary became as familiar as the one she'd used in advertising and the words tossed around so easily in the labs and fields actually made sense.

Many nights she fell asleep on the sofa in Michael's old office, a book on fungus or bunch rot or problems that occurred during fermentation propped open on her lap. Come morning she would go home for a shower and something to eat and be back at her desk before the office staff arrived.

Consuela worried that Elizabeth was pushing herself too hard. Every time Alice called, she somehow managed to bring the conversation around to "there being more to life than work." Even Tony Reynolds, who quietly and unobtrusively put in almost as many hours at the winery as she did, found it necessary to chide her gently now and then about too much work and too little play damaging the spirit. Elizabeth listened patiently to the well-intended advice, agreed she needed to slow down, thanked everyone for caring, and then went back to work.

It wasn't that she didn't appreciate their concern or believe what they were trying to tell her; her reluctance stemmed from an almost desperate need to be where the work would lead her. She was in the process of building a new life for herself, one that was complex and fulfilled and rewarding, a place where there would be no need for anything or anyone else.

The month after Amado died she began looking at applicants for the wine master position Amado had steadfastly refused to fill after Michael left. She'd interviewed a dozen men and half that many women but still hadn't found anyone. David Robertson, who had sent several highly qualified people her way, finally stopped doing so out of frustration. He insisted she wouldn't be happy until she found another Michael, and since there wasn't one to be had, she was wasting everyone's time in the search. The accusation had hit too close to home for her to ignore, and she'd promised herself she would take a less critical view of the next applicant.

Half a year had passed without Amado's guiding hand at the winery, and it was the morning of a clear September day that promised to turn blistering by afternoon when a knock sounded on Elizabeth's office door. "It's open," she called.

Tony Reynolds stuck his head inside and smiled. "You gotta come outside and see the results of the Brix test on the Gamay Beaujolais they just brought in."

"That good, huh?"

"Jack said not to tell you, that you had to come see for yourself."

She pushed her chair back and stood, inordinately pleased to be included. When she'd officially taken over the winery, the feeling of unity and family that Amado had fostered had not transferred to her automatically. In subtle and sometimes not so subtle ways, she'd discovered her employees' loyalty and respect were two things they expected her to earn for herself.

As she rounded the desk, her private line rang. She reached for the receiver and told Tony, "Give me a second to get rid of whoever this is."

He nodded. "I'll be in the yard."

She waved in acknowledgement and put the receiver to her ear. "Elizabeth Montoya," she said.

"Elizabeth, it's Jim."

"Jim—what can I do for you?" In the months since Amado's death, Jim Webster had become as much friend as attorney.

"You sound as though you've had a good morning."

"Unlike you. What's up?"

"I'm afraid I have some disturbing news. Are you free to come to my office this afternoon?"

"I wish I could. It would be nice to get out of here. Is it something we could handle on the phone?"

There was a long, disturbing pause. "I'd rather not. How about if I come there?"

"What time?"

"Lunch?"

She had planned to work through lunch. "I'll have Consuela fix something. Sandwiches okay?"

"Anything, as long as it's accompanied by a bottle of that wonderful Chardonnay you sent over last month."

His attempt at lightness fell flat. Elizabeth fought an urge to insist that he not wait to tell her what was going on. "I'll see what I can find in the cellar."

Jim arrived at eleven-thirty. Elizabeth was in the yard, watching a load of grapes being dumped into the crusher. She waved when she saw him and excused herself from the men she'd been talking to.

As she approached, she extended her hand. "If it was your intention to scare the hell out of me," she said, her smile in place for anyone who might be watching them, "you succeeded."

"I'm sorry, Elizabeth, but it couldn't be helped. I

didn't want to dump the news on you without being here to go over your options with you."

"If you don't do something about the look of doom on your face, someone is going to make up a story to match. Rumors grow faster than the grapes around here."

He didn't say anything more as he followed her into her office.

When they were inside, Elizabeth motioned Jim to a chair. She sat on the edge of her desk, her hands propped on either side as she leaned forward expectantly. "All right, you've got my attention."

He took a deep breath. "Felicia and Elana have received an offer to purchase their forty-nine percent of Montoya Wines."

If someone had told her to write down the problems she could possibly face her first year of operation, this one wouldn't even have made the list. She was too stunned to say anything for several seconds. Finally her mind settled on the obvious. "Who?"

"Hicks and Brody."

"The tobacco company? What do they want with a winery?"

"I called Joan Walker—a broker I know—and had her do some checking around before I came over. According to what she was able to find out, they've been looking to expand in this direction for a long time."

"But what gave them the idea Montoya Wines might be for sale?"

"Actually, from the pieces I've been able to put together so far, it looks like it was Elana and Felicia who approached them. Or at least they had their attorney do the actual approaching."

Her anger was swept away by fear. "Can they get away with something like—"

"I'm afraid so."

"And there isn't anything I can do to stop them?"

"According to the terms of the will, you have first right of refusal and the option to meet any offer."

"How much are we talking about?"

He made a face. "I'm afraid it's several more million than you have liquid, Elizabeth."

She left her perch on the desk and began pacing the room. "How long do I have to come up with the rest?"

"Amado must have anticipated something like this because he made it clear he didn't want me to stipulate the normal ninety days in the clause."

"Which means?"

"You have whatever the court decides is 'reasonable time.' Considering the circumstances, we'll probably get the one hundred and twenty days."

"Another month—I don't understand how that's supposed to be such a big help." The smile he gave her touched on menacing. She was glad he was on her side.

"It all comes down to how long the court appearance can be delayed."

"So the time isn't retroactive?"

"You've got it."

"My God, Jim. Can you imagine what would happen if I allowed a company like Hicks and Brody to come in with their flow charts and management teams? Even with controlling interest I'd be spending more time doing battle with them than I would running the winery."

"There's another option we haven't talked about, Elizabeth. It isn't necessary for you to do battle with them at all. Hicks and Brody would prefer a complete buyout. From what I've been able to learn so far, they don't want to deal with you any more than you want to deal with them. Their attorney authorized me to tell you they were willing to match the offer they made to Felicia and Elana and throw in a nice bonus for your additional two percent. You would be an extremely rich woman."

"You can't be serious. How could I do that to Amado?"

"I understand your sense of loyalty, but it's time you recognized that Amado's gone, Elizabeth."

"But I promised him I would never sell—"

"Look, I'm sorry, but someone needs to say this to you, and it looks like I'm elected. You know as well as I do that you're in over your head here. This offer is a legitimate way for you to get out while you've still got your head above water. I'm not going to let you dismiss what could very well be your best chance for a secure future out of some misguided sense of loyalty." When she started to answer him, he put up his hand to stop her. "That old saying about the one sure way to make a small fortune in the wine business is to start with a large one didn't come out of a comedy routine. Just because Montoya Wines has been around five generations doesn't mean it's invincible. One or two bad years and all of this could disappear. And then where would you be?"

"Back in advertising. Look, I appreciate what you're trying to do for me, but you're wasting your time. There isn't anything you can say that will change my mind."

"I could get them to make concessions." He went on

as if he hadn't heard her. "You could keep the houses. And if you're worried about the people who work here, I can have it written into the contract that no one would be let go for at least a year. That would give everyone plenty of time to look around for—"

"You aren't listening to me, Jim. I'd rather see the place closed down than sold to someone like Hicks and Brody."

"You sound like a petulant child who's been told she isn't going to get her way no matter how big her tantrum." After several thoughtful seconds passed, he put his hands on the arms of the chair and pushed himself up. "If we're going to stand a chance of winning this thing, you're going to have to come across as one hell of a businesswoman. You can't be the first one to blink."

She frowned, not quite sure how to interpret what he was saying. "Does that mean you're going to help me?"

"To tell the truth, I'm looking forward to it. It's been a long time since I've been in an old-fashioned, bare-knuckled fight." He started toward the door. "I have a feeling this one is going to more than make up for the dry spell."

She followed him. "If you really feel that way, why were you trying to get me to sell?"

"Because you pay me to give you the best advice I can. What we're about to do isn't it."

She rocked back on her heels and smiled with relief. "I didn't want to lose you."

He chuckled. "But if I hadn't agreed to your terms, you were ready to send me packing."

"In a minute."

A wicked smile lifted the corners of his neatly trimmed mustache. "Which is precisely why I'm sticking around. There's something about a really tough and determined woman that makes me respond to the call to arms. I think I must have been a general or something in Joan of Arc's army."

"What's our next step with Felicia?"

"Don't you mean Felicia and Elana?"

"Elana's a puppet. It's Felicia we have to worry about."

"Leave Felicia to me. Your job is going to be rounding up the money."

"How much do I need?"

"I figure you need another ten million on top of what you've already got in liquid assets."

She caught her breath. The sum was three times what she'd expected. How could she be so out of touch with the market? "You're kidding."

"Just be glad it's a take-it-or-leave-it offer and we don't have to get involved in a bidding war with Hicks and Brody."

"What if they change their mind and up their offer?"

"They won't."

"How can you be so sure?"

"Because they aren't the ones who initiated the action. They may be lusting after Montoya Wines, but they aren't in love. If this deal falls through, there's another one ready to take its place."

"I see you've already started working out a strategy."

"I knew you wouldn't sell."

"Am I that transparent?"

He reached for the doorknob. "That stubborn."

"I thought you were staying for lunch."

"Can't—too much to do." He grinned. "I will take that bottle of Chardonnay you promised me, though."

Elizabeth went to the lunch room to retrieve the bottle of wine, then walked Jim to his car and waited for him to drive away. When she returned to her office, she stood at the doorway for several seconds, staring at her desk and the work awaiting her there.

How was she ever going to come up with another ten million dollars? The sum was mind-boggling, almost more than she could comprehend. If she'd paid more attention to the weekly reports from her accountant, she would never have been caught off guard this way. Surely she'd paid inheritance taxes on the winery that were based on an assessed valuation. How could she not know something like that?

Obviously she was not yet the hotshot businesswoman she'd pictured herself.

26

Elizabeth propped the phone on her shoulder while she reached across her desk for her calendar. "How soon do you expect to close?" she asked.

The woman on the other end of the line was an attorney from Los Angeles, representing an up-and-coming rock singer who was anxious to invest a large part of his newfound riches by buying a winery, and wasn't it lucky Elizabeth's just happened to be available? Needing every dime she could raise, Elizabeth had decided to try selling the property without hiring a Realtor. She'd given herself four weeks and was only three days away from the deadline when the rock star called and asked for a personally guided tour.

"As soon as we've come to an agreement on the terms, I'll start putting the papers through," the woman replied.

"I told you last week, the terms are set. Get back to me when you're ready to sign and I'll take the property off the market."

"I can assure you my client is not going to change his mind. After his visit to the winery he is satisfied it meets his investment needs."

"That's all well and good, but there's no way I'm pulling the property off the market until I—"

"Would ten thousand dollars earnest money convince you?"

Elizabeth laughed. "Try adding another zero and tie it to a timely closure and we have a deal."

"I'll have to get back to you on that."

"To be fair, I should tell you that I'm expecting another offer to come in this afternoon. If they're ready to go forward . . . What can I say? I haven't tried to hide the fact I want this sale handled quickly." She put her hand to her chest as if she could physically contain the swell of fear that her bluff wouldn't work. The woman might not be a specialist in real estate, but she wasn't stupid. December was hardly a prime time for moving property.

"Surely you don't expect me to—" There was a long pause. "What the hell," she said, her words punctuated with a sigh of resignation. "I'll express the signed papers to your attorney this afternoon. As soon as you've approved them, the check will be deposited in escrow."

It was everything Elizabeth could do not to let out a whoop of joy. "It's been a pleasure," she said. She hung up the phone, sat back in her chair, and smiled.

She was getting closer. Once Amado's collection of Fabergé cigarette cases and his Remington bronzes were auctioned, she would be closing in on what she needed. In order to cover legal expenses and the incidentals that kept popping up, her jewelry was scheduled for private sale later that week. Another month or two and she'd know exactly how much she would have to borrow to complete the deal.

And then it would be just her. Elizabeth Mary Montoya, sole proprietor of Montoya Wines. Finally, after more than thirty years, she would have an identity that wasn't tied to, or dependent on, anyone else.

It was almost nine o'clock when Elizabeth arrived home that night. Her initial surprise at seeing Consuela's car still in the driveway had turned to concern by the time she opened the front door.

She walked down the hallway toward the back of the house. "Consuela?" she called out.

"In here," came the answer.

Elizabeth went into the living room and found Consuela holding a shiny silver ornament in her hand, putting the final touches on a perfectly formed blue spruce Christmas tree. The remnant of child still left in Elizabeth wanted to clap her hands in delight; the woman who had known so few years of the familial happiness and joy associated with the season was annoyed at the reminder.

As if she understood what Elizabeth was feeling, Consuela explained gently, "Alice called today and said she was going to be able to come early for Christmas after all. I knew you wouldn't want her to see . . ." She shrugged. "I just thought it would be easier this way."

Elizabeth's first inclination was to protest Consuela's assumption that she had purposely ignored the holiday, to offer the defense that she'd simply been too busy to put up a tree herself. Consuela would accept the excuse because she respected Elizabeth's right to privacy. But they would both know the truth. "It looks beautiful. I would never have done this for myself. Thank you."

Consuela placed the silver ornament near the top. "It is good that you have found the strength to begin again, Elizabeth, but you must not let the memory of having Amado with you last year keep you from making new memories. You do not honor those who are gone when you stop living yourself."

Unknowingly, Consuela had provided Elizabeth with an excuse she would not have thought of herself. "It's just that it seems so pointless to go to all the bother without anyone here to enjoy the effort."

"Are you no one?"

"You know what I mean."

Consuela began gathering empty boxes. "It is too bad Michael is not here."

The words echoed in Elizabeth's mind. "Why would you say that?"

"He loved Christmas. He was like a little boy the way he would drop hints and tell me to try to guess what he'd put under the tree for me. If he were here, he would have been the first one to insist you begin again."

Elizabeth could think of one Christmas that had been less than wonderful for Michael. The memory of that night filled her with a desperate longing. She crossed the room and stood in front of the tree, letting her gaze take in the individual ornaments. They were lovely, handcrafted pieces of art. How could she not have noticed them before? She held an angel up for closer inspection. "Where did this come from?"

"Amado brought them as gifts to Sophia and Felicia and Elana whenever he traveled. Even after Sophia went back to Spain he would add new ones to the tree for her. I don't think he ever stopped hoping."

"If they were gifts—"

"Why are they still here?" She shrugged. "I can only guess why Sophia refused to take hers with her. It is easy to understand why Felicia would not take those that belonged to her, she knew it would hurt her father. Each Christmas I have seen Elana look longingly at those that belonged to her, but she will do nothing to risk her sister's disapproval."

When it came time to take down the tree that year, Elizabeth would package up the ornaments and send them to Elana. What she did with them then was up to her. And then next year Elizabeth would follow Consuela's advice and begin anew, gathering her own decorations. The thought pleased her. "I've never even bought a piece of garland for myself before," she said.

"Well, you own an attic full now. Michael used to hang it everywhere."

Would she never escape him? The doorbell rang. Elizabeth looked at her watch. "Who do you suppose that is?"

Consuela grinned and gave Elizabeth a little push. "You'll never find out if you don't answer it."

"You know who's out there, don't you?"

Consuela went back to picking up the boxes. "I'm not saying."

For one unguarded, breathtaking moment, Elizabeth let herself believe it was Michael, that he had come home for the holidays. She had to force herself not to run down the hall.

But it wasn't Michael, it was Alice. "Grandma! Consuela told me you were coming, but I had no idea it would be tonight. What a wonderful surprise." And it was, just not the one she'd been hoping for.

Alice stepped inside and gave Elizabeth an even longer than usual hug. "I know how busy you've been and I didn't want to intrude, but it seemed everywhere I went this year they were playing 'The Little Drummer Boy.' I tried, but I just couldn't stay away any longer."

Their first Christmas together Elizabeth had played the song so often that Alice had hidden the tape. She hugged her grandmother again, especially tight this time, her instant of disappointment forgotten. "If I'd known that was what it would take to get you here, I would have sent you a copy for Halloween."

"Then you're not upset that I've come early?"

"It's the best present I could have hoped for." Out of the corner of her eye she saw Tony head up the walkway, Alice's luggage in tow. Behind her, Consuela came down the hall, preparing to leave.

"Alice, how good you look," Consuela said.

Alice gave the other woman a warm smile. "It's been too long."

"Where do you want me to put these things?" Tony asked.

"Just leave them here in the hall," Elizabeth told him. "I'll put them away later."

The cold air hastened the good-byes. Consuela promised a long visit with Alice the next day, Tony said he would see Elizabeth in the morning, and seconds later Alice and Elizabeth were alone.

"Why didn't you tell me you were coming?" Elizabeth asked as she closed the door. "I could have picked you up."

"I knew how busy you were, and Consuela said Tony wouldn't mind."

There was more going on than Alice was admitting. "Let's go in the living room. There's some spiced cider in the refrigerator. It will only take me a minute to heat it up."

When they were settled on the sofa, Elizabeth focused her attention on Alice, making it clear she wanted an answer as direct as the question she was about to ask. "All right. You want to tell me the real reason you're here early, or are you going to make me work it out of you?"

A slow, sheepish smile formed. Alice wrapped her hands around the mug of cider. "I told Consuela we'd never get away with it."

"So what is it now?" When Alice didn't immediately answer, Elizabeth prodded her again. "Don't tell me she thinks I'm working too hard again and you're supposed to get me to slow down."

"I wish it were that simple." There was a long pause. Alice took a sip of her cider and then settled the mug in a coaster. "I'm not sure how to say this."

Whatever was bothering Alice, she wasn't going to be put off with light-hearted reassurances. "When did it become necessary for us to dance around a subject with each other?"

"It's just that I can't help feeling I'm intruding on something that's really none of my business."

"There isn't anything—"

"It's about Michael."

Elizabeth caught her breath in surprise. "What about Michael?" she asked carefully.

"Consuela seems to think there might have been something going on between the two of you before he left."

"What makes her think that?"

"The reasons aren't important. Is she right?"

"Yes, but it's not something I want to talk about. Besides, what possible difference would it make now?"

The confusion Alice felt was reflected on her face. Yielding, at least temporarily, to Elizabeth's refusal to talk about Michael, she said, "All right. Then why don't you tell me how it's going with the Felicia and Elana thing."

"Jim told me the other day that he's run out of ways to delay, and that from the looks of it we'll be keeping the January court date. He seems pretty confident the judge will grant us the six months we're requesting."

"Did you ever get a chance to talk to Felicia about this?"

"I've tried, but she never returned my calls."

"I still don't understand why she would want to do this to you."

"The forced sale has nothing to do with me. It's just a continuation of the battle between her and Amado. What better way to get back at him for Sophia?"

"She must have been beside herself when you didn't cave in and sell your half, too."

"I'm sure she thought that once all those millions were dangled in front of me I would jump at the opportunity to become a woman of leisure."

"I've never asked, but I've wondered why you didn't." She hesitated. "Is it because this was Michael's home and you want him to always have a place to—"

"If Michael were ever going to come back, he would have been here for the funeral." She picked up her cider and tipped the cup back and forth, watching the spices gather at the bottom. She was torn between the release talking about Michael to Alice would bring and an almost overpowering shame that made her want to deny everything. "In the beginning I told myself I was hanging on to the winery because I'd promised Amado I would. But I discovered I like what I'm doing, Grandma. And for the first time in my life, I actually like who I am. It's an incredible feeling, one I'm not about to give up without a fight."

"I understand that. But can you win?"

It was a fair question, and Elizabeth knew why Alice had asked. If she didn't win, what would happen to her then? Where would she go? More important, who would she be without the winery providing her identity? "I don't think Felicia would have taken me on if she'd known the emotional stake I have in the winery."

"Don't underestimate her, Elizabeth. You may have determination on your side, but she's the most calculating, manipulative person I've ever seen."

"In a peculiar way, she comes by it honestly. Amado was a master at getting what he wanted. The longer I knew him, the more I realized he never did anything by chance or on impulse. I used to wonder why he took the

Fabergé collection and the paintings out of the winery showroom and moved them back to the house when we got married, and why he insisted the Modesto Winery be put in my name. None of it made sense until Felicia made her move. Amado anticipated what could happen long before he even knew he was sick. He worked to instill the sense of family heritage in me and then gave me the means to buy out his daughters."

Elizabeth had done a lot of thinking since Amado's death. More than once she'd wondered about their serendipitous meeting and their whirlwind romance. Amado had found something in her that went deeper and was far more complex than love at first sight. He'd recognized her need to belong to something and her tenacity when it came to hanging on. Not once in his final months had he reminded her how important it was to him that the Montoya legacy remain intact. He knew without being told that his dream, his commitment, had become hers and that she would do whatever it took to see the Montoya tradition continue at least one more generation.

"You forgot to mention the jewelry," Alice added. "Amado just didn't seem the type to give those great big gaudy things he was always coming up with."

"Oddly enough, I think he actually came to enjoy it. At least I hope he did because something tells me I'm going to take a real beating on the resale."

"What are you going to do if you come up short?"

"I'll worry about that when the time comes."

"I could sell my house if you think it would help. It won't bring much, I know, but you're welcome to anything and everything I have."

Elizabeth leaned forward and took her grandmother's hand. Alice wouldn't sleep for a week if she knew how much money Elizabeth still had to raise. "When I went into this I told myself that your house and Great-Grandma Boehm's china were off limits." She stood. "I could use another cup of cider. How about you?"

Elizabeth had intended the physical action to mark the end of the discussion about her finances. When she returned she handed Alice her cider and, with a determined air, asked, "How's Mr. Benson doing?"

Alice gave her a look that said she wasn't having any of it. "Same as he was my last letter. Now let's get back to—"

"Can we let my problems go for tonight? It's been months since we've been together. Surely we can think of something else to talk about."

"We don't have to talk at all," Alice said. "We can just sit here and admire that beautiful tree." She brought the mug to her lips and blew softly on the steaming liquid.

Elizabeth's defenses crumbled, and she was hit with an all-pervading loneliness. "I think I would like to tell you about me and Michael after all," she said. "Is that all right?"

"Of course it is," Alice said. And then, in the special, caring voice Elizabeth remembered from her childhood, the one she would use when Elizabeth came home from school in tears at yet another slight, she added, "There is nothing you could do or say that would make me think less of you."

Elizabeth tucked her legs up underneath her and settled deeper into her corner of the couch. For the next half hour, in fits and starts and several pauses to regain her composure, Elizabeth talked about how she and Michael had gone from being adversaries to loving each other and how Amado's hand had guided them along the way.

"Did you ever find out what happened between Michael's brother and this Susan person?" Alice asked as Elizabeth came to the end of her story.

"Not for several months. I couldn't bring myself to ask Amado about it, and he didn't volunteer. Then one day we were having breakfast on the deck and Amado mentioned that he had run into Paul in town. Paul told him that he'd heard Michael was gone and wondered if anyone had heard from him." Elizabeth shifted positions, stretching her legs and then tucking them back under her again.

"Had they?" Alice asked.

"As far as I know, no one around here has heard anything from him or about him since the day he left. If they have, they don't talk about it, at least not to me."

"So it was running into Paul that led to the discussion about Susan?"

"It was as if a dam had broken inside Amado. He couldn't stop talking about Michael. I think he'd finally realized how much he'd lost, and he was trying to find a way to deal with it." In all of his planning, Amado had forgotten the most important detail—how deeply Michael would feel his sense of betrayal and how it would affect him. Amado knew what kind of man Michael was. If he had just stopped to think of all the potential consequences of his manipulations, he would have known that leaving was the only honorable thing Michael could do.

"How sad you both must have been, sharing your feelings about Michael."

Elizabeth mentally shook herself in an attempt to escape the resurrected emotions. "Anyway, about Susan. She and Michael went together all through high school and became engaged the day they graduated. . . ." Elizabeth told Michael's story in a flat, tight voice, the heartache coming through in the story itself.

"But the farm was still there for Paul to inherit." Alice sighed. "I've seen it happen over and over again— good, loving families torn apart by as little as an acre of land."

"According to Amado, Susan came from a family that had trouble putting food on the table every day. She was determined to escape that environment, and when it began to look like Michael would have to drop out of school and take a laborer's job, she was beside herself. She knew that Paul had been attracted to her the whole time she and Michael were going together, so . . ."

"She traded brothers."

"One way or another, Michael has been made to feel second best all of his life." She didn't say anything for several seconds. When she did, her voice was as soft as a whisper. "He can't go through it again. Not even for me."

"If you still love him—I know it sounds terrible to talk about this so soon after Amado—but there really isn't any reason, you know what I mean. Have you thought about trying to contact him?"

Elizabeth plucked at the seam on her wool slacks. "It's the way I put myself to sleep at night."

"Then I don't understand what's keeping you here."

"I don't know where to look. And even if I did, I'm

not sure I would do anything about it. I love being in charge at the winery, Grandma. The hours I put in there aren't because I'm trying to run away or hide from something, or someone. I'm there because of the sense of accomplishment I feel at the end of the day."

"But wouldn't it be even better if there was someone to share those feelings with you? What are you afraid of, Elizabeth?"

"Losing the one thing I have left where Michael is concerned."

"And that is?"

"Hope."

"That surprises me."

"Why?"

"I've never known you to take the coward's way out before."

Elizabeth brought her knees up and pulled them tight against her chest. "I've never had so much to lose."

"Michael means that much to you?"

"More."

27

Elizabeth pulled into the parking lot at the winery. It was the first day of work in the new year, and she was determined to start it in an upbeat mood despite several setbacks the previous week. Amado's collection of cigarette cases hadn't brought in as much as she'd counted on, and her jewelry had sold for less than half of what she'd expected.

The worst news had been the judge's decision to give her only three months to come up with the money, instead of the six Jim Webster had requested. Sanders Mitchell, the attorney for Felicia and Elana, had argued successfully that since the court date had already been delayed three months, to give Elizabeth yet another six months would be unconscionable. To Jim's consternation, the judge had agreed.

The phone greeted Elizabeth as she entered her office. "Elizabeth Montoya speaking."

"I tried you at home," Alice said. "But Consuela told me you'd already left."

"Grandma." Elizabeth glanced at her watch. Even taking into account the time difference, it was early in Kansas. "Is something wrong?"

"I don't know. I got a call from George Benson a couple of minutes ago. He said there was a man at the school yesterday asking about Elizabeth Preston."

A chill stole through Elizabeth's body. "Who did he talk to?"

"Besides George, you mean?"

"Yes." It didn't matter, anyone in town could have told him about the Preston family's tragic accident. Fifteen years wasn't near enough time to dim the memory of the loss of the town's most prominent citizens.

"I don't know. George said he was afraid that if he questioned him too closely, it might make him suspicious."

"Does Mr. Benson know who he was?"

"Some private detective out of Kansas City."

"Did he happen to mention who'd hired him?"

"George asked, but the detective wouldn't say."

Elizabeth swallowed the lump of panic that threatened to choke her. "What kinds of questions did he ask?"

"Pretty general, until he found out about the accident."

"And then?"

"He wanted to see the annual for the year you graduated."

"Did Mr. Benson give it to him?"

"George told him they didn't keep them around that long, that someone would have to check the storeroom and it could take a week or more. The detective said he'd be back."

"It's been so long . . . I never thought . . ." Elizabeth leaned forward and covered her eyes with her hand. She needed time to think, to try to make sense out of what was happening. But time was her most precious commodity.

"George wanted me to tell you that you weren't to worry about him, that he knew what he was doing when he helped you back then and he hasn't regretted it one day since."

"I'm going to call Jim Webster and see if there's something he can do."

"Let me know if you hear anything on your end."

"You too." Elizabeth said good-bye and reached for her phone directory. She had Jim Webster's number half dialed when she remembered most people were just getting out of bed.

"Dammit," she said out loud. "Why now?"

She looked at the papers on her desk. There was no way she could concentrate on shipping schedules and acreage yields, but she'd go crazy if she didn't have something to keep her occupied until Jim got to work. Better to do something—anything—than sit there and wait.

Five minutes later she was on the road, headed for Jim Webster's house to try to catch him before he left for work. Mandy, Jim's wife, answered her knock, clearly surprised to find Elizabeth on her doorstep so early in the morning.

"Elizabeth, what a lovely—"

"I apologize for barging in on you this way, Mandy, but I have to see Jim. Is he still here, by any chance?"

"He won't be leaving for work for another hour or more, and there's no apology needed. It's always a pleasure to see you, no matter what time of day. Come in, we were just about to have breakfast. Why don't you join us."

She stepped inside. "Thank you, but I've already eaten."

"Coffee, then?"

"Yes, please."

Mandy took Elizabeth's coat and hung it in the closet. "I'll have Margaret bring a tray to the sunroom for you and Jim. It's beautiful out there in the morning."

Either Mandy was completely oblivious of the urgency in Elizabeth's voice or hoped to put her at ease with social banalities. One possibility was as disconcerting as the other. "Mandy, I don't mean to be ungracious, but this isn't a social call."

"No, of course it isn't. I should have guessed you wouldn't drop in for a chat at this hour. I'll get Jim for you. Why don't you wait in his office?"

"But your breakfast . . ." She followed the words with an apologetic smile.

"It's not Jim's favorite meal anyway. He's always preferred brunch." She pointed down a hallway. "It's the third door on the right. I'll make sure you're not disturbed."

"Thank you."

The room where Mandy sent her was a duplicate of Jim's office in Napa. Elizabeth passed on the overstuffed white sofa and headed for the chair opposite the desk. She'd been seated only a few minutes when Jim came in, carrying a tray with coffee. He poured the rich brown liquid into a pair of heavy mugs and looked at her, an eyebrow cocked in question. "A splash of cream, no sugar?"

They had had coffee together only once in all the time they'd known each other, and that had been months ago. "You're remarkable."

"Just observant." He came around the desk and sat opposite her. "And right now I'm not sure I like what I see. What's happened to bring you out so early this morning, Elizabeth?"

"There's so much to tell, I don't know where to begin."

Jim picked up his mug and settled deeper onto his chair. "I hate to be obvious, but there's no place like the beginning."

At first Elizabeth stumbled in the telling of her life story, rushing forward with details and then remembering something that made her go back. After a while she managed to distance herself from the autobiography, and it almost seemed as if she were talking about someone else; then the telling became easier. Jim seemed to sense when she was giving short shrift to something that made her uncomfortable and would stop her with pointed questions. Otherwise he let her continue uninterrupted, saving his comments for the end.

By the time she'd brought him up to that morning and the conversation she'd had with Alice, Jim was sitting back in his chair, his elbows propped up, his hands pressed together tent fashion. He tapped his index fingers to his chin as he listened to Elizabeth tell him that she would do whatever it took to protect George Benson and her grandmother, even if it turned out that Felicia was behind the investigation and the only way to stop her was to sell the winery.

"Do you think that's what Felicia is after?" he asked.

"I don't know. I keep telling myself I'm being paranoid where she's concerned, that it's possible she isn't even involved. But then if she's not the one snooping into my background, who is? And, more important, why?"

"What do you think the chances are that the Elizabeth Preston the detective was looking for isn't you at all, but another woman with the same name?"

"I don't believe in coincidence."

"Neither do I." He let out a long, exasperated sigh. "The trouble with secrets is that the longer they're kept, the more important they become. Yours are so old they've grown all out of proportion to the truth. Let's forget about the college thing for a minute. You were a young girl when your parents died. What possible influence could you have had on them? Without influence or control, how can there be guilt?"

"Almost everything I know about my parents' capture and trial and escape attempt I read in old newspapers and magazines in the library at college. At the time it all actually happened, my grandmother refused to let me watch television or read what was being written."

"As I recall, they never really had a chance. The escape plan wasn't very well thought out, and their friends abandoned them at the first sign of trouble."

"Alice tried to protect me from the reporters, but they knew she couldn't be with me all the time and they just waited until she wasn't around." She felt a need to explain how it had been for her back then. "I remember one woman who asked me how I felt when I found out my mother had been shot in the head so many times they had to use her fingerprints to make a positive identification." Elizabeth had tried to keep her mind from forming an image of what her mother must have looked like, but it was like trying to dodge raindrops. And then when she was in college, thanks to one of the old newsmagazines she looked up, she no longer had to rely on her imagination. The photograph was indelibly printed in her memory, as fresh as if she had seen it yesterday instead of all those years ago.

"When Mandy's and my first child died crossing the street in front of our apartment in San Francisco, I learned not to question the whys and wherefores of losses. Eventually I even discovered there was good that could come out of the worst tragedies. Without the push to reevaluate my life, I'm convinced I would still be caught up in the pressure-cooker law firm I was with at the time. Mandy feels that with the way I was back then, our marriage would never have survived. If she's right, our two youngest boys wouldn't have been born. Do you see what I mean?"

"What you're telling me is that you think I should let go of my past."

"Unless there's some good you haven't told me about that comes from hanging on."

"I'm not 'hanging on' to anything, Jim. It's just there. It follows me around wherever I go."

"Did you ever tell Amado about your parents?"

"No." Only Michael, she added silently.

"What about the scholarship?"

She shook her head.

"Did you ever tell anyone?"

"You."

"Why only me?"

The question was so fundamental, the answer so obvious, she was momentarily at a loss for what to say. Finally she told him, "It was my silence that bought me freedom from my past."

"You're wrong, Elizabeth. Your silence has imprisoned you."

How could she make him understand? "One of the basic tenets of advertising is that image supersedes substance. It's not a supposition, Jim, it's a fact. It's how you're perceived that counts, not who you are. It just so happens that the image I have now is also the person I really am. But none of that would matter if I told the truth about my background. Who I am would be lost in the way people perceived me. I would become the child of murderers who grew up to become a thief and a liar herself."

"Do you really think anyone in this valley cares who your parents were? It's been fifteen years since you left Farmingham, Elizabeth. The curious stares, the gossip, wouldn't last a week."

"Maybe not, if that was all there was to it. But I don't think people around here would be quite so quick to forgive me for what I did all on my own."

Jim's eyebrows drew together in a puzzled frown. "What are you talking about?"

"Why mince words? I stole Elizabeth Preston's scholarship. There's no way to pretty it up. The sad part is that if I don't find some way to stop whoever's checking up on me, the lives of two innocent people are going to be as messed up as mine will be."

"From what you've told me, George Benson isn't exactly innocent."

"All George Benson did was come up with the idea and assume the risk for helping me. I was the one who profited."

"There are lots of people who would admire you for what you did. And rightfully so, as far as I'm concerned."

"And there are those who would want to see me lined up right alongside all the other thieves. I don't fool myself about this, Jim. Even if I could find a way to protect Mr. Benson and my grandmother, there's the winery to think about. If this gets out, I won't be able to hold on long enough to survive the bad publicity."

"My God, Elizabeth, you were just a kid, and a desperate one at that."

"Somehow I don't think I would get off with that kind of defense. I may have been a kid, but I knew what I was doing." She leaned forward to put her mug back on the tray. "Listen to us. We're beginning to sound like I'm the attorney and you're the client."

"I'm sorry, Elizabeth. You came here for help, not a lecture." He reached in the drawer and brought out a tablet and pencil. "What do you want me to do?"

"Find out why I'm being investigated."

"Something tells me the 'why' will take care of itself once we discover the 'who.'"

28

Two weeks after Elizabeth's meeting with Jim, the detective he'd hired to find out who was investigating her still hadn't come up with anything. George Benson had called to tell her he'd discovered that one of the secretaries had handled a request for Elizabeth Preston's high school records, sending them in a return envelope to a post office box in Chicago. She hadn't thought to write down the number.

The waiting turned Elizabeth into a nervous wreck. Her heart jumped every time the phone rang; her hands trembled when she picked up each day's mail and sorted through it. Her sole island of sanity was the office after everyone else had gone home for the day. It was the only time she could concentrate enough to get any real work done.

Turning over the last page of a report that had

arrived that day from the lab at Davis, Elizabeth saw that the charts Charles Pinkley had told her had been enclosed were missing. She started rummaging around her desk to find them and spotted the sandwich Tony had brought her from the deli before he left for home.

She picked up the bundle, peeled back the wrapper, saw that it was pastrami, and made a face. It wasn't her favorite, but she was hungry enough that it didn't matter. She grabbed some change from her drawer and headed for the soda machine in the employee's lunch room.

On her way back to her office, she saw headlights swing across the windows in the reception area and heard a car pull into visitor parking. Curious, she went to investigate.

She arrived in time to see Edgar get out of his car. He immediately headed for the office, his stride purposeful. She flipped the lock and opened the door, not wanting to give him the satisfaction of summoning her with a knock.

"Edgar—" She was brought up short by the look on his face. "Not a social call, I take it?"

"Can we go inside?"

"Of course." She moved to the side to give him room to enter. It had been months since they'd seen each other. "And to what do I owe the honor of your visit?"

"I have something for you."

"Oh?" It was then she noticed the large manila envelope he had tucked under his arm.

"Why don't we go to your office?"

"All right," she told him, her curiosity growing.

He followed her down the hall and waited until she

was seated before he tossed his package on the desk. "This makes us even," he said.

Elizabeth met Edgar's gaze, but the look on his face told her nothing. "I don't know what you're talking about."

He sat down, yielding his advantage. "I think you do, but I suppose in your position I'd want proof, too. Go ahead, look at it."

She opened the metal clasp and slid out the contents. A copy of the *Farmingham Daily News,* its banner headline announcing the fiery car crash that killed the Preston family, lay on top. So, it was Edgar who'd been investigating her. She leaned back in her chair. She didn't have to look at any of the remaining material.

"Now what?" she asked.

"As I said, we're even."

And then it hit her. That day at the apartment. "I never considered you in my debt."

"You could have said something to Elana, but you never did. Your reasons are your business. I just figured I owed you one."

Elizabeth couldn't believe what she was hearing. Edgar was the last person she would have expected to exhibit a code of honor. "I don't know what to say."

"I wish I could tell you that my giving you the file put you in the clear, but knowing Felicia, she's going to keep on until she finds something she thinks she can use against you."

"So the investigation was Felicia's idea?"

"Who else?"

"She's going to get her money one way or another. Why is it so important that she take me down in the process?"

"It doesn't have anything to do with you. It's her father she's after. She won't be happy until everything he built and everything he stood for is dismantled. You just happen to be standing in her way."

"Why does she hate him so much?"

"He never told you?"

She shook her head. Since Amado's death, she'd discovered there were lots of things he'd kept from her.

"Felicia blames Amado for her mother's suicide."

"That doesn't make sense. Sophia and Amado had been separated for years when she—"

"Logic doesn't have anything to do with it. Sophia poisoned Felicia's mind where Amado was concerned. I don't think there was anything Amado could do or say to erase the image of Felicia finding her mother the way she did, and quite honestly, I think Sophia planned it that way. Felicia swore she'd find a way to hurt her father as deeply as he'd hurt her mother. Selling Montoya Winery to Hicks and Brody is the way to do it."

"But Amado is gone."

"It doesn't make any difference. Felicia wants his memory and everything he stood for gone, too."

"And any means justifies the end."

"That's why Felicia put me in charge of checking you out."

"You're telling me that she doesn't know what's in here?"

"She thinks the detective couldn't come up with anything. But I wouldn't be surprised if she decided to check with him herself. Which is why I decided to come here tonight to show you what he'd found. I suggest you do whatever it takes to get Felicia off your back and that you do it as soon as possible. If she gets her hands on this, she won't hesitate to use it any way she can. My guess is that she'll say you tricked Amado into marrying you the way you tricked the people at Safford Hill into believing you were Elizabeth Preston. I wouldn't put it past her to try to get the will set aside."

"If she succeeded, half of the money that's now mine would be Elana's. . . ." And whatever came to Elana benefited Edgar.

"The implication being why am I giving the file to you instead of Felicia?"

"The thought must have crossed your mind."

"I'm content with what I have, always have been." He chuckled. "Which is just one of the things that drives Elana nuts about me."

She picked up the papers. "'Thank you' seems a little inadequate considering what would happen if this ever got out."

"I don't know that I would have come here tonight if you hadn't paid the scholarship money back."

"How did you know that?" She'd made the contributions anonymously.

Edgar smiled. "Robert Sidney is the best detective in the business. About the only thing he didn't bother reporting was where you buy your groceries, and that was because I didn't ask."

It gave her an eerie feeling to know how thoroughly she'd been investigated.

Edgar slapped his hands on his knees and stood up. "God willing, we won't be seeing each other once this thing is settled." He headed for the door. "If it turns out

Felicia finds out about this anyway, I'll do what I can to warn you, for all the good it will do."

"Take care of yourself, Edgar."

"Now don't go all soft and consider changing your opinion about me. I'm still the same old philandering son of a bitch I always was. Lucky for you, I happen to believe in paying my debts."

Elizabeth was at the bank when the doors opened the next morning. As soon as Edgar had gone the night before, she'd called John Sordello, the manager, at home to set up the appointment. John had handled Montoya Winery's banking needs for over two decades, and his familiarity with the winery allowed Elizabeth to skip the formalities and go directly to the reason she was there.

John listened intently as she told him how much money she needed, why she needed it, and how she intended to pay it back. She'd considered acknowledging that the reason she hadn't come to him earlier was that she already knew the odds against the bank lending her the money she needed. But then why admit something like that?

John didn't say anything right away. It was everything Elizabeth could do to keep from filling the silence with persuasive arguments why the bank should be thrilled she'd come to them for the loan.

When he finally leaned forward, his body language was folksy and open. "Let me apologize ahead of time for asking this, but I feel it's something that has to be addressed. Are you sure it wouldn't be in your best interest to go ahead with the Hicks and Brody sale? It's a generous offer, especially in today's market."

Before she could answer, he added, "Amado told me about your promise to carry on for him when he was gone and asked me to do what I could to help. Personally, I thought at the time that it was unrealistic to expect you to handle the day-to-day operation by yourself, and I haven't seen or heard anything today that made me change my mind. There isn't another winery close to Montoya's size that doesn't have at least two wine masters. You don't have one."

She couldn't argue the point and didn't blame him for questioning her ability. The odds were against her. Every year saw the failure of wineries run by men who had a lifetime of experience. What made her think she could succeed, especially alone? "I'm willing to secure the note with a first deed of trust."

"How are you going to do that while Felicia and Elana still own forty-nine percent?"

She was so used to thinking of Montoya Wines as hers, she hadn't taken them into consideration. "Can't it be set up where—"

"A few years back we could have worked something out, but nowadays everything we do is scrutinized, especially when it involves this kind of money. I'm sorry, Elizabeth, I really wish I could help you."

She wasn't going to be dismissed that easily. "What if I used the operating capital to fill in the remainder of what I need to buy them out? Would you take a first then?"

He thought a minute. "Do you realize what a risk you're taking?"

"What difference does it make whether I lose the winery to Hicks and Brody or bankruptcy? It's as finished one way as the other."

"You can't be serious—if you sell, you're set for life."

"That's not what I'm looking for. If I need a roof over my head, I can always go back to advertising." How was she going to get through to him? "Look, I know it sounds corny, but I'd rather go down fighting. I can't imagine anything worse than being a rich widow with all that empty time on my hands."

"There are a hundred things you could do with—"

She was wasting her time trying to make him understand. "Back to my question, John. Would you give me the loan?"

He scratched his chin as he considered how to answer her. "I'll go the equivalent of two years' operating capital, no more. And . . ."

"Yes?"

"Before I put the loan up to the board, I want to be able to tell them you have a wine master capable of pulling this off." He got up and came around the desk. "I know it sounds like I'm being a real stiff-necked bastard about this, but there's nothing I hate worse than foreclosures, especially when they involve a friend."

Why was it the expedient path was never the easy one? She waited until she was sure she wouldn't choke on the words before she told him, "I'll have a list of candidates on your desk tomorrow morning."

"How badly do you want this loan to go through?"

"Meaning?"

"I can guarantee the board will go along with whatever

I recommend if I can tell them Michael Logan is the wine master. Amado always swore there was no one better."

Elizabeth stood outside the bank and studied the grocery store across the street, trying to remember if she'd ever seen a telephone inside. She could have used John's, but the call she had to make required the privacy that came with a public phone.

If she had any hope of finding Michael in time to head off Felicia, she needed someone who was good at what they did. She smiled. Not just good, the best. Robert Sidney.

What beautiful irony it would be if, in the end, it turned out Felicia's Machiavellian behavior provided the means for Elizabeth not only to find Michael, but to keep Montoya Wines, too.

Amado would be pleased.

29

Elizabeth maneuvered the rental car she'd picked up in Milan around a hairpin turn as she moved deeper into the vineyards of the Piemonte wine region of Italy. According to the map she'd picked up at the airport, she was still several miles from Michael's house.

More than enough time to change her mind, go home, quietly and quickly sell her shares to Hicks and Brody, and disappear, escaping the possibility that her past would come back to haunt her. It was insanity to risk everything on a loan that needed only a couple of bad harvests to ruin her, even with Michael as wine master.

No one believed she could make a go of the winery, not even the people who worked for her. They cared enough to try to hide their feelings when she was around, but she knew they were almost as worried about their jobs with her in charge as they were with the possibility that Hicks and Brody might take over.

Tony Reynolds had been more subtle than the rest, expressing his doubts with stories seemingly casually integrated into their conversations about farmers and would-be vintners who had flocked to the valley in the flush of the seventies and how few were still there.

The road she'd been traveling for the past half hour narrowed abruptly, forcing her to slow down. In less than an hour it would be dark and easy to miss road signs. She could be wandering around the countryside for hours.

She should have spent the night in Milan and started out in the morning. But then Michael would undoubtedly be at work, and she would either have to search for him there or wait for him to return home. Another day would be gone, another day to think and to question what she was doing. If only she could shake the feeling she was wasting what little time she had left chasing a dream.

Michael had made a new life for himself. According to the detective report, after more than a year at sea, Michael had finally settled in Italy. Why would he want to come back to a place that held so many painful memories? She'd thought she knew him, but in reality it seemed she hardly knew him at all. Not once had he mentioned a love of sailing or the sea. She would never have thought to look for him there.

The slender thread of confidence she'd used to sustain her through the long trip snapped. With sudden clarity she saw that it didn't matter how wonderful her offer was; nothing she had to give would entice Michael to come back with her.

Michael opened the front door to the old brick farmhouse. "Angelina, I'm home." He removed his jacket and paused to take a deep breath, savoring the spicy smell coming from the kitchen.

A willowy woman came into the room, wiping her hands on a towel, her cheeks flushed from the heat of the stove. She gave Michael an expansive smile, clearly pleased to see him. "How did the tasting go?"

"Fantastic. I think I've actually got Guido talked into making the change." He looked around the living room. "Where's Antonio? I have something for him."

She shot him a scolding look and clucked her tongue. "How many times must I tell you he will be spoiled if you keep bringing him presents?"

He held up his hands in surrender. "It's the last time. I promise."

"Uh-huh. I think I should believe the sun if it told me it will stop rising in the morning before I believe such a thing from you."

Coming home to Angelina's three-year-old son was the highlight of Michael's painfully ordinary workday. "So, where is he?"

"At his grandmother's, being spoiled by her," Angelina said. "He had a fever this morning. I think he might be getting his father's cold."

"You should have stayed home with him today. You know I wouldn't have minded."

She laughed as she reached for the tie to her apron. "You need a wife and a bambino of your own to spoil."

He dug in his coat pocket for the hologram of Big Bird that he'd picked up for Antonio on his trip into Milan. "It will never happen," he said, handing it to Angelina.

"If you would just let me introduce you to my cousin Constanzia. I know you would change your mind."

A knock caught Michael's attention before he could parry Angelina's oft repeated thrust that he and her cousin were perfect for each other. He went to the door, thinking it was Liborio, Angelina's husband, coming to pick her up.

His smile of greeting faded when he looked into the dim light and saw who it really was looking back at him. Seeing Elizabeth so unexpectedly was like a physical blow, and he took a step backward. At the same time a compelling urge to close the door and pass off what he'd seen as an apparition came over him. But even as the thought formed, on its heels was the knowledge that it was already too late. The painful memories hadn't lessened in the almost two and a half years since they'd seen each other; they'd only lain dormant.

Elizabeth flinched at his reaction. "I'm sorry. I should have called to warn you." She offered him a quick smile of apology. "To be honest, I was afraid if you knew I was coming, you wouldn't be here."

He scanned the space around her, sweeping the yard and her car. She'd come alone. He settled on her again, taking in every detail while telling himself to do so was insanity.

She'd changed since he'd last seen her. The most obvious—she'd cut her hair. It was short and full and easily caught in the wind swirling around her. His hand formed into a fist at his side as he fought to keep from reaching out for the curl that lay against her cheek. He could almost feel the softness. "Why are you here?"

She hugged herself against the cold.

Or was it the defensive anger in his voice? Goddammit, he'd worked hard to put her out of his mind. And here she was, back in again. And there he was, back where'd he'd started.

"I need your help," she said. "I know I have no right to ask—" Her gaze fixed on something behind him, and the rest died unspoken.

Michael turned to see what had caught her attention.

Angelina came up to stand beside him and gave him a gentle nudge with her elbow. "What's the matter with you?" she whispered. "Where are your manners? It's freezing out there. Ask your friend inside."

He'd traveled thousands of miles to get away from Elizabeth Montoya. She had no right to do this to him. He didn't want her in his house. He didn't want to picture her there when she was gone. He didn't want to imagine he could smell her perfume or hear her laughter.

Angelina elbowed him again, an older sister chastising an errant sibling. "For shame, Michael. What a way to behave."

"If I've interrupted your dinner, I could come back later," Elizabeth said.

Michael moved out of the doorway. As the light from the entry fell on Elizabeth's face, she looked down at the ground. But not before Michael saw the fear in her eyes. An unreasoning swell of triumph hit him. It had been as hard for her to come as it was for him to have her there.

"Michael will not have his dinner for an hour or more," Angelina answered for him.

A car pulled up behind Elizabeth as she looked to Michael for confirmation. Angelina grabbed a heavy shawl off a peg on the wall and threw it over her shoulders. "Perhaps you will be here when I return, and our Michael will introduce us then," she said to Elizabeth.

Michael ignored her blatant hint. He would not get off so easily tomorrow. "Give Antonio a hug for me," he said. "And tell him I hope he's feeling better."

Angelina looked at Elizabeth and started to say something, then glanced back to Michael and plainly thought better of it. She ran to the car and, as Liborio drove them away, stuck her hand out the window and waved.

"You have a housekeeper?" Elizabeth asked. It was as much statement as question.

"What did you think she was?"

"It's been a long time . . . you've never wanted for female companionship."

"Times change. People change." As his shock at seeing her there began to diminish, curiosity took its place. What had brought her all this way? And why now?

"Coming here tonight was a mistake," she said. "I should have known better."

"Meaning you think the morning would have been better, or that you shouldn't have come at all?"

"I should have realized how deeply you'd be involved in your new life." She brushed her wind-tossed hair from her face. "I pictured seeing you a lot of ways, Michael, but I never imagined that you'd simply gone on as always." She shrugged helplessly. "I'm sorry. I didn't mean that the way it sounded."

"What did you expect?" Why did he care that she couldn't see the hell he'd gone through? What possible difference could it make now?

"Please, Michael. There's so much you don't know."

The catch in her voice shattered the invisible barrier he'd put up to protect himself. "It's cold out there. You might as well come inside."

They moved into the living room. Michael turned to her. "Do you want a drink?"

"Something hot would be nice."

"Coffee?"

She nodded.

When he returned from the kitchen she had taken off her jacket and was standing with her back to the fireplace. He set the tray on a table, poured the coffee, and handed her a cup. "You said there was something I didn't know," he prompted.

Elizabeth brought the steaming liquid to her mouth and took a sip. She'd rehearsed for days the actual words she would use to tell Michael about Amado, but now she couldn't remember any of them. "The night you left, Amado told me he was dying," she finally blurted gracelessly.

Michael stared at her through narrowed eyes. "What did you say?"

"It was congestive heart failure," she went on. "Slow but unstoppable."

"You said *was*. What does that mean?"

She wrapped her hands around the cup and stared at it, not wanting to see the pain in Michael's eyes when she answered him. But at the last moment she looked up again, unable to shield herself. "He died last spring."

The color drained from Michael's face. "No one told me. Jesus, how could I not have known?" He sent her an accusing look, and she saw there were tears mixed with the anger and confusion. "Why didn't you—"

"I didn't know where you were."

"You found me now."

"I hired a detective."

"It took him all this time?"

"I only hired him a week ago. Before then I thought you stayed away because you wanted to." She put her cup back on the tray and reached out to touch his arm. "It wasn't until the detective told me about the year you were on the boat that I realized you couldn't have known what was happening to Amado."

Michael sank into the chair beside him. "All this time . . . and he's been gone. I've never pictured him any way but healthy, in the winery working, the two of you . . ." He shook his head as if to clear it. "How could I not have known?"

"You left before he began to fail. The only sign there was anything wrong—" She stopped herself, but it was too late.

"What?"

She could sidestep his question with something that would satisfy him, but there had already been too many secrets and half-truths in her life. Michael deserved more from her. She deserved more from herself.

After several minutes Elizabeth walked over to the fireplace and held her hands out to the flame. Her back to Michael, her voice low but steady, she began. First she told him the reason for Amado's impotence—that it had nothing to do with her and that he had never stopped loving her. She left nothing out, no matter how painful or awkward or embarrassing. She even went back to fill in the details she'd left out the night she come to his room to feed the kittens. She told him about Amado's misguided manipulations to bring them together, about Felicia's duplicity, and about Edgar's peculiar form of chivalry.

Michael listened without comment, stopping her only when her voice became too soft for him to hear. As she neared the end, she turned to look at him. "The last thing he said to me was to tell you that he was sorry for the way things turned out."

Seconds stretched into minutes as Michael sat and stared into the fire. "I never wrote to say good-bye. I tried, but I couldn't find the right words."

She'd had years to come to grips with Amado's illness and death. It was still new to Michael. "He understood."

He looked up at her. "You left out something."

She frowned. "I don't know what you mean."

"Why you came here tonight."

She picked up her cup but saw the coffee had grown cold and put it down again. "The bank won't help me unless I have someone who knows what he's doing running the place."

He sat back in his chair. "Why me? There are dozens—"

"John Sordello seemed to think that with your experience, the board would move more quickly with its decision."

"So it was John's idea to use me as the collateral, not yours?"

She swallowed. "What do you want me to say?"

He stared at her long and hard. "Just tell me the truth."

"It was his idea to go with the best."

"I see."

"But I was the one who hired the detective to find you."

"So what you're telling me is that you came all this way just to offer me a job? Am I supposed to be impressed?"

His anger confused her. "Is it so terrible to know someone thinks so highly of you?"

"Hell no. I live for it."

Pride had been her only companion for so many years, the thought of putting it aside to tell him how she felt, the reason she was *really* there, terrified her. If he rejected her, what would she have left? "I'm in trouble, Michael."

"Yeah, I can see that you are. It must be hell knowing if you don't get what you want, you'll have to put up with becoming part of the idle rich."

"You know I don't give a damn about the money."

"How would I know that?"

"Because I'm here."

An ironic smile formed on Michael's mouth. He shook his head slowly and looked down at his folded hands. "Amado really knew what he was doing when he married you. He spent half his life trying to instill a sense of family in Felicia and Elana, and it got him nowhere. Then you come along and a couple of years later he has you willing to do whatever it takes to keep Montoya Wines out of Hicks and Brody's evil hands, even if it means you could lose your shirt in the process." His gaze swung up to meet hers.

"I'm not doing anything you wouldn't do in my place," she shot back at him.

"So he found there were two of us cut from the same cloth."

"So where does that leave us?"

"I don't know."

"Will you at least listen to my offer?"

"Sure, why not?"

What had seemed like such a good idea on the plane over suddenly seemed all wrong. If Michael came back, it would be because it was something he wanted to do, not because she had made him an offer he couldn't resist. She was rescued from the need to answer immediately when a scratching sound on the window drew Michael's attention. He got up and crossed the room. Seconds later cold air swept past Elizabeth, followed by a thumping sound as something hit the floor.

She caught her breath in surprise when a large black cat pressed itself against Michael's legs and circled several times before lifting its head to peer at her. "Howard?"

He brought his ears forward at the sound of his name. It was too much to expect that he would remember her; he'd been little more than a kitten the last time they saw each other. But the year had done nothing to dull Elizabeth's memory. Howard had been the connecting link for so much that had happened between her and Michael. "I told you he would be a beautiful cat," she said.

Michael responded to the hunger in her voice and became her friend again, the one who had listened and shared the inconsequential until it became important. "He prefers 'handsome.' It's a male ego thing."

Howard circled Michael once more, rubbing against his legs while keeping his attention focused on Elizabeth. "I was afraid you'd given him away."

Michael smiled. "I considered it—for about ten seconds, then came to my senses. Who in his right mind would take in a cat like Howard?"

With a haughty flick of his tail, Howard left Michael and came across the room. He hesitated several seconds, then jumped on the sofa beside Elizabeth and leaned forward to sniff her outstretched hand.

"I wouldn't try to pet him if I were you," Michael warned. "He still doesn't like strangers touching him."

Even though it was true, the "stranger" hurt. She glanced up and caught Michael looking at her, his gaze enigmatic. "I thought about getting a cat after Amado died," she said. "But . . . I didn't."

Howard made a tentative step closer, his nose actively working the air.

Michael moved to stand over Howard, as if ready to ward off an eminent attack. Elizabeth welcomed the change in Michael that Howard's appearance had created. The protective shell was still there, but cracks had appeared.

As if prodded by a long dormant memory, Howard moved onto Elizabeth's lap, came up on his hind legs, touched noses with her, and then butted the top of his head against her chin. A loud purring sound burst forth.

"I'll be damned," Michael said.

She looked at him. A pain of longing went through her. "At least one of you is glad I came."

Time stood still. "What do you want from me, Elizabeth?"

She ran her hand down Howard's back and finally admitted the real reason she'd come. It had nothing to do with protecting her secret or saving the winery. She'd come there because she loved Michael as much now as she had the day he'd left. Time and distance had done nothing to ease his loss or the longing that had become as familiar to her as her face in the mirror each morning. "More than you're willing to give, I'm afraid."

"How do you know?"

Howard settled deeper into her lap. She ran her hand down his tail and felt the familiar bump.

"You're stalling," Michael said.

She looked up at him. God, she was such a coward. Why couldn't she just tell him she loved him? Instead she said, "I came here to offer you twenty percent of the winery or five hundred acres if you would stay with me four years."

He let out an appreciative whistle. "Are you sure I'm worth it?"

"Without you I won't get the loan."

"What if I told you I could get someone the bank would accept?"

That possibility had never occurred to her. "Does that mean you don't want the job?"

"Not on those terms."

Even if his answer wasn't what she'd really wanted to hear, it wasn't no. "What terms do you want?"

He lowered himself to his haunches to look directly in her eyes. "All I want now is what I've always wanted," he said. "You."

The answer was on the tip of her tongue when somewhere in the back of her mind she heard Amado's voice sound a warning. Not even to gain what she wanted more than anything else in the world could she let Michael perceive himself second best. In an entire lifetime there were only a handful of moments when what was said or done made any real difference. To let one pass because of inattention or cowardice was to forever live with regret. Never again would Elizabeth let that happen to her. She would seize every precious moment given to her from then on and treat it as the gift it was. "On one condition."

"Which is?"

"That you marry me."

Michael's answering smile told her that he understood what she was doing. "You drive a hell of a bargain."

Her heart took a funny beat that left her light-headed. "It's a take-it-or-leave-it deal, Michael. No counteroffers."

He reached for her hand, brought it up to his lips, and kissed her palm tenderly. Howard let out a disgruntled sound as he was nudged from his position on Elizabeth's lap. "How about December?"

He was asking for time to mourn Amado. "I like December," she told him.

She closed her eyes to press the memory of the moment into her mind to take out and hold again and again, a talisman for whatever hard or lonely times were ahead. When she opened them again, Michael was looking at her.

"You don't have to do that anymore," he said. "This is real." He put his hand on the back of her neck and brought her forward. She opened her mouth when their lips met, and he brought the touch and feel and taste of her into him. His head swam with the reality of having her in his life again. "And it's forever," he murmured as he moved to kiss her again.

AVAILABLE NOW

CHEYENNE AMBER by Catherine Anderson

From the bestselling author of the Comanche Trilogy and *Coming Up Roses* comes a dramatic western set in the Colorado Territory. Under normal circumstances, Laura Cheney would never have fallen in love with a rough-edged tracker. But when her infant son was kidnapped by Comancheros, she had no choice but to hire Deke Sheridan. *"Cheyenne Amber* is vivid, unforgettable, and thoroughly marvelous."—Elizabeth Lowell

MOMENTS by Georgia Bockoven

A heartwarming new novel from the author of *A Marriage of Convenience* and *The Way It Should Have Been.* Elizabeth and Amado Montoyas' happy marriage is short-lived when he inexplicably begins to pull away from her. Hurt and bewildered, she turns to Michael Logan, a man Amado thinks of as a son. Now Elizabeth is torn between two men she loves—and hiding a secret that could destroy her world forever.

TRAITOROUS HEARTS by Susan Kay Law

As the American Revolution erupted around them, Elizabeth "Bennie" Jones, the patriotic daughter of a colonial tavern owner, and Jon Leighton, a British soldier, fell desperately in love, in spite of their differences. But when Jon began to question the loyalties of her family, Bennie was torn between duty and family, honor and passion.

THE VOW by Mary Spencer

A medieval love story of a damsel in distress and her questionable knight in shining armor. Beautiful Lady Margot le Brun, the daughter of a well-landed lord, had loved Sir Eric Stavelot, a famed knight of the realm, ever since she was a child and was determined to marry him. But Eric would have none of her, fearing that secrets regarding her birth would ultimately destroy them.

MANTRAP by Louise Titchener

When Sally Dunphy's ex-boyfriend kills himself, she is convinced that there was foul play involved. She teams up with a gorgeous police detective, Duke Spikowski, and discovers suspicious goings-on surprisingly close to home. An exciting, new romantic suspense from the bestselling author of *Homebody.*

GHOSTLY ENCHANTMENT by Angie Ray

With a touch of magic, a dash of humor, and a lot of romance, an enchanting ghost story about a proper miss, her nerdy fiancé, and a debonair ghost. When Margaret Westbourne met Phillip Eglinton, she never realized a man could be so exciting, so dashing, and so . . . dead. For the first time, Margaret began to question whether she should listen to her heart and look for love instead of marrying dull, insect-loving Bernard.

COMING NEXT MONTH

THE COURT OF THREE SISTERS by Marianne Willman
An enthralling historical romance from the award-winning author of *Yesterday's Shadows* and *Silver Shadows*. The Court of Three Sisters was a hauntingly beautiful Italian villa where a prominent archaeologist took his three daughters: Thea, Summer, and Fanny. Into their circle came Col McCallum, who was determined to discover the real story behind the mysterious death of his mentor. Soon Col and Summer, in a race to unearth the fabulous ancient treasure that lay buried on the island, found the meaning of true love.

OUTRAGEOUS by Christina Dodd
The flamboyant Lady Marian Wenthaven, who cared nothing for the opinions of society, proudly claimed two-year-old Lionel as her illegitimate son. When she learned that Sir Griffith ap Powel, who came to visit her father's manor, was actually a spy sent by King Henry VII to watch her, she took Lionel and fled. But there was no escaping from Griffith and the powerful attraction between them.

CRAZY FOR LOVIN' YOU by Lisa G. Brown
The acclaimed author of *Billy Bob Walker Got Married* spins a tale of life and love in a small Tennessee town. After four years of exile, Terrill Carroll returns home when she learns of her mother's serious illness. Clashing with her stepfather, grieving over her mother, and trying to find a place in her family again, she turns to Jubal Kane, a man from the opposite side of the tracks who has a prison record, a bad reputation, and the face of a dark angel.

TAMING MARIAH by Lee Scofield
When Mariah kissed a stranger at the train station, everyone in the small town of Mead, Colorado, called her a hellion, but her grandfather knew she only needed to meet the right man. The black sheep son of a titled English family, Hank had come to the American West seeking adventure . . . until he kissed Mariah.

FLASH AND FIRE by Marie Ferrarella
Amanda Foster, who has learned the hard way how to make it on her own, finally lands the coveted anchor position on the five o'clock news. But when she falls for Pierce Alexander, the station's resident womanizer, is she ready to trust love again?

INDISCRETIONS by Penelope Thomas
The spellbinding story of a murder, a ghost, and a love that conquered all. During a visit to the home of enigmatic Edmund Llewelyn, Hilary Carewe uncovered a decade-old murder through rousing the spirit of Edmund's stepmother, Lily Llewelyn. As Edmund and Hilary were drawn together, the spirit grew stronger and more vindictive. No one was more affected by her presence than Hilary, whom Lily seemed determined to possess.

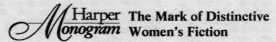